I0629367

# Praise for Jessica Tilles

". . .destined to yield high fruitage — powerful work, from a powerful writer."
– Michelle McGriff, author of *Obession 101*

"I applaud Tilles' boldness and her ability to cut to the chase."
– Linda Washignton-Johnson, Founder of Jackson Mississippi Readers Club

"Tilles writes with style and pizzazz."
– Black Men In America.com

"Strap yourself in for one hell of a ride!"
– Gayle Jackson Sloan, author of *Saturday's Child*

"Tilles engrosses the reader in vivid, shocking situations that are sure to stir a well of emotions."
– Tahira Chloe Mahdi, author of *God Laughs Too*

"Riveting, sexy, edgy. . .will have you squirming in your seat."
– Diane Dorce', author of *Devil in the Mist*

# Also by Jessica Tilles

*Anything Goes*

*In My Sisters' Corner*

*Apple Tree*

*Sweet Revenge*

# Fatal Desire

## Jessica Tilles

Xpress Yourself Publishing

Xpress Yourself Publishing, LLC
P.O. Box 1615
Upper Marlboro, MD 20773

www.xpressyourselfpublishing.org

For information about special discounts for bulk purchases, please contact Xpress Yourself Publishing Special Sales: 1-301-404-5615, Fax: 1-530-685-5346 or info@xpressyourselfpublishing.org.

Manufacturered in the United States of America

ISBN 0-9722990-5-X

Distribution by:
Baker & Taylor and Ingram Book Group

Visit Jessica Tilles at www.JessicaTilles.com

*Desire is addictive*
*It feels good*
*Then it hurts like hell*
*Before it becomes fatal*

# Acknowledgments

Finally! I e-mailed the last chapter of *Fatal Desire* to my editor, two weeks before its release. I really pushed the envelope. Now comes the tough part — the acknowledgments. This is going to be short and sweet. I can barely keep my eyes open. So, if I omit someone, please blame it on my tired mind and not my heart.

Jesse and Wallace Wright, my wonderful mom and dad. Thank you for giving me life and being proud of me. Both of you keep me on my toes, daily. I love you with all of my heart and all that I am.

Herbert Lipscomb, my brother and friend. Thank you for being my biggest supporter. *Last Request* is next up! Also, to my handsome nephew, Christopher Coles-Lipscomb. I don't know what God has planned for you, but I know it's going to be truly awesome. To be so young, you are such an old soul.

John Wooden, author of *A Moment of Justice, A Lifetime of Vengeance*. Thank you for taking on the project of editing *Fatal Desire*. You challenged and pushed me to write my best work yet. I cannot thank you enough.

Janet West-Sellars, author of *Quiet As It's Kept*. Thank you for being my third set of eyes. I appreciate all you have done on *Fatal Desire*.

Gary Johnson, the mastermind behind *Black Men In America.com*, my ace in the hole, my crispy chicken, salty shrimp eating partner in crime, thank you for being a wonderful business partner, confidant and friend. Your keen business sense and advice has kept me on track and focused. Thank you for having more faith in me than I had in myself. Your picture should be in Webster's next to the word *friend*.

Bill Holmes, author of *One Love*, thank you for allowing me to introduce your debut to the world. Be proud of your work and never write as though someone is looking over your shoulder. No matter where your literary travels take you, always know you will have a huge fan and supporter in me.

Victor Tilles, once again, I would not be an author had it not been for the tough love. We are connected for life. You are my friend and your Porcshe is on lay-a-way. :-)

A special, heartfelt thank you to Bernice Rowe, my cousin. I just love you so much. You never comment on the contents in my books, especially the sex scenes. I know how those scenes make you blush. You are always so proud of me and it shows, especially when you take me by the hand and introduce me with, "This is my cousin, the author, I was telling you about." That means the world to me. Remember how Darlene and I used to wear your clothes and dance and sing in your high heel shoes? Okay, I am beginning to cry. Moving right along. . .

I haven't forgotten about you, girl. Darlene Rowe Stukes, thank you for being my muse. You are a bad bitch and Raven's twin. Love you!

Derek McGinty, thank you for being my friend, lending me your ear, a strong shoulder to cry on, and sound advice. When I call, you always answer. Just like a true friend.

A big thank you to book clubs every where, way too many to name. Your support is insurmountable. Especially, a group of phenomenal women who are doing the damn thing down south: The Divas of the Jackson Mississippi Readers Club. Thank you for supporting me from day one.

A sincere thank you to some wonderful people in the literary industry. In one way or another, your advice, friendship, or words of kindness changed my life. Thank you Carla Dean, Eric Pete, Janet West-Sellars, William Frederick Cooper, Yonder One, Meisha Camm (I'm so proud of you!), Crystal Ellis, Michelle McGriff, Gayle Jackson Sloan, Harold L. Turley, Michael Baisden, Collen Dixon, Denise Campbell, Misherald Brown, Monica P. Carter, Jonathan Luckett, Delores Thornton, Maxine Thompson, Tracy Price-Thompson, Bill Holmes, John Wooden, Tahira Chloe Mahdi, Gerald Malcolm, Brenda L. Thomas, Karen E. Quionnes Miller, Lawrence Wayne, the members of Writer's Rx and The Writer's Hut, Lee MacDonald (truly a wonderful beautiful sister) and the entire staff at Karibu Books, and all of the wonderful book stores that continue to support me.

I saved the best for last. Leslie Ramos Walker… what can I say that I haven't said during the thirty-nine years I've called you big sister? I love you and am so glad I have you (and Glenn) to dance and grow old with.

To all of my sisters — stay strong, proud & phenomenal!

Jessica Tilles
April 23, 2006, 1:23 AM
Upper Marlboro, Maryland

# Fatal Desire

# 1

Smooth as silk and equally enticing, "Good evening," said the soft, sensual voice, pulling her full rose-painted lips to the microphone. "Welcome to *Sexual Desire*, an evening of pleasure. I am your host, Simone Kelly, here to help you wind down from your day and rev up your night with love, sex and fantasies. Tonight, I want to hear from my sisters. Ladies, if you had one wish for tonight, what would that wish be? Then, we will turn it over to those brothers who feel they can step up to the plate and grant the sisters' wishes. Is that cool?"

Simone stretched her arms out and dropped her head back. She let out a deep-throated moan and said, "The lines are lighting up. We have wishes to be granted tonight," she softly chuckled. "My brothers, my brothers, pull up a seat and listen carefully. This game is for the big dogs. No puppies allowed." Simone adjusted her headset, moved closer to the microphone and nodded toward Leon, her producer.

Leon smiled and returned the nod.

Simone glanced at the switchboard in front of her and shook her head. "Oooh," she cooed into the microphone, "it's going to be hot tonight!"

Teddy Pendergrass crooned *Love for Two* in the background as Leon held up one finger and mouthed, "Line one."

"Welcome to *Sexual Desires*. What's your wish, sister?"

The whiney, gum-popping voice said, "I'm tired of these weak ass men!"

"Now, now, sister, let's not down the brothers tonight."

"I'm just telling it like it is. The sorry mother—"

"Ouch!" Simone quickly disconnected the call. "No, no, my sister, so much negativity spoils my mood. Let us move on. Hello caller, you are on the air. What's your wish?"

Jamaica clutched the phone tight.

"Are you there?"

Jamaica gathered herself and stumbled on her words. "Ye...ye...yes. I'm here." She was so nervous, she could hardly lift her voice above a whisper.

"Speak up, sis, and tell me your wish."

"Hello, Simone," Jamaica said, clearing her throat. "I'm a little nervous. I've never called into a radio station before."

Simone softly chuckled. "Just relax, take your time and tell me what's on your mind."

"Well, okay." Jamaica cleared her throat again and positioned herself comfortably on the bed, with her legs folded beneath her. She took a deep sigh, closed her eyes and went for it. "I'd like to meet someone who is kind, caring, gentle and most importantly, consistent."

"You're not asking for too much, caller. Let's see if there is a brother in Chocolate City tonight who is capable of fulfilling your fantasy. We're going to put you on hold and Leon, my producer, will take down your name and number. If someone calls, we'll connect you. Is that cool?"

Jamaica perked up. "Yes," she said, barely able to control her excitement. "That's cool, Simone. Thank you!"

Simone chuckled at Jamaica's excitement. "You have a blessed night, girlfriend, and I wish you luck."

"Thank you. You do the same." Jamaica anxiously waited to give Leon her phone number.

"Alright, we're going to take a little break and pay a few bills. Brothers, don't sleep on the last caller. Give me a call at

202-555-2525. This is Simone Kelly and I'm going to fulfill your sexual desire tonight."

Simone flipped a switch on the console and smiled at Leon.

## 2

It took ten minutes for Jamaica's phone to ring. She sat on the bed, Indian-style, contemplating whether to answer it. She was nervous as hell and could not believe she had done such an idiotic thing. What self-respecting woman would do such a thing? Lately, men had not been her strong suit, let alone a stranger she would possibly meet over the airwaves.

The phone was on its fourth ring when she snatched it from its cradle.

She hesitated.

"I can hear you breathing," came from the other end of the phone line.

Jamaica took a big sigh of relief. "Oh, hey girl, whew..."

Maxine chuckled. "No, I ain't the man from the radio," she blurted out, barely aware of how loud she was talking, causing Jamaica to hold the phone an arm's length away from her ear. "Jamaica, what were you thinking?" The tone of her voice turned to a scolding parent.

"I don't know. I guess I wasn't thinking."

"No you weren't. You can't be that desperate for a man to put yourself out there like that," Maxine said without an ounce of inflection.

Jamaica slouched and fell back onto the bed. "Max, there is nothing desperate about me," Jamaica said in a voice that seemed to come from a long way off.

Maxine and Jamaica had been friends since Howard University. Even then, she knew how to choose the right words to make Jamaica feel like a complete idiot.

"Jamaica, you don't need to meet men that way," she scolded.

"Uh huh," Jamaica replied. "How am I supposed to meet them? At the club or on the Internet?"

"With patience, honey," Maxine retorted with cold sarcasm. She did not appreciate Jamaica's snide remarks, but she was cool. She recognized that Jamaica did not see how desperate she was coming off and it was her duty, as her best friend, to let her know, whether she liked it or not, how much like an ass she sounded.

Maxine continued. "I know you want someone in your life," she chuckled, "But that's not the way." Her chuckle turned to laughter. "You could end up with a pervert or something worse." Her words were playful but the meaning was not.

Jamaica caught the sarcasm in Maxine's voice, which was something that continuously annoyed her to no end.

"Yes, I know. Oh well, I am sure they haven't received any calls anyway. I wasn't freaky and nasty enough."

Maxine let out a long audible breath. "Girl, no man wants a freak in public no way."

Jamaica was inclined to change the topic. She knew if she did not, Maxine would be scolding her for the next three hours.

"Have you talked to Tillie and Randy yet?"

Maxine sighed. "Not yet, have you?"

Jamaica shook her head no, as if Maxine could see over the phone.

"Jamaica?"

"I'm here...no, I haven't spoken with Tillie, but I've spoken with Randy. He wants to hit Zanzibar tonight."

"Eww, why Zanzibar? I can't stand that place. It's always like a meat market and packed, too."

Jamaica grabbed the Emory board from the nightstand. "I don't know," she said, filing her nails, which was more like a nervous condition when she was on the phone. "I don't feel like a club tonight." A beep alerted Jamaica that she had another call. She put Maxine on hold and clicked over. "Hello?"

"Hey, Ma, what's going on with ya?"

"Not much, Randy. We were just talking about you."

"We?"

"Maxine is on the other line. She wanted to know what we were getting into tonight. It's Friday you know."

"Word, that's why I was calling, I'm down with whatever, Ma. Call me back and let me know what you two trick divas decide."

Randy hung up before she could respond to his tacky comment.

When she clicked over, there was dead silence. She figured Maxine had put her on hold, so she held tight for a minute, before hearing Maxine clear her throat.

"Jamaica, you there?"

"Yeah, that was Randy. He said he's down with whatever."

"Cool. I just got off the phone with Tillie. She basically said the same thing."

"Well, I guess the choice is ours."

"Looks that way...I hate when they do that mess. All they are going to do is complain anyway."

"Hey, let's go to the Chart House in Alexandria."

Maxine hissed. "Girl, I *do not* have Chart House money. I get my check next week. Are you treating?"

"Moving right along," Jamaica chuckled. "How about we go to the Cheesecake Factory?"

"Sounds good," Maxine said.

"Call Randy and Tillie and let's meet there about eight."

"It's seven o'clock now, Jamaica!" Maxine exclaimed in irritation.

"So what? You can't get there in an hour?"

"I'd like to wash my ass first, if you don't mind," she said in a raw, sarcastic manner.

"What time do they stop serving?"

"It's Friday night. They stop seating people around eleven. Let's meet at nine-thirty."

"See you then," Jamaica replied.

"Check caller ID the next time you get a call. If it is a strange number, don't answer it. No men from the radio station, Jamaica," Maxine scolded, once again, in her motherly tone of voice.

"Yes, ma'am. See you later."

Jamaica smiled and returned the phone to the cradle. She knew better than to sit by the phone and wait for a stranger to call. Besides, her wish had absolutely nothing to do with sex. She shivered at the thought of having unbridled, passionate sex with a stranger. She shook the arousing thoughts from her head. Those thoughts did nothing but frustrate her. It had been a minute since her last rendezvous with herself. She reached under the pillow and grabbed a man's biggest nightmare — the silver bullet!

She stepped out of her panties and slightly squatted, before the hum of the stimulator connected with her fleshy clitoris. Shuddering at the pulsating pleasure, she fell back on to the bed and raised her muscular thighs in the air. Her legs hung at an angle, while her foot arched and her toes pointed like a ballerina. Using the stimulator as a speculum, she inserted it inside her wetness, easing it upward toward her erogenous zone. She wanted the feeling of anticipation to go on forever and feeling as if in another second she would surely explode. It was wonderfully blissful.

Jamaica had not planned to shower, but since she felt like she had the best sex in the world, a hot bath would be the icing on the cake.

Once inside the bathroom, she turned on the hot and cold water and tossed bubble bath tablets into the bath. Standing before the mirror, she slipped out of her clothes and pinned her hair on top of her head. She stepped out of the mound of clothes around her feet, stepped into the tub, and slowly lowered herself into the cloud of bubbles. The hot water stung her skin and immediately relaxed her tired muscles.

She looked down at herself through the bubbles and admired the finely trimmed patch covering her pasture. She played in it. She twisted it. She was ready to give herself to the right man. *If he ever comes along*, she thought, followed by a deep, heavy sigh. She leaned her head back against the tile wall and immersed in the water, up to her neck. She closed her eyes and relaxed until her fingertips and toes looked like prunes.

Pulling herself from the tub, she reached for the thick, lime-colored terrycloth towel and wrapped it around her dripping, sudsy wet body. She stepped out of the tub onto the plush bathroom carpet that felt like cotton beneath her wet, sudsy feet. Once again, she stood before the mirror and dried herself off. As she reached for her toothbrush, the shrieking of the phone startled her. She jerked her head toward the bedroom. Instantly, she felt the warmth of menopausal hot flashes. It felt like her blood was running hot through her veins. She was scared shitless. Maxine's words, "Check the caller ID," ran through her mind like wildfire blazing through the California Hills. She could not move. Her feet were planted where she stood. She stared wordlessly in the mirror. On the fifth ring, the answering machine picked up.

"Hi, this is Jamaica and here is your chance to leave me a message!" BEEP!

"Jamaica, this is Simone Kelly. I have a connection for you. Please give me a call at the station when you have a chance. Peace." BEEP!

Should she return the call? Thanks to Maxine filling her head with all kinds of crazy thoughts, she was terrified and stood as frozen as an ice sculpture.

Once she melted, she slowly walked toward the phone, as though it was infected with the plague. She reached out her hand, almost afraid to touch the phone. Was it going to bite her?

Finally, she pressed redial and spoke directly with Leon, the producer.

"His name is Derek and he asked that we give you his number or whatever makes you comfortable."

"Oh? Well, I don't know. I mean I don't know anything about this Derek."

"Use your call block and he won't get your phone number. He sounds nice. Give him a call. You never know. This may be the man of your dreams."

"Did he tell you anything about himself?" Feeling like the most desperate woman on the planet, she decided against her question. "Never mind."

"Do you want his number?"

Jamaica retrieved a pen and pad from the drawer of the nightstand. She jotted down the number, said thank you and ended the call. She looked at the clock and decided to call Derek tomorrow.

## *3*

Fall in Washington, DC was Jamaica's favorite time of the year. Leaf-covered sidewalks and mild winds were a welcome from the hot and hazy summer. She didn't know about anyone else, but she was one Black woman that could not stand heat, except for the heat that warmed her home during the ice-cold winter months. *In a few months, there will be snow-covered everything*, she thought, so it was time to take her Chevy Tahoe in for a tune-up as well as new tires. She knew you could not live on the East Coast and not have a four-wheel drive during the winter months. It's unbearable.

The Tahoe pulled into the underground parking garage of Mazza Gallery. After driving down three levels, she finally pulled into a tight space. *This garage is not meant for trucks*, she huffed to herself, before climbing out of the truck and locking all of the doors. Although she was in downtown Chevy Chase, she wasn't going to chance having her truck stolen.

Once the doors opened to the mall level, she stepped off the elevator and immediately caught sight of her crew.

"Hey, Ma," Randy called out.

*I wish he wouldn't call me that*, she thought, frowning up her face.. She loathed it, but never uttered a word about it. She didn't know why all of a sudden, or even where, Randy adopted the thug mentality. All that were missing were the cornrows and pants hanging off his ass.

"Hey Randy, Tillie, Max."

"Hey girl." Tillie greeted her with a warm embrace. "How's it going?"

"Same shit, different day. You know how it is," Jamaica chuckled.

"Don't I know it, too," interjected Maxine, followed by a warm embrace around Jamaica's neck. "Good to see you, girl." She released the embraced and nudged Jamaica. "You get any calls before you left home?"

Jamaica remained silent. She didn't want Randy or Tillie to know she was so desperate she had to call into a radio station for a man. However, if she knew Maxine, she knew it was going to come out sooner than later.

"Y'all should've heard your girl on the radio this evening," Maxine said.

*Can't hold water*, Jamaica thought.

"Was that you, Jamaica? I thought the voice was familiar," Tillie said, smiling widely, almost excited by the idea of her best friend making her debut appearance on the radio.

"What were you doing on the radio?" Randy asked, adding to the bombarding questions.

"Nothing," she replied.

"Nothing my ass. That girl was on there looking for a man," Maxine said.

Jamaica's body stiffened in shock, causing the words to wedge in her throat. She couldn't speak.

*That damn Maxine*, Jamaica thought, as she cleared her throat and pointed towards the restaurant. "Look at the people waiting. Did anyone put our name on the list?"

"Yes we did and answer my question," Randy said.

Jamaica's defenses were up. She opened her mouth and spoke loudly. "Do you know how to mind your goddamn business?" The words that rolled off her tongue felt strange.

She'd never spoken them to her friends before, and definitely not in such a harsh manner.

Tillie's mouth fell open.

Maxine stood still. Her lips were pressed shut so no sound would burst out.

Randy showed no signs at all.

Jamaica's defenses began to subside. "Sorry, guys. To be honest, I'm quite embarrassed by it all."

Maxine nodded her head and poked out her bottom lip.

"I feel you, Jamaica," Tillie consoled. "It's all good. Besides, we don't need to talk about it now. We'll wait until we are seated," she said, bursting out with laughter.

Maxine cracked a smile.

"I've never heard you curse before, Jamaica," declared Randy.

Jamaica rolled her eyes upward and walked towards the restaurant.

"Randy, I don't know what rock you've been hiding under, but that trick curses like a damn sailor," Maxine corrected him, with laughter. "Don't believe me? Keep on asking her about the radio station!"

Jamaica turned on her heels to face them. "Shut the fuck up, Max!"

"See? What did I tell you? A damn sailor!"

# 4

Jamaica decided to forego the club scene and climbed into bed around midnight. TV Land had started the *Good Times* weekend marathon an hour earlier. She finally fell off to sleep when members of the Junior Warlords shot J.J. It was almost a guarantee she'd spend the weekend watching the marathon, unless a miracle happened and she actually had a real, live date. Since it had been almost a year since her last date, she was sure there was no chance of that happening.

At three in the morning, the telephone rang. Even though she was dead to the world, Jamaica picked up before the end of the first ring. Late night calls always put fear in her heart. She thanked God it wasn't her parents or any of her siblings.

"Yes, who is this?" She was groggy and irritated.

"This is Derek Braxton."

She leaned up on her elbow and yawned, wiping the sleep from the corner of her eyes. "Who?"

"I'm sorry for calling so late."

"If you don't tell me who you are, I'm hanging up this damn phone!"

"I responded to your plea on the radio the other evening."

Jamaica shot straight up in the bed; eyes wide open like a deer in headlights. "How did you get my number?"

"From the radio station."

"What in the fuck?"

"Wow..."

She was too concerned with her number being offered up to strangers to offer a reply.

He continued. "I guess they didn't think..."

"You're goddamn right they didn't think!" she yelled into the phone. "You didn't think either. Do you know what time it is?"

He was taken aback. This surely wasn't the attitude he expected from what appeared to have been a very levelheaded woman who made a plea for a good man?

Derek thought him calling her was a bad idea and apologized. "I won't bother you again," he said, hanging up in her face.

"No, he didn't hang up on me," she shouted. A war of emotions ran rampant through her. Her biggest pet peeve was to be hung up on. "How dare he hang up on me, after calling me at three in the morning, with no rap." Despite her better judgment, she found herself reaching for his phone number and dialing like a mad woman. Before he could speak, she yelled in his ear, "You are very rude!"

Her angry retort hardened him. "Look, lady. I apologized for calling you so late. I don't appreciate the language you're using either. I'm not interested in a woman with a potty mouth!" he barked.

*Potty mouth*, she laughed to herself before she threw back her head and released a great peal of laughter.

He sighed with annoyance.

She brought her hand up to stifle her laughter. "Are you still there?" she asked, slightly chuckling.

"Yes," he responded sternly.

"You have to admit it. Potty mouth sounds pretty funny."

His voice softened. "You're right, it does," he said, then laughing in a deep, jovial way.

She liked his laugh. It was warm and inviting.

Once he settled his laughter, he said, "I am really sorry for calling so late."

"It's no problem. It merely shows that you have no sense of timing."

"More like being excited to connect with you, but I'll let you get back to sleep. Maybe I can call you some time tomorrow."

"No," she responded quickly. "I don't mind talking for a bit, now that I'm up."

"Are you sure?"

"Yes, I'm sure. So, what's your name again?"

"Derek Braxton and Jamaica is a beautiful name. Were you conceived in Jamaica?"

She tried to suppress a giggle. "No, I was conceived in Washington, DC. I don't think my parents have ever traveled outside of the Metropolitan Area, and my last name is Kingston."

"You've got to be kidding me!"

"Nope. Are you kin to Toni Braxton?"

He chuckled. "Funny. Are your parents still with you?"

"Yes, they are."

"You're very blessed."

She assumed by his response that his parents might have been deceased. She didn't quite know how to approach that topic, so she left it alone. "Do you have sisters and brothers?"

"One sister, Gina."

"Is she older or younger than you?"

"I'm the oldest..."

"And how old are you?"

"Does it matter?" There was a trace of laughter in his voice. "How old would you like for me to be?"

"Yes it does matter and I'd like for you to subtract 2005 from the year you were born and come up with your correct age," she retorted.

"I see you're always on your toes," he said.

"Uh huh and how old did you say you were?"

"How old are you?" he asked.

"Old enough," she said, rocking back and forth with laughter.

"From the looks of my birth certificate, I'm forty-five years old. How about you?"

"I'm thirty-four, turning thirty-five soon."

"Oh my, a tenderoni."

"Absolutely! What do you do for a living?"

"I work..."

"Okay, smart butt, enough of that or I'm hanging up the phone."

He laughed, sincerely amused by the slight annoyance he was causing. "I'm self-employed. I own a construction business."

"That's cool," she said, holding the phone away from her face. She couldn't believe she had just said that. "So, how long have you been in business for yourself?"

"Oh, about ten years."

"Wow, that's a long time. Business is good?"

"I've had my good times and I've experienced the bad. It all comes with the territory when you want to work for yourself."

Jamaica yawned and crawled under the covers.

Derek reacted to her yawning. "Listen, get some rest. Let's talk tomorrow."

"Okay, that sounds like a great idea." She yawned again.

"Actually, I'd like to meet you tomorrow. If that's okay with you."

"Sure, but it has to be in a public place. A girl can't be too cautious."

"No problem. That is what I was going to suggest. How far are you from downtown DC?"

"Not very far, why?"

"Let's meet in McPherson Park, across from the White House."

"McPherson Park?"

"Yes. Is that okay with you?"

"I cut through that park every day, going to work."

"We can meet some where else, if you'd like."

"Nope, McPherson Park is just fine. Plus, I like for the man to take charge."

"Be careful what you ask for, lady."

"*You* better be careful. As I said before, I'm one of a kind." She was flirting and it felt good. She hadn't had anyone to flirt with in such a long time.

"I love a confident woman," he said, flirting in return.

"A perfect combination, wouldn't you say?" Her mouth flew open. She couldn't believe the words that escaped from her mouth, easy as one, two, three. Her frisky side was showing and she liked it. She planned to show it more often.

# 5

McPherson Park, located in the nation's capital, directly across the street from the White House, was home to the homeless, the have-nots and the not wanted.

Walking through McPherson Park saddened Jamaica deeply. It was a short cut she loathed taking to work, but she loathed walking the extra six blocks out of her way even more. However, she enjoyed having lunch there because it was her way of keeping herself grounded, recognizing that all of the blessings she'd received should not be taken for granted.

It was a hot, muggy August day in the Chocolate City sitting on the park bench. The tall shady trees cooled off the park and she felt serenity. She felt at peace.

She stared across the street at the White House, glaring into a window on the second floor, where the curtains appeared to be drawn back. She leaned forward, trying to get a better look. She could've sworn she saw someone standing in the window, looking out at the park.

She grunted and mumbled, "Probably Bush smiling down at the homeless, thanking his lucky stars it's not him out here. I'm sure he thinks just like his mama, 'they are better off in the park'."

She sighed heavily, stretched out her legs, and leaned her head back, allowing the sunrays to beam down on her face. She closed her eyes and held tight to her purse. She felt eerie, as though someone was watching her. However, it was broad daylight, so she kept her worries to a minimum. Derek would be showing up any minute.

With an average build and a pink complexion, the man looked across the park and smiled. He thought it was amusing that someone would take a nap in the park, while clutching to their purse, for dear life. However, this wasn't the first time he'd seen her in the park nor was it the first time he lost his nerve to speak.

He folded his paper and stood to his feet. He placed the folded paper under his arm and walked across the park toward the bench occupied by Sleeping Beauty.

He thought she was beautiful—and peaceful. He cleared his throat.

She was startled, quickly opening her eyes and sitting erect on the bench.

"Do you mind?" he asked, pointing at the empty space beside her.

She looked around the park and wondered why, of all the empty benches, he chose to sit with her. When she should've been flattered, she was annoyed. This was her time to herself. To reflect on life in general and she didn't need any interruptions.

"There are other empty benches you could sit on," she said, looking up at him, her hand shielding her eyes from the sun.

He clasped his hands together and looked around the park, regretting his approach. "Yes, you're right. There are several benches…"

"If you don't mind, I'd like to sit alone," she snapped.

He said, "I'm a good listener."

"No, you're not. If you were, you would move on."

"Whoa!"

"Sorry. Don't mean to be rude."

"Of course not, it appears to come off naturally from you."

She sighed heavily. She surely wasn't in the mood to deal with a whiney ass man, whose ego had been crushed because he'd been shot down.

"Fine," she said, sliding over toward the other end of the bench.

"Thank you," he smiled, before sitting at the other end. "After all, it is a public bench."

She ignored him. She positioned her body, with her back slightly toward him.

He removed the folded paper from under his arm and placed it on the bench, between them. He looked at her and then placed his hands in his lap. He was at a loss for words and she surely didn't want to hear any words he had to say.

"Lovely day, isn't it?" he said.

An annoyed look spread across her face. She sighed heavily and watched the homeless man lying in the middle of the park.

He looked in the direction of her stare. "Right in front of the White House, of all places," he commented.

"Where else are they going to go?" she snapped.

"There are shelters throughout the city," he retorted calmly.

"That is easy for you to say. You have a roof over your head, food on your table, clothes on your back…"

"You're absolutely right."

"Yes, I know I'm right. Right across from the damn White House, nonetheless. I think he was looking out the window anyway—probably laughing at them."

"Who is he?"

"The man you voted into office."

He chuckled. "I didn't vote for him."

She faced him. "Now that surprises me."

Feeling relaxed, he slightly turned his body towards her. He had had this conversation many times before. Because he was a Caucasian in his late-thirties, everyone took him for being a member of the Republican Party. He smiled.

She continued. "I just knew you were a Republican."

"How so?"

She lifted up her chin. "You look like one."

"What does a Republican look like?" he asked sarcastically.

"Don't get smart and you know what I mean."

"No, I don't and I'm not getting smart..."

"Your shoes," she replied in a snobbish manner.

He looked down at his shoes and crossed his leg. "I beg your pardon."

"You're wearing wing-tipped shoes. All republicans wear wing-tipped shoes, especially in black. A dead give away." She rolled her eyes and looked the other direction.

"Darren Kent, Democrat, and you are?"

She looked at him, smiled and then lowered her head. "Jamaica Kingston, idiot, nice to meet you."

"You said it, not me." They both laughed. "You have a beautiful name, Jamaica Kingston."

"Thank you and no I wasn't born in Kingston, Jamaica," she blushed. Now it was her time to become relaxed as she sat her purse on the bench between them, on top of his folded paper. "I must advise you that I am meeting someone here."

"Thanks for the heads-up."

He started to get up before she stopped him.

"We can chat until he arrives," she said.

He smiled and nodded in agreement. "So, do you think that all homeless people should sleep in the park and not in shelters?"

"No. Shelters are for their own safety and good. But, there are so many who refuse to seek shelter, especially at night, during the cold winter months."

"I guess they feel safer in the park," he said.

"They'll freeze in the park."

Jamaica shook her head in disagreement and decided to change the topic. The last thing she wanted to discuss on such a beautiful afternoon was the homeless situation in the nation's capital.

She continued. "So, Darren, are you married, single, widow, or divorced?"

"I've been divorced for eight years."

"How many children do you have?"

"I don't have children. My ex-wife was barren."

Jamaica tilted her head to the side. Confusion was written all over her face.

He said, "My wife was unable to have children."

"Oh, I see. I'm sorry to hear that. How old are you?"

"I'll be forty on Saturday."

"Oh wow, Happy Birthday in advance," Jamaica cheered.

"You're not going to spend my birthday with me?" he asked.

His question shocked her like a jolt of lightning. She searched his face for sincerity. She searched his eyes for game. She couldn't see his heart.

She twisted up her face and said, "You're good," before turning her back towards him, again. She was in no mood for games, let alone wanting it in her life.

"What do you mean?"

"Honey," she said, sticking out her leg. "I paid a lot of money for these Jimmy Choos and I'm not trying to walk in your bullshit and fuck them up."

Darren was taken aback. He wasn't sure what to make of her Dr. Jeckyll and Mr. Hyde impersonation. His gut was telling him to get up and leave the wacko sitting there, with her Jimmy Choo knock-offs. His heart was telling him to see what she had to offer.

"May I be frank with you?" he asked, talking to the back of her head.

"If you must."

"You come to the park just about every other day. Each time I'd see you, I'd try to muster up the courage to speak to you. Today, I got the courage and now I've offended you. Although, I don't know what I said to have offended you, but whatever it was I said, I am truly sorry and wish I could take it back. The last thing I'd want to do is upset you."

Jamaica turned her head towards him, her body slowly followed. "It's okay. I guess I need to relax."

He smiled and said, "Thank you for being so kind and forgiving a jackass."

Jamaica fell out with laughter. "You're being way too hard on yourself."

His smile turned to warmth. "You have such a beautiful smile."

"Thank you," she blushed. She looked at her watch. "My friend is ten minutes late."

Darren stood to his feet. "Do you think I could call you?"

"Why would you want to do that?"

"I find you intriguing and very attractive."

"Thank you very much, but I don't date outside of my race."

"Oh, I see."

Darren smiled and shook his head with disappointment.

"What's that for?"

He forced a smile. "It's a shame you would limit yourself."

"It's more of a preference," she said, looking around the park for Derek.

"I see. Have a wonderful day and I hope your friend shows up soon," he said as he walked away.

She hoped he showed up too.

Jamaica watched him walk away and wondered if she could really see herself with a pink man. Darren was a nice person, but she could never bring herself to date a white man. Although he did have a nice ass.

# 6

Jamaica sat impatiently on the bench, waiting for Derek to show. Her frustration grew as each second passed. In a disgusted huff, she grabbed her purse and walked toward McPherson Square Metro. Refusing to allow Derek to monopolize her day or anyone else for that matter, she decided to take the Blue Line to Pentagon City. She'd used the last of her Mac Studio Fix and could stand to buy a new pair of shoes. With a shoe fetish in comparison to Imelda Marcos, Jamaica needed a new pair of shoes like she needed a huge hole in her head. Some people use food for comforting. Jamaica bought shoes.

Actually, she wasn't depressed. She was more disappointed. So far, Derek had shown himself to be a nice person. She never expected he would stand her up. But then again, this was their first meeting. Therefore, her expectations shouldn't be too high.

As she walked toward 15th Street, she felt her cell phone vibrate inside her purse. She reached in, pulled it out and read the Caller ID. The number was not familiar to her. Typically, she would've allowed the call to go to voicemail, but her gut instinct was nudging her to answer.

"Jamaica Kingston," she answered in her most professional voice, not sure who was calling. She wanted to play it safe.

"Hi Jamaica, this is Derek."

Her heart skipped at the sound of his voice. "Where are you?"

'I'm home, waiting for you."

"Oh, I don't have time for games. We never agreed to meet at your house. I would *never* agree to meet at your house in the first place. I don't know you that well to be coming to your house. You have some nerve to stand me up and then call me with this lame ass excuse. How dare you? Who in the fuck do you think you are?" She stopped short and inhaled deeply.

"Jamaica, you really need to calm down. You may pop a vessel. I know we didn't make plans to meet at my house. I changed the plans. Now, will you come over?"

"No. Did you not hear anything I just said?"

"Don't ruin things for me, Jamaica," he pleaded. "I promise you that you will not be disappointed."

"It is too soon to come to your home, Derek. Sorry, but it's a rule I live by."

"Rules are made to be broken."

"Not my rules."

"Come on, Jamaica. Please," he begged.

She smiled. For her, hearing a man beg was pleasing to the ears.

She said, "I don't have my car."

"Where are you? I'll pick you up."

"Can I hop on the metro to get to you?"

"Yes! Take the Red Line to Friendship Heights and call me when you get there. I'll pick you up.

"Okay…"

"Wait, better yet. What Metro stop are you about to get on?"

"McPherson Square."

"Great, I can time you. I'll see you when you get to Friendship Heights."

"Okay. I'll see you then. Bye."

He said, "Bye, bye, baby," before ending the call, and the hair on the nape of her neck rose, sending chills throughout her body.

She smiled broadly. She liked the sound of it—baby. She liked him. She had to play it safe. She couldn't let him know that. If he wanted the upper hand, he could probably get it with little struggle from her.

The fresh air was a welcome pleasure compared to the smell of urine she had to endure during her escalator ride from the bowels of the underground Metro. Jamaica wasn't a huge fan of public transportation. She only partook in it when coming downtown, because she loathed trying to find a parking space.

The black Mercedes SL 230 convertible pulled up to the curb, with the finest, baldheaded man she'd ever laid eyes on. She could hardly contain herself. She giggled and did a little skip before making her way to his car.

"Hello, beautiful!" Derek smiled. His teeth were white as snow, enhanced by a perfectly trimmed mustache.

"Hiya, handsome. Are you going my way?" she flirted.

He leaned over and opened the door.

She hopped in, leaned over and kissed him on the cheek, which was something she would have never done. However, she felt comfortable in his presence.

"Thank you," he said. "Buckle up, sexy. I don't want anything to happen to you before I get you home."

"I am not having sex with you, Derek," she declared.

"Who said anything about having sex? Although it wouldn't be such a bad idea."

"No one, but making sure you don't get any funny ideas, Mister."

"You got it, baby. No funny ideas from me," he smiled and pulled into traffic.

The Mercedes drove up Wisconsin Avenue and made a right turn onto Nebraska Avenue.

Jamaica was dumbfounded. She'd lived in Washington, DC all of her life and she had never ventured past Georgetown. This area was new to her.

"Hey, there is NBC!" she shouted.

Derek smiled and said, "Yes, that's NBC. You'd never seen it before?"

"No. I've never been over here before. It's sad I know. Can we stop there?"

"For what?"

"I want to see Jim Vance!"

Derek fell out with laughter. "You're too much. We'll take a tour of NBC some other time."

"Do you promise?"

"Woman, you're just like a kid at an amusement park." He wasn't complaining. On the contrary, he loved a woman who wasn't afraid to show the little girl in her.

Jamaica settled herself in her seat and, with wide eyes, admired all of the beautiful homes on Nebraska Avenue. When Derek made a left onto Fox Hall Road, she damn near pissed her pants.

"Oh my God. Look at these homes!"

Derek glanced at her. The top was down and he thought how lovely she looked as the wind blew her hair all over the place.

She looked at him, smiled and pulled the hair from her eyes. "Derek, do you live over here?"

Derek made a right turn off Fox Hall Road and stopped at the stop sign. He looked at her, leaned over and kissed her on the cheek.

"What was that for?" she asked.

"No reason."

He made a right turn and entered Fox Hall Estates.

"Damn!" she blurted out, quickly bringing her hand to her mouth. "Are these town homes?"

Her reaction amused him. "Yes, I suppose you could call them town homes."

Her mouth fell open when he pulled into a driveway and the garage door opened. She didn't see him push any buttons.

"How did you do that?"

"Do what?"

"Open the garage door without pushing any buttons?"

"Sensors, baby."

She sat back in the seat and rested her arm on the armrest, careful not to let her fingers touch his. She didn't want him getting any ideas.

Once inside the house, her mind was blown. She stood in the foyer of the mini mansion, trying to contain herself.

Derek's home was quite masculine, not filled with unnecessary pieces of furniture. There was exquisite artwork hanging on the walls, several pieces by Karmella Haynes. Hardwood flooring, covered with expensive Oriental rugs. Definitely not the imitation Oriental rugs she'd seen in department stores. They were the real things.

"I love Karmella Haynes. I have a couple of her pieces, too."

"Yeah? My buddy turned me on to the sister a couple of years ago."

She breathed heavily and followed Derek into the kitchen. Everything was black—from the stove to the refrigerator to the cabinetry and the flooring. White appliances stood out, especially the white pots and pans that hung from the ceiling rack. She frowned, forming a questionable look on her face.

"What's wrong?" he asked.

"I've never seen white pots and pans before."

Derek was amused and said, "I picked those up in my travels. I believe I found them in Italy."

It was obvious to her that she was not his type of woman. She wasn't well traveled or well versed nor was she physically fit. She could stand to lose a little around the mid-section. Exercising was never her forte and she hadn't planned to start any time soon. However, she also felt if she was going to be with a man like Derek, who stood six-feet-one and weighed in at a firm and muscular two-hundred-ten pounds, she needed to, as Beyoncé so eloquently put it, "Work it out."

It was obvious Derek was sitting on bank and she tried like hell to push those dancing dollar signs out of her head. She wanted to like him for him. Lord knows it was extremely hard to not think about what he may get her for Christmas — shopping on Rodeo Drive, Cartier and Tiffany's. She had always wanted to receive a little blue box for Christmas or her birthday.

She raised her right hip and slid up on the black wooden stool. She rested her purse on the black marble island that stood in the middle of the massive kitchen. She looked around, her eyes landing on Derek reaching into a small glass encased refrigerator with at least twelve bottles of wine. He pulled out a black bottle with an ethnic looking label. It was obvious his favorite color was black. *Power to the people*, she giggled to herself.

"Wine?" he asked, holding the bottle towards her.

"That would be nice. Thank you."

He pulled opened a drawer from the bottom portion of the refrigerator. Something else she'd never seen before. He pulled out two chilled wine glasses.

"I had put these in before I picked you up," he said, placing the wine glasses on the counter. As he uncorked the bottle of wine, he asked what was going through her mind.

"I'm taking in your beautiful home."

"Thank you," he said, pouring the wine. "You're welcome to visit any time you'd like."

"You're kidding me, right?"

"No," he smiled.

"Derek, let us be straight with each other."

Derek nodded and handed her a glass of wine. "Before we become straight, I'd like to make a toast."

Jamaica smiled and held up her glass, making a point not to raise it too high in the air. She didn't want it to appear as if she didn't know what she was doing, even though she didn't. The only time she toasted was at weddings and never in a mansion, with a man who was obviously a millionaire in her eyes.

"Here's to a lasting friendship, and possibly much more."

Their glasses gently touched and the clinking sound could be heard through the house.

*Definitely not dollar store glasses*, she surmised.

She sipped her wine and looked him square in the eyes. "Are you a player?"

His smile turned upside down. "No, I don't play any kind of games, Jamaica. As you can see by my home, I don't have time for games or drama."

"That's not what I meant," she said, thinking she may have offended him with her off-handed comment.

"I know what you meant. You think that because I'm well off, I have women knocking down my door."

"Well, yes."

"Baby, I am a single, forty-five-year old man who has never been married. Does that sound like a man who has women beating down his door?"

"I'm sure you have women knocking down your door. But I'm also sure you are a man who is quite selective when it comes to women."

"I have to be. Everyone should be selective about who they allow into their lives."

"I agree."

"That's called settling and I don't settle in my professional life, so I'm certainly not going to settle in my personal life."

"So, let me ask you a question."

Derek opened the refrigerator. "Ask away," he said. "Are you hungry?"

She shook her head no and proceeded to ask her question. "I can knock on your door any time of the day or night, without calling?"

"That would be rude. You should call first to make sure that I am home."

"Oh."

"No, I'm not seeing anyone, Jamaica. No, I don't have regular company." He chuckled and bit into an apple. "So much for being straight with each other," he chuckled with a full mouth.

Jamaica waved her hands in the air and surrendered. She smiled and said, "Okay, you've got me. My question was pretty premature."

He shook his head. "No, it wasn't. There is no such thing as a premature or dumb question, in my opinion. If you want to know something, you had better ask it. I do not volunteer any information." He finished off his apple and said, "Let's start a fire."

Jamaica raised one brow. "You want to start a fire at the end of September? We're having an Indian Summer, Derek."

"Yes. I'll turn up the A/C so it'll feel more like January," he laughed.

Hopping off the stool, she looked around the room, turning herself in circles. She stopped and faced him. She propped her hands on her hips and frowned.

"What's wrong?" he asked.

"I can't find it."

A quizzical look crossed his face. "What are you looking for, Jamaica?"

"The helmet you wear on the little yellow bus that will be picking you up in the morning, because your ass is crazy to want to start a damn fire in the middle of a heat wave!" She bent down to her knees with laughter.

As much as he tried to suppress his laughter, Derek laughed so hard he let out a fart, causing Jamaica to laugh harder.

"Oh, Jesus!" she screamed.

"I know, I'm sorry," he laughed. "That was rude of me, but I was laughing so hard it just slipped out. I was trying to hold it, too."

She raised her hand toward him. "No, you're sharing way too much information with me right now." She pulled herself upright and sipped her wine.

Derek rested his hands on his hips and stared at her, making note of the deep dimples in her cheeks, her cute pudgy nose and tempting red gloss highlighting her lips. He smiled and said, "You are so beautiful when you're laughing."

"And I'm ugly when I'm not laughing? Is that what you're trying to tell me?"

"Woman, please!" he chuckled. "You sure know how to blow a moment." He grabbed the bottle of wine and his glass. "Grab your glass and follow me," he politely ordered with a warm smile that gave her a slight chill. She was so aroused, it wasn't funny.

Jamaica kicked off her shoes and got comfortable on the sofa as she watched Derek build the fire. As he bent over, adjusting the wood logs in the fireplace, she enjoyed watching his behind. She was tempted to grab it; it looked so juicy to her. Temptation took over. She lunged towards him and palmed his behind.

He jumped. "Hey, watch it now," he smiled. "You're getting a little too familiar. You're not respecting me," he teased, with his hands on his hips.

"Whatever!"

He lit the fire and took a seat beside her on the sofa. He sat as close as he felt she would be comfortable with, not wanting to make her feel uneasy. Although, since she had just grabbed his ass, he was quite certain she was very comfortable. Nevertheless, he wasn't going to make any assumptions.

Jamaica was working on her third glass of wine. She felt warm, not sure if it was the fire, wine or Derek.

"Why are you sitting all the way over there?" she asked, amazed at her ability to be so forward. *Definitely the wine*, she concluded.

He looked at her and smiled. Their legs were practically on top of each other. He wondered how much closer she wanted him to be. Mind you, he wasn't complaining, but didn't want to scare her off by moving too fast. Little did he know, and despite her "take it slow" motto, that cherry was ripe and ready to be popped.

Jamaica leaned into him and laid her head on his shoulder.

Derek wrapped his arm around her shoulder and caressed her tightly.

"This is nice," she said.

"I told you it would be."

"Yes, you did," she smiled. "I'll never second guess you again."

"Liar, liar, pants on fire." They both chuckled. "Women always second guess a man."

She winced at his chauvinistic remark. She raised her head, looked at him and said, "What is that supposed to mean?"

"Nothing," he said, kissing her on the forehead.

She pulled away from him.

He continued. "Oh, come on, Jamaica. I don't know what I meant by it."

"That's bullshit and you know it."

He shook his head. "There goes that potty mouth again."

"Oh, I'll give your ass a potty mouth all fucking night!"

Derek lowered his head and directed his stare toward the fire. He was not an argumentative man and didn't care too much for women who were. As far as he was concerned, anyone who used vulgarity, repeatedly, had a very limited vocabulary.

"Are you ignoring me now?" She was angry as hell.

Derek continuously shook his head. He was really digging Jamaica, but her aggressive behavior had turned him off for the moment.

"Derek?"

"Yes, Jamaica."

"Answer my question."

He looked up at her. "Sweetheart, I meant nothing by the comment, other than in a joking manner. You took it personally and I'm sorry. I don't like arguing or any type of confrontation. I'd rather you be in my arms than standing over me yelling. I won't deal with this kind of craziness." He reached out for her. "Please, Jamaica, let's not go there."

She reached for his hand and sat on his lap.

"If I offended you, I'm sorry," he apologized.

She wrapped her arms around his neck and kissed him on the forehead, on the bridge of his nose and on his lips, before his tongue.

"You didn't offend me. I'm sorry, *baby*," she cooed.

Her emphasis on the word baby kicked his testosterone into overdrive.

In a swift motion, Derek swept Jamaica beneath him and smothered her with kisses. Their pants were hot and heavy, almost demonic sounding.

Swelling at top speed, Derek's hardened penis bulged against her abdomen as his hand slid between the warmth of her skin and the elastic in her gym pants.

"Ohhhhh," she moaned. Her juices oozed from her opening, moistening her inner thighs.

Wiggling inside her pants, his fingers found her bud and stroked it, until it swelled between his fingers tips.

Her lips parted and spoke the words that all men feared. "Rape me." He didn't respond. "Force-fuck-me, Derek." His finger stopped wiggling around in her wetness. "Don't stop fingering me," she demanded.

Derek pulled himself up and looked down at her. "I don't do the rape thing, baby. Not trying to go to jail."

"I don't want you to really rape me, silly. I like to be fucked with force."

"That's not the kind of loving I do," he said as Anthony Hamilton crooned *Can't Let Go* through the eight tiny Bose speakers positioned in each corner of the room. "Do you here those lyrics?"

She shook her head yes.

"That is the kind of loving I make. If you want something other than that, I'm not your man."

She gazed into his eyes; her smoldering look revived his erection.

She slid her pants down around her knees, allowing one leg to escape.

Swiftly, his pants were unzipped and his penis inside of her, losing himself in her love.

Her hand drifted down around his thigh to his testicles, where she stroked him as he stroked in and out of her.

"Turn over, baby," she whispered in his ear, as he pounded her walls, swooshing around in her juices. He shook his head no, not wanting to pull out of her. "Yes, turn over. Let me ride you," she insisted.

With hesitancy, Derek withdrew and allowed her to slither from beneath him. Sitting upright on the sofa, he gasped. She was the most beautiful creature he'd seen in quite some time. His heart raced at top speed, fast enough to win the Indy 500.

Jamaica straddled him, slowly slid down on his hardness, and started bucking him like a wild rodeo horse. Her head was going round and round, arms flailing in the air. "Woo yeah," she cooed. She grabbed her breast and licked her nipple.

Derek stopped moving, his eyes wide as if he'd just seen a ghost. "Wait a minute," he said. "Please stop, Jamaica."

She stopped and looked into his eyes. "What's wrong?"

"Are you clean?" he asked.

"Are you?"

"Yes I am."

"So am I," she said, as she proceeded to ride his now soft dick.

With frustration, she dismounted her wild buck and asked, "May I take a shower, please?"

"Yeah, sure. Up the stairs, the first door on your right is my bedroom. Help yourself."

"Thanks," she huffed as she gathered her clothes and marched up the stairs. The bedroom door slammed closed.

Derek's head fell back against the sofa. He closed his eyes and sighed heavily. "Women," he mumbled.

## 7

Derek had fallen asleep on the sofa. The sound of the running shower upstairs woke him. He stretched his arms above his head and looked towards the stairs. He had felt awful about earlier and wanted to make it up to Jamaica. Even though it was too soon to know if she was Ms. Right, he really did like her.

He crept upstairs to the bathroom and peered through the gap in the door. The full-length mirror on the wall gave him a perfect view of Jamaica. The sponge glided over her size twelve body, as the soapy bubbles slid down her plump round behind.

Jamaica wasn't the type of woman he was used to dating – not the statuesque model type. However, something intrigued him about her. She was very curvaceous, even though her up tilted breast was less than the desired mouthful and she carried around a slight pooch, He watched as her curved hips swayed seductively. He grabbed his crotch and gently squeezed, trying to suppress his desire to take her. Her hair wasn't shoulder length, as he preferred. She carried herself with confidence, filled with an air of arrogance that aroused him. She was gentle and beautiful, and could be playful as a girl or as composed as an intelligent woman.

Turning slowly, showing a full frontal view, the soapy sponge washed her breasts, as her other hand rubbed the suds off gently over her silky skin. Her fingers traveled down her stomach and below her abdomen. As her legs parted, her fingers lathered, concentrating on cleansing her full vaginal lips. Her body shivered from the arousal that came from the tips of her fingers. Much attention was paid to her clitoris as her head fell back under the running water.

Derek's attempt to suppress his arousal was invalid. His arousal grew more intense as he watched the water trickle down and over her beautiful body. His pants fell to the floor.

He pulled off his shirt and tossed it to the floor. He climbed into the shower and pulled her into him. Kissing her softly on the lips, his hands felt the curves of her body, as they gently wrapped around her. His fingers stroked up her back, then back down to her ass. He gently squeezed and pulled her cheeks apart. The hot water rolled down her back and flowed between her crack, making tiny streams around her vagina, blending with her sweetness, and down to her thighs.

She turned her back to him.

His hand drifted between her legs as he kissed his way around to her back.

She bent over into an L-shape and pressed her palms flat against the brown marble tiled wall. She raised her leg up to her chest.

He knelt down behind her and planted kisses on her buttocks and thighs. He spread her sweet lips apart and extended his tongue toward her clitoris. When he gently stroked her swelling, she arched her back and released a passionate coo.

She had lost her grip to the wall and slipped down to the shower floor.

Derek licked and sucked on her swell as the water splashed on his head and trickled to his busy tongue.

The intensity had become unbearable. She contracted her muscles, released them and then let out a shrill scream of ecstasy. She dropped to her knees and pressed her face against the wall.

He rolled his tongue up and down her back.

Jamaica faced him and kissed Derek with passion, from his lips to his neck and his chest.

He stood to his feet.

She kissed his stomach.

He stroked her breast in a circular motion.

His love pulsated and tightened as she kissed his thighs and fondled his sack. She grabbed him firmly and slowly worked the base, as she tasted and sucked the tip. When his love tensed, she gripped tightly and sucked him vigorously; opening her mouth wide as his seed oozed over her face, dripping down her chin and onto her breasts.

Derek leaned into the waterfall and moaned deeply, while Jamaica released her grip and planted her behind on the floor of the shower. She leaned against the wall, pulling her knees into her chest.

He looked down at her, the stream of water running over his shiny dome and down over his face, his mustache doubled as a waterfall. "Are you okay?"

She nodded and smiled. "I've never felt anything like it before."

Derek smiled widely.

"Oh, you're good," she continued. "But I had an orgasm while giving you head."

Derek tilted his head to the side with a questionable look on his face.

"My sentiments exactly," she chuckled.

Derek sat on the floor of the shower, circled his legs around her and rested his head against the wall.

"I still can't believe you're single," she said.

He pressed his fingers against his lips to shush her and closed his eyes.

*8*

Jamaica woke from a restless sleep feeling queasy as she sat up in the bed. She pulled aside the curtain. Her neighbor, Mrs. Johnson, was hanging laundry – socks, a bra, men's boxers and linens that unfurled like flags in the wind. Mr. Johnson lounged in the chaise lounge, with his pipe pressed between his lips, engrossed in the morning paper. Jamaica raised the window and inhaled the cool morning breeze.

As she wiggled out of bed, she stood to her feet and stretched her arms high above her head. Immediate thoughts of Derek smothered her. She smiled. Her panties rode between her butt cheeks. She pulled them out and sluggishly walked to the kitchen, where she started a pot of coffee. As it brewed, she searched the refrigerator for breakfast. She forgot to go grocery shopping. She shrugged and turned on the radio. The station was tuned to 96.3 WHUR FM. Audrey Chapman talked about cheating spouses.

From the alcove of her living room, which served as an office, Jamaica could look through the window to see Maxine, Randy and Tillie approaching the front stoop. She raised the window and yelled down to them. They smiled and waited for the buzzer to allow them entry.

As usual, Maxine walked through the door, without so much as a "hello" and into the kitchen, making her direct aim to the refrigerator.

"Hello to you too, Ms. Lady," Jamaica said to Maxine as Tillie and Randy both greeted with their usual hugs and kisses on the cheek.

"Oh, hey girl," Maxine said with her face buried in the refrigerator. "Got anything to nibble on?"

"I need to hit the grocery store this weekend."

"You sure do. This joint is empty!" Maxine retorted, looking through the cabinets.

"Don't you have food at home, damn? Get out of my kitchen," Jamaica jokingly snapped.

Randy sat on the sofa across from Tillie. "She does the same thing at my place too," he said.

"Uh huh, mine too," Tillie chimed in. "No home training, but I love her just the same."

Maxine walked into the living room with her middle finger extended. "This is for all of y'all," she pouted, plopping down on the sofa next to Randy. She caressed his legs. It's no secret that Maxine had a thing for Randy, her friend for the last fifteen years.

Randy smiled and removed her hand from his knee. "You're treading in dangerous territory," he joked. "Friend or no friend, I'll fuck you in a New York minute."

"Damn," Tillie laughed. "Give her what she wants then maybe she'll leave you alone."

"Or stalk you," Jamaica chimed in.

Again, Maxine extended her middle finger.

They all chuckled.

Unable to pinpoint exactly what was going on, but Tillie knew something wasn't right with Jamaica. She seemed happy. She was glowing like a fly in shit.

"Jamaica, what's been going on with you? We haven't seen or heard from you in a couple of weeks," Tillie said.

"Yeah, Jamaica, we missed you the last few Fridays," Randy added.

Maxine said, "She's getting dicked down real good. That's why we haven't seen her."

Of the four of them, Tillie was the nosiest, wanting to know about any and everything that wasn't any of her concern. "Who is he and when are we going to get to meet him?"

"He's that guy she met from the radio station," Maxine responded.

Jamaica shot Maxine an annoyed look. "Could I please tell my own business?"

Tillie perked up in the chair and said, "You're holding back on us, Jamaica?"

"His name is Derek and yes, he's the guy I met from the radio station."

"Word? I need to call in to the station myself. See if I can get me a honey to open her legs up for me."

Jamaica's head snapped toward Randy. "What the fuck are you implying, Randy?"

"He was very clear," Maxine answered on Randy's behalf. "If this Derek guy could find a woman from the radio to open her legs, just as you did so easily, then he could find a trick, too."

It was obvious Maxine was envious. Since her divorce three years ago, when her husband left every morning with *The Washington Post* tucked under his arm and a cup of coffee in his left hand, and never returned, she'd knock down every positive thing that happened to her girlfriends.

Jamaica's jaws clenched, her eyes slightly narrowed. "Go to hell, Maxine!" She gave Randy a hostile glare. "And you can kiss my ass, too!"

Randy stifled a grin, which softened Jamaica's hardened face.

"I met someone," Tillie blurted.

All eyes focused on Tillie.

"The first thing he said to me was, 'You're amazing.' I have learned that when they tell you you're amazing, it's over before it starts." She turned to Randy and eyed him up and down. "Isn't that right, Randy?"

Randy evaded the question and looked in the opposite direction. "What's on the agenda for today, ladies?" he said, changing Tillie's chosen topic of discussion.

"Why did you do that?" Tillie asked Randy. "You are the most evasive person I know."

Jamaica looked at Randy, then at Tillie. "What's going on between you two?"

"Nothing," Randy responded. "Your girl is always trippin' on something."

Tillie stood to her feet. "This guy I met," she said. "I've known him for years, but we recently connected."

Maxine leaned forward in her seat and clasped her hands together.

"We had always been attracted to each other," Tillie continued. "But wasn't sure how to approach it, so a few months ago, he came by my apartment. For nothing special, just to hang out, as he would usually do."

Randy became restless and fidgety.

Maxine turned her glare from Tillie to Randy.

Tillie walked toward the window and looked out, her back to everyone. "One thing led to another and we made love." Her voice began to crack. "It was wonderful. He took me to levels I never knew existed." She turned to face Jamaica. "I had anal sex for the first time!"

Maxine's anger toward Randy was at an all time high. "You nasty motherfucker," she said under her breath. Jamaica and Tillie didn't hear her, but he heard her loud and clear.

Jamaica reached out at Tillie and said, "Tillie, honey…"

Tillie pulled away and continued. "It's been three of the most wonderful months of my life."

"Three months?" Jamaica asked. "Three months and you're just telling us?"

"I love him, Jamaica," she smiled. "But," she said, the smile leaving her face and her head lowered. "Randy doesn't love us."

Jamaica's mouth hit the floor.

Maxine was speechless.

Randy walked toward Tillie and caressed her shoulders. "What do you mean by 'us'?"

Tillie yanked away from him and yelled, "Yes, Randy, I'm going to have your baby!"

"It's not mine," Randy retorted.

"Just like a no good motherfucker!" Maxine shouted.

"We never used a condom," Tillie cried.

"You said you couldn't get pregnant," Randy snapped.

"I never said that!"

"Yes you did. It's not mine. I know I wasn't the only one you were fucking."

Tillie stood still. A terrifying realization overcame her. Randy was no different from the rest of the dogs, who lifted its leg and pissed where they lay.

"For the last three months, every single night, you and only you were in my bed. Not another soul." She quickly turned around and pointed her finger in his face and yelled, "You! You were the only one I fucked, you bastard!" Tillie gathered herself and faced Jamaica. "I am sorry you had to witness this. I hope Derek is a much better man than that sorry ass over there." She walked toward the door.

"Where are you going?" Maxine asked.

"It's too early for this shit," she said, as the door closed behind her.

Jamaica and Maxine looked at Randy.

"I'll take care of it," he said.

"Yes, you do that," Maxine ordered. "Go after her!"

Tillie heard Randy yelling her name from down the street. He was hot on her heels and angry as hell.

"Tillie! Tillie!"

She ignored him and picked up her pace.

"Tillie, damn it!" His pace quickened, then he started jogging. "Tillie!"

Tillie jogged up the hill, turned the corner and ducked into the alley. She watched Randy run past the alley.

She relaxed her body and walked toward the opening of the alley. As she turned the corner, Randy stepped out in front of her.

She stumbled backward.

"I know you heard me calling you!" he said, spit splattering in her face.

She wiped his residue from her face. "Leave me alone, Randy!"

"Why didn't you tell me you were pregnant?"

Tears poured from her eyes and danced down her cheeks and around her nose.

He grabbed her by the arm and yanked her into him. He leaned in close. He seethed with mounting rage. "Get rid of it," he said between clinched teeth. "I don't care how you do it, but you'd better do it. This is one nigger you won't trap."

"No," she said with a slight smile of defiance. "I'm not killing *our* baby." She yanked from his grasp and pushed by him. Looking over her shoulder, she smirked, rubbed her belly and spewed, "You're going to be a father, whether you like it or not," and walked away.

"Tillie!"

"Go to hell, Randy!"

# 9

He had no expectations. He wanted nothing. It was good to have someone in his life. He did not intend to fall in love. He'd been down that bumpy road before and liked living a drama-free life. He was forty-five years old and had enough serious relationships to last a lifetime. Besides, his business kept him away too much to nurture a relationship. Marriage was definitely not in his future. Having someone to keep the right side of his bed warm and wonderful conversation was all he needed.

Meanwhile, it had been two months and he was acting like those men who could no longer dress, without consulting their wives. Although he was adamant about not diving into a relationship, he found himself with constant thoughts of Jamaica. Even now, he could smell her scent and hear the softness of her laughter. He was missing her. He was in love. Damn!

October fifteenth was right around the corner and Jamaica would be celebrating her thirty-fifth birthday. He wanted to do something special for her. Something she would always remember.

Derek was never afforded the luxury of planning big parties on his own. He always delegated that responsibility to his sister, Gina. He wanted to plan something big for Jamaica and he knew Gina was the perfect person to plan it. She had grace and style, and just happened to be his personal assistant. Even though he had an office manager, Gina was the only one he trusted with his personal and sensitive business affairs.

From his home office, he leaned back in his chair and called out to Gina, who sat in a small cubicle outside of his office.

"Derek, why do you insist on yelling? I'm not across the street. I'm right outside of your door," she chuckled, but still irritated with having her name yelled at the top of his lungs.

"Yes, so you keep reminding me."

"What can I do for you?"

"Jamaica's birthday is on the fifteenth of October and I'd like to plan an intimate evening with her friends."

"Great, I'll finally get to meet this woman who has your attention," Gina said, straightening the papers on his desk.

"No, she doesn't have my attention. She's only a friend and…"

"Tell that to someone who doesn't know you from a bowl of grits, Derek."

Derek laughed and shook his head. "That's why I wouldn't trade you for anything in the world. I would be lost without that sassy mouth of yours."

"This much I know. Now," she said, taking the seat in front of his desk, "give me something to write on."

He raised his brow.

She sighed and said, "Be right back," and returned with a ruled Steno pad and her favorite purple ballpoint pen. "Okay, date and time?"

"October fifteenth at eight o'clock."

"Who would you like to cater the dinner?"

"B. Smith, in person."

"Get real. B. Smith's restaurant it is. Would you rather have it there or here?"

"Here, with a quartet of some kind."

"Oh my, you're going all out for this 'friend'," she teased.

Derek cleared his throat. "As I was saying, I'd like for it to be intimate, with only a few people. She has a small circle of friends, so that should do it."

"I'll need the guest list so I can mail out the invites. Oh, and for the record, you're only giving me a few weeks to plan this shindig. We are practically in the middle of September."

"I know, but I know that you, better than anyone, can pull it off."

"Flattery will get you everywhere," she smiled. "Okay, not to worry. I'll handle it."

"I appreciate you for this," he said.

"Yes, I know you do. By the way, I'll need her home and work address."

"Why?"

"Well, Mr. Big Spender, if you're going to do it up, you might as well do it up right. The week of her birthday, I'll send flowers each day."

"You're in the wrong business," he smiled.

"Yes, I tell myself that every morning I have to get up and sit outside of your office." She looked at her watch. "It's a quarter to five. Mind if I leave early?"

He shook his head no. "See you tomorrow and thank you."

"Anytime."

"Hey," he said as she reached the hallway. "I love you, little sister."

"Yes, I know. Ditto, big brother."

# *10*

Ever since her unexpected divorce three years ago, Maxine had been living in a glass bubble. Not like John Travolta and *The Boy in the Plastic Bubble*. This bubble wasn't visible to anyone else except Maxine. She never ventured outside the circumference of that bubble. She never let anyone in either. Her friends knocked. She could see them, but she couldn't let them in, no matter how much she loved them. They were human and were capable of hurting. She didn't want to be hurt ever again.

Long ago, she'd come to the realization that if she was going to keep men at a three-thousand-mile distance, then she might as well learn how to date herself. She ventured to the movies, which was easy. Many people go to movies alone. However, she didn't know too many women who ventured to bars, clubs, concerts, plays and restaurants alone. Eventually, she got used to it and had no problems keeping her Saturday night date with herself at her favorite watering hole, Martini's.

When Maxine saw the brown envelope in the mailbox, her heart sank. She could see the postmark. She knew whom it was from — her friend, Frank, whom she'd formed a bond with over the Internet. It was the only relationship where she felt comfortable. He was miles away in Germany and there was no possibility of her becoming attached. At least, that's what she thought. After several years of communicating and occasional long-distance phone calls, she felt herself slipping into the abyss of love. Then, one day, the communication stopped. No e-mails, phone calls, signals, snail mail, nothing.

Reluctantly, she tore open the envelope, unfolded the pages and lifted them to her nose. She inhaled the masculine aroma. She sat down on the stoop and her lips moved as she read the letter.

*Dear Maxine,*

*How are you? It's been a long time. I'm sorry I have not been able to call you or even get online. It has been quite hectic here. Where is here? Well, I can't tell you. Unfortunately, in my line of work, I hardly know where I am. However, I am safe.*

*I've been thinking of you, wanting to hear your voice. I miss you. I miss our conversations.*

*I'll be coming home for the Holidays and I wanted to stop through DC for a few days to spend with you. I hope that would be all right.*

*I'll try to call you as soon as I can. Right now, there is no phone where I am...please don't stop sending me e-mails. I'm not able to read e-mails every day, but I have been receiving them. They make life here so much easier.*

*Well, until next time, be good.*
*Love,*
*Frank*

The letter fell into her lap. "He's alive," she whispered. A lonely tear splattered onto the letter, slightly smudging the ink.

After the demise of her marriage, Maxine suffered a serious bout with depression. Taking leave from her job, she ate, slept, drank and smoked herself into an ugly stupor, gaining a whopping fifty pounds. Locking herself in her room for days, surrounded by piles of trash and not bathing until the funk kicked her butt, she decided to check her e-mail. That was when she ventured into the Black Voices chat room.

The chatting addiction was instant. Before she knew it, she was chatting daily. Then she received an instant message from someone who went by the ID, Bad4Ya. She was instantly pulled out of her slump and allowed her to feel whole again. The online chats with Frank, Bad4Ya's real name, turned into a fulfilling relationship, lasting several years. It was a regular dose of daily e-mails, sporadic phone calls, and hopes and dreams of one day meeting.

Her dream of meeting her online lover was nearing. Her excitement grew as she made plans for their meet. Then she received the devastation of her life.

*December 22, 2004*

*Dear Maxine,*

*You don't know me, but I know a lot about you. My name is Patsy and Frank is my brother. I don't know how to say this, so I'll come right out with it. Please forgive my bluntness, but I'm failing at finding a more subtle way to tell you.*

*Several months ago, Frank was diagnosed with cancer. I had no clue nor did anyone else in our family. Frank is a very private person. It doesn't surprise us he would keep this kind of news to himself, thinking he could beat this thing.*

*Last week, I received a call that my brother was in the hospital, with only three months to live. Of course, I rushed to his side, mad as hell at him for not telling us and living with this secret.*

*I asked him if I should tell you and he said no. He said he didn't want you to know. That he doesn't want you to worry about him. I knew he loves you. He keeps harmful things from those he loves. I am going against my brother's wishes. I found your e-mail address taped to the monitor. Maxine, you should know what is going on with Frank. Of course, I will tell him about my e-mail to you. He's not going to like it, but at the same time I believe he will be relieved that you know.*

*I'll be in touch with you and keep you updated as to his health. Please know you will always be considered part of the family.*

*Take care,*
*Patsy*

That was the last she had heard of Frank, until now. Maxine brushed away her tears and tossed the letter to the side. "Fuck him," she mumbled, as she gazed out of the window. It had been one long year without a word from Frank. She wasn't thinking about him. She could care less if he came for a visit, so long as he didn't visit her. It was half-past nine and she needed to get ready. She couldn't be late for her date. Time is money and she had more time than money.

# 11

The hooker knocked on the door twice, fast and rapid, just as she was instructed. Without hesitancy, the door opened quickly, showing a room as faded and worn as the rest of the hotel.

She paused, looked around the room and thought, *What a dump.* "You couldn't have found a better hotel than this?" she said, looking at the tattered, spotted chair, a throwback from the mid-seventies. She turned to the bed. "This doesn't look clean at all."

Walking slowly inside the room, her hips swaying, she noted the sour yellow curtains heavy and closed, thick and stained by too many years of not being cleaned; a chipped and marred press-board dresser; a chipped gold-flake lamp; and a heavy, dark television set with stains from too many burned candles. She turned up her nose at the lingering smell of mold and mildew.

He stood behind the door, quiet as a piece of furniture. "You're not living here, so what's the big fucking deal?" He swung the door shut just as quickly as he'd opened it.

She jerked around to face him. She looked at his face. He was tall, broad shoulders, evenly distributed muscles under a fitted body shirt and blue jeans. Laced up Air Jordan's covered his huge feet. This might be worth her while. She wondered if the myth about men with big feet having big dicks were true.

"The big fucking deal is that I deserve better than this shit," she said, popping the gum she stuck in her mouth before her car pulled into the Drake Motel.

"You're a whore. You deserve what you get paid and that's about it." His words were stern and without sympathy.

A smile graced her lips as she thought about bashing him upside his big ass head with the lamp. She tossed her purse on the chair and broadly looked him up and down. "So, you're the guy looking for company."

He snatched her purse and flipped it upside down, his eyes never leaving hers.

"Hey, what are you doing? All you had to do was ask and I would've shown you what was in it."

He pushed the rattail comb to the side as the tube of lipstick rolled off the bed and onto the floor. "You're a dirty whore," he said, still glaring into her eyes.

Her body stiffened. Her weight shifted as she tugged at her short, satin skirt. She started toward the door.

"Where are you going," he said, grabbing her by the elbow.

"I don't want any trouble," she said, her voice trembling.

"Am I scaring you?"

She nodded wooden like, as though her neck was thick. Her fear was increasing, but she knew she needed to relax. "I don't quite understand."

"I won't hurt you. Don't leave."

She relaxed her shoulders and took a deep breath.

"What's your name?" he asked, wrapping his thin lips around a Marlboro cigarette.

She sat quietly on the bed, looking around for objects she could use to end his life if this encounter got out of hand. "Maxine," she whispered.

"How long have you been trickin'?"

She folded her arms across her chest. "Not very long."

He sat down beside her and slightly stroked her thigh.

She stiffened at his touch.

"You seem like you're an intelligent woman. You running low on cash or something?"

"I ain't here to tell you my business." She rose in one fluid motion. "I have to go."

"Take off your clothes," he demanded. "Then tell me why you're doing this."

She didn't budge. Instead, she pondered his question. Why was she there? She had a job, stocks, an IRA, a retirement fund and her rent was paid up for the next six months.

"No particular reason," she said. "I like sex."

He reached inside his pocket and pulled out crumpled up bills. "For your honesty," he said, tossing the crumpled up bills to the floor.

She slowly reached around to the back of her skirt and lowered her zipper.

"Dance for me," he said, smiling at her, exposing a rotted front tooth.

She turned her back to him. If she looked at that rotted tooth again, she was going to throw up. She reluctantly swayed her hips.

As she closed her eyes and slipped her fitted top over her head, she became aware of another kind of excitement—dancing. She imagined pulling up on a pole and wrapping her legs around it, twirling down to the floor.

A clammy paw, groping at her thigh interrupted her dream.

"Max, is it true what they say about black women?"

Maxine faced the low life and retorted, "Is it true what they say about white men?"

He chuckled and stood to his feet. "Not all of us have little dicks," he said as he unzipped his pants and pulled them, along with his boxers, down around his knees.

"Yes, it's true. All black women have the golden pussy."

He grabbed her around the waist and pulled him into her, his cigarette dangled from his pasty lips.

Maxine pushed away from him and stripped down to her thong. She wanted to get it over with, so she laid down on the bed and raised her legs up, the heels of her feet rested on the edge.

"Damn it, little mama, you don't waste any time."

"I have things to do and since you have emptied out my purse, fished through my things, find the condom and put it on."

He knelt down before her gapped open legs and peered at her thick thighs and fleshy mound.

Maxine looked down between her legs, rolled her eyes up toward the ceiling and plopped her head back onto the seedy mattress. *Crazy motherfucker*, she said to herself when she felt his dirty fingers pulling her thong to the side. She slightly cringed.

"I've never seen a black pussy before," he admitted, glaring into the unfamiliar orifice. "Wow, I don't know why I expected the lips to be pink. I thought all pussies had pink lips. Why are yours so black?"

Maxine sighed heavily and lowered her legs to the floor, pulling herself upright. Face to face to the freak, she held her breath. She didn't want to inhale the hot bacteria that escaped from his mouth or come too close to his sore-infected lips she didn't see when she first entered the room.

"Oh, hell no," she said in a huff, pushing him to the side and rising to her feet. "I'm not fuckin' you. Not during this lifetime."

"I ain't paying you if you don't."

"Keep your money," she said slipping into her clothes. She reached for her purse, sweeping up her loose belongings.

"Go see a dentist, buy some soap and wash your nasty ass before you even think about fucking a black woman. Even then, you probably won't get fucked," she said as the door slammed behind her.

Maxine took off running down the hall toward the stairs. Nothing was going to hinder her from getting the fuck out of that seedy ass place, not even waiting on the elevator. Her descent from the fifth floor to the lobby took all of a minute, as she skipped steps and slid down railings from one level to the next, practically shredding her pantyhose, and enduring metal splints poking her in the ass.

She dashed through the lobby, out the door and picked up speed, sprinting towards her car. She did not know if the freak was on her heels or not. She never looked back.

"Fuck this shit," she said, as she jumped inside the car, out of breath, panting and heaving so hard, her breast touched her chin with each inhale.

What in the hell possessed her to want to try prostitution? Her bank account may not have been bursting at the seams, but she could eat out every night of the week, if she chose to do so. She was determined to experience everything life had to offer, no matter how ridiculous. Put a checkmark beside prostitution. Pole dancing in a topless bar is next. It appeared to be less life threatening.

As Maxine's Mazda Miata sped North on Route 301, toward Pennsylvania Avenue, Nelly's *Hot In Herre*, alerted her to answer her cell phone. She pressed the speaker button. "What's up, Randy?"

"How did you know it was me?"

She looked down at the phone, frowned and shouted, "Caller ID, you jackass. What do you want?"

"Tillie is trippin'."

"What else is new?"

"I tried calling Jamaica, but she ain't answering the phone."

"She's probably got her ass tooted up in the air," Maxine replied with envy.

"Ugly is so hideous on you, Max."

"Whatever, Randy, where are you?"

"Home."

"Doing what?"

"Nothing, just chillin'. I'd like to see Tillie tonight, but she's trippin', man, and I don't feel like being nagged tonight."

"You've yet to tell me exactly what she's tripping about."

"I'm not ready to be a father, Max."

"You should've thought about that before you fucked her."

"Uh huh, okay, I'll check you later. I'm not in the mood for your shit, either."

"Okay, okay…sorry. What do you have to sip on over there? I could use a drink right about now."

"You know my bar is always stocked."

"Cool. I'll see you in fifteen minutes."

"Right. I'll unlock the door. Just come on in. I'll be in the basement."

"You got any smoke?"

"Don't I always?"

"Peace, baby," she said, ending the call.

Maxine increased the volume on *Best of My Love*, by The Emotions. Then she reached inside the glove compartment and pulled out a pack of Newport cigarettes she had hidden away for two weeks. She had been trying to quit smoking for six months and so far, so good, until she needed to take the edge off. However, it was either keep a stale pack in her glove compartment to take the edge off or eat herself to a size twenty.

# 12

The three-level, refurbished row house sat on Capitol Hill, nestled on a quiet side street. Maxine stood in the small foyer of Randy's refurbished row house on Capitol Hill and observed the impeccable living space. In her estimate, it was quite unusual for a bachelor. She was not a regular visitor of Randy's to know that his place was always spotless – you could eat off the floor, but who really does that?

"Anal ass," she mumbled, walking toward the door leading to the basement. "Randy," she yelled. "Why don't you dirty this place up some time," she chuckled.

"What's up, girl?" he yelled up the stairs. When she descended to the basement, he continued. "You know I can't stand a lot of clutter."

"I see you've been busy since I was last here. I love the hardwood floors."

"Thanks. Rest your coat. What're you drinking?"

"Rum and Coke." Maxine pulled off her wrap and tossed it on the leather sofa.

Randy was filling the glass with ice when his mouth flew open at the sight of Maxine's attire.

Maxine saw his shock and said, "Don't even ask."

"Why are you dressed up like a two-bit hooker?"

"I said don't ask," she huffed, sitting on the sofa with her legs gapped open.

Randy chuckled and shook his head. "You never seem to amaze me with the crazy shit you do, Max."

Maxine nodded and kicked off her shoes. "You wouldn't believe me if I told you."

"Try me," he said, handing her the Rum and Coke, and then sitting beside her.

"Okay, but promise you won't laugh. You have to promise you will NOT tell Jamaica or Tillie. I surely wouldn't hear the end of it from those two."

"I'll try my best not to tell it," he chuckled.

"Randy, promise me!"

"Max, whatever it is, it can't be all that bad."

She raised her head up and squared her shoulders. "I had a trick tonight."

Randy fell into a hearty laugh.

She continued. "Trust me, it's funny now, but it sure as hell wasn't funny an hour ago."

"You're right. I don't want to know," he laughed, bending over, his chin touching his knee.

"It's not that funny, Randy. I could've been killed or something," she pouted, not liking him laughing at her, making her feel more like a stupid ass fool.

"Seriously though, Max, if you are in a financial bind, you should've said something? You know we've got your back."

"That's just it," she lowered her head. "I have more than enough money."

He leaned back on the sofa and crossed his leg over his thigh. "Then I don't understand why you would degrade yourself"

She took a gulp of her drink. "I received a letter from Frank today."

Randy tilted his head to the side.

"You know," she continued. "Remember the guy I was communicating with over the Internet for over a year?"

Randy twisted up his mouth and then poked out his bottom lip. "I don't think you ever told me about him. You know you never share things with me as you do Jamaica and Tillie. That *girlie* stuff."

She smiled and slightly shoved him on the thigh. "I'm sorry. We don't want you to feel left out."

"Nope, it's cool. Sometimes, I prefer to be *left out*," he chuckled. "What about this guy?"

"I received communication from a relative that he was dying…cancer."

"I'm sorry to hear that, Max," he consoled, resting his hand on her thigh.

"It's cool, Randy. I mean, after I didn't hear anything for a while, I thought he was dead. At least, that is what I told myself in order to deal with my loss, if you will."

Randy nodded in agreement. "So, you heard from him today. That must've made you happy to now know that he's not dead."

"Yeah, I suppose I should be happy, but I don't know how to feel, to be honest."

"Okay, so you still haven't told me how you ended up as a street walker."

"Not a street walker, Randy."

"All the same."

"Because of Frank, I realized I wanted to experience all that I could in life, before my time comes. Randy, before I die, I want to be happy in knowing that I've done all the things I have ever wanted to do. You know what I mean?"

"Yeah, well, tomorrow isn't promised, that's for sure."

"Exactly!" She stared ahead. "That is why I am here."

Randy looked puzzled.

"I just hope she'll be able to forgive me," she said, taking her drink to the back of her throat, emptying her glass.

"Who? What are you talking about?"

She faced him and leaned into his face. She could smell the brandy on his breath. "I've always wanted to be with you."

Randy leaned back. "Hold up, Maxine."

"I'm here. No one has to know, Randy. Do it for me. I want to know how you would feel inside of me."

"No, Maxine," he said sternly. He shook his head from side to side. "It ain't happening here, baby."

She stood up and undressed before him. She propped her hands on her hips. "Okay, so you are telling me, right here and right now that you don't want to taste this pussy? You're telling me that you don't want to fuck me?"

"That is exactly what I'm saying. Put your clothes on and we'll forget all about this…this…your temporary loss of sanity."

She chuckled loudly. "Bullshit! Your dick is hard now. I can see it." She turned around and bent over. With her fingers, she spread her ass cheeks apart and wiggled her ass in his face. "Taste me," she said. For some reason, Maxine had a fetish with bending over and having people kiss or taste her ass.

Randy smacked her on the ass, as hard as he could. Maxine jumped forward, losing her balance. "Get your clothes on and get the fuck out. Some kind of friend you are. Your girl is about to have my baby…yeah; you are dressed for the occasion. You fucking whore." Randy was seething mad. He stood to his feet, coming eye level with her. "Goodbye, Maxine. You can show yourself out."

As he walked away, Maxine ran behind him and pushed him against the wall, his face pressed against the cedar paneling. She grabbed his wrists and plastered his hands against the wall. Her hot breath warmed his ear. "Fuck me, Randy. Fuck me now and I'll never, ever bother you again."

"No," he said between clinched teeth. "I don't want to hurt you, Maxine. Get your hands off of me."

"What are you going to do, beat me up?"

His breathing was heavy and his voice began cracking. "I don't hurt women."

She kissed and gently bit his neck. "Fuck me, Randy."

Randy broke free of her grasp and shoved her toward the steps. "You need help, Maxine." He grabbed her things and tossed them at her. "I won't tell Tillie how her *best friend* tried to fuck her man."

Maxine's mouth flew open. What was she doing? Deep inside, Maxine was torn. She couldn't believe what she had done. What had gotten into her? Tiny rivers streamed down her face. "I'm sorry, Randy. I...I don't know what got into me. Don't hate me."

He placed his hands on his hips, stuck out his left leg and turned his face away from her. "Get some help, Maxine."

# *13*

With one hand placed firmly on the curve of her neck, he pinned her down to his mattress. Her heart raced in the connection where skin met skin and she knew if he pressed any harder against her throat, she would not be able to breathe.

"You like it, don't you?" he whispered, his hot breath on her face and charcoal eyes focused intently on her face. She couldn't have answered if she tried, her voice silenced by the placement of his steady palm. Her body trembled as a rush of pleasure slid through her. Without words, she told him everything he needed to know. The sweet scent of her arousal surrendered her, and she sighed and bucked her hips forward, wanting him inside her.

"You like being had?" he asked, pressing harder against her throat.

She mouthed, "Yes," as she continued bucking against him.

The bedroom door flung open and the faceless being stood naked, his flaccidity called out to her.

The pressure on her neck stifled her. "Help me," she mouthed.

Jamaica shot up in the bed, her heart raced as sweat poured over her body. She looked around, with her hand tightly affixed to her throat. Her body trembled. She'd just had the worst dream of her life. However, it wasn't the first time she'd had this dream. What did it mean?

At one o'clock, the phone rang. When she answered it, there was silence, followed by static, which really spooked her. She hung up the phone. It rang again. She waited until the third ring to pick up. She was on a speaker phone, but didn't' recognize the voice.

"Hello? Jamaica?"

Speaking," she answered. Her voice was raspy.

The caller hesitated.

"Hello, gorgeous."

Jamaica was still uneasy from her dream, struggling to respond. "Who is this?"

"Do I sound that bad," the voice chuckled.

Jamaica turned on the lamp on the nightstand next to her bed. "Could you take me off speaker, please?" She could hear as the handset was picked up.

"Woman, it's Derek."

"Hey, you." She felt a sigh of relief. "What're you doing up?"

"I couldn't sleep."

"Oh. Well, I was sleeping pretty good," she lied.

"I didn't get to see you today."

"I'm sorry, Derek. I had so much running around to do."

"You can make it up to me."

"Okay," she said, leaning back against the headboard.

"Do you want to catch a movie?"

"At one in the morning?"

"Yep, at one in the morning."

"Honey, you want to tell me what movie theater is open at one in the morning?"

"Yep, your place. I'll bring the movie and the wine and you pop the corn."

"Derek, I have to work in the morning."

"Call in sick."

"I can't do that. I don't have the leave. If I call in, I won't get paid."

"I'll pay you for the day."

"Derek, don't be silly."

"Baby, haven't you ever just wanted to do something silly, without putting any thought to it at all?"

"Of course, but I have bills to pay."

"I'll pay your bills. Now, no more excuses. Go brush your teeth, I can smell your hot breath through the phone," he teased.

Jamaica laughed. "Go to hell, damn it."

"We'd have a lot of fun if we went together," he laughed. "So, do we have a date?"

Jamaica bit down on her bottom lip. It was the end of the company's fiscal year and reports needed to be ran. She hesitated before responding, "What the hell? Come on over. Don't forget your checkbook."

By two-thirty, Derek appeared with a bottle of wine, a couple of steak and cheese subs from Eddie Leonard's and her favorite movie, *Sparkle*.

Impressed at his listening skills and his ability to be very attentive, Jamaica kissed him on the cheek and emptied his arms.

"I chilled a couple of glasses in the freezer," she said.

"I figured you might be hungry."

"You figured right," she yelled from the kitchen. "Make yourself comfy and put the movie in. The DVD player is in the unit under the television."

Derek accepted the invite and slipped out of his shoes.

Entering the living room, Jamaica handed him a chilled glass of Riesling. "What's on your mind?" she asked, heading back to the kitchen for the subs.

He watched her hips sway from side to side.

"What makes you think something's on my mind?"

"You couldn't sleep. There must be something on your mind."

"You were on my mind. I wanted to see you."

She placed the plate of subs on the coffee table. She moved beside him, sat down and stretched her legs under the coffee table. Her toes touched his toes.

"You know all of the right things to say," she smiled. "You really know how to pile it on."

He grabbed her around her shoulders and pulled her into him. He blew in her ear.

She laughed. "That tickles." She shooed him away with her hand. "Cut that out." She used the remote to turn on the DVD.

"I want to make a toast," he announced.

"Again?" she chuckled.

They raised their glasses.

"To us!" he toasted.

She frowned. "That was original," she said sarcastically.

He turned up his lips and rolled his eyes up toward the ceiling, as if in contemplation. "You're right. Okay, how's this?" He cleared his throat. "To the best pussy I've ever had!"

Jamaica fell over with laughter. "Here, here!"

*Precious Lord* came from the opening scene of *Sparkle*.

Jamaica closed her eyes and mouthed the words to her favorite gospel hymn. She found herself swaying from side to side and clapping, eventually belting out *Precious Lord*, then going into a loud hum because she didn't know the rest of the lyrics.

Derek looked at her and asked, "Where do you see yourself in five years?"

Still clapping, she looked at him. "That's a good question."

"Do you have any goals?" he asked.

"Yes, I do."

"What are they?"

The corners of her mouth turned up. What a fine time to start asking questions about her future.

"I want to be a writer," she said, to shut him up. She wanted to watch the movie.

"What's stopping you?"

"Man, will you hush so we can watch the movie?"

"Alright," he said, burying his face in her neck. "But we will finish this conversation later."

She giggled, he smiled, and their tongues danced and frolicked, missing the first thirty minutes of the movie.

# 14

The morning after, legs intertwined as Derek stroked quickly and deeply into Jamaica. Sweat poured down his face and onto her heaving chest. Her erect nipples yearned to be tasted.

"Ohhhhh," she moaned, with each long, deep stroke. "Take your pussy, baby," she said.

"It's mine, baby?" he whispered into her ear.

She nodded and then said, "Yes, Daddy."

"Daddy's about to work that ass," he said. "Um huh, yeah," he groaned.

The phone rang.

"Shit!"

"Let it ring, baby," she pleaded.

Derek ignored the phone and continued stroking his woman. When the phone stopped ringing, he said, "Turn over."

She turned over and pushed herself up on her hands and knees.

Derek fingered her pussy to ensure wetness before he drilled into her again.

The phone rang as he began insertion. "Shit!" He collapsed on her back.

Jamaica rolled from beneath him and reached for the phone. "Hello?"

"What're you doing? I'm downstairs," Maxine said.

"Give me a few minutes and come on up." She hung up the phone and rolled onto her back. She was immediately pissed off at Maxine when she looked down at his used to be hard as a rock dick. "Her timing is shit," she said.

"What? Who is it?" Derek was annoyed by the interruption.

"Maxine."

"How does she know you're home?"

"I don't know. She must've called the office."

"Forgive me if I'm not very hospitable," he said, pulling the covers over his shoulders.

"Don't be like that, baby. I'll get rid of her. She won't be here long."

She walked toward the door, slipping into her robe. She looked over her shoulder and said, "I'll miss you," and blew a kiss.

He hadn't been asleep for long before he was awakened by the noises. Jamaica and Maxine were in the kitchen. Derek heard them thumping around, opening cupboards and speaking in muffled voices. He looked at the clock and saw that an hour had past. So much for getting rid of her. He wondered for a moment if Jamaica had forgotten about him. Once out of bed, he slipped into the bathroom and turned on the shower.

Jamaica's ear perked up when she heard the shower running. Maxine looked puzzled.

"Girl, do you have company?" Maxine asked.

Jamaica brought her hand up to her mouth. "Oh, shit. I got so caught up in talking about Randy and Tillie, I forgot about Derek."

"What? Why didn't you tell me I was interrupting your flow, girl," Maxine said. "Girl, bring the radio man out here and let me see what's got your nose so wide open."

Jamaica shushed her and said, "I don't think it's a good time for you two to meet. He's probably a little miffed with me, since I forgot about him."

Maxine chuckled. "Girl, how can you forget about your man? Alright then, I'll meet him some other time." She grabbed her purse and headed for the door. "I'll call you later, chick."

"Okay. Love ya, girl."

"Love ya back!"

After Jamaica closed the door, she turned her back and leaned against the door, gently banging the back of her head against the door. "Damn, damn, damn," she mumbled. She walked toward the running water and entered the bathroom. "Hey, babe."

"Hey you! You forgot about me."

"I'm sorry, baby. I got so caught up with talking about the Randy and Tillie situation, time got away from me."

"Randy and Tillie?"

"Yes, my two friends. Remember, I told you about them."

"Oh, yeah," he said, lathering Dove all over his body. "What's going on with them?"

"Well, it appears that Randy and Tillie have hooked up."

"That's a good thing, right?"

"No, not a good thing. She's pregnant."

She could hear the shower turning off. She reached for the towel and held it up in front of her.

"Damn. So what are they going to do?"

"Don't know," she said, handing him the towel as he stepped out of the shower. "That is what me and Maxine were talking about. We haven't heard anything from them since Tillie announced the new arrival."

"I'm sure things will work out for them," he said, wiping water from his chest, abdomen and between his legs. What a man. Derek worked out five times a week and it showed. He was cut in all the right places. "So, you're going to make it up to me, right?"

"What are you talking about?"

"You forgot about me. You have to make it up to me."

Jamaica smiled and refused to complain about having to do make-up sex.

He wrapped the towel around his waist. "I want to try something and see if I can make you come."

"You haven't had any problems with making me come so far," she confirmed.

Derek told her to slip out of her robe and squat down to the floor. He made it clear that under no circumstances should she touch herself. He wanted to do all of the work. He lubricated two of his fingers with the Vaseline that sat in the caddy over the top of the commode. He squatted down next to her, held her around her shoulders to brace her, and inserted the two lubricated fingers into her rectum. He wiggled them vigorously, pushing hard against her perineum, rubbing the wall of muscle with all of his strength.

"Oh, God," she squealed in sheer ecstasy. Clutching his arm tightly, a stream of urine suddenly squirted from her, forming a puddle on the bathroom floor.

"Let it go, baby. We can clean this up later. Bear down on me."

She did as she was told, pushing down around his fingers, never dreaming she could be launched into orgasm like a rocket without clitoral stimulation. Her thighs shook as she squatted and bore down. She pushed down so hard, she felt like she was pushing out a baby. More fluids gushed out of her. Her body was overwhelmed with waves of pleasure as his fingers rubbed more vigorously against the pressure of her now frantically contracting sphincter.

"*Ooh, shit!*" she exclaimed. She felt herself hyperventilating and convulsing like a crazed nut.

Derek was still holding her, smiling. "Did you come?" he asked, laughing and extremely pleased with himself at the successful completion of the maneuver he had learned from watching dirty movies.

She was unable to form words. She slightly shook her head, then collapsed to the floor.

# 15

After dinner, they had a glass of wine. Tillie appeared on the karaoke floor of Whispers Lounge and managed to raise the volume as she belted out *Nobody's Supposed To Be Here*, by Deborah Cox, followed by an ugly imitation of Patti LaBelle, with her arms flailing in the air, and head and neck bobbing back and forth like a chicken, trying to sing, "*You Are My Friend*."

"This is embarrassing," said Randy as he waved for the server.

"Who in the hell told her she could sing?" Maxine chuckled.

"Leave her alone," Jamaica said. "Let her have a good time. She's not hurting anyone…"

"Just our ears," Randy interjected. "Tillie is always singing. I'm telling you, she thinks her ass is Mary J. Blige or somebody."

"She sounds like a cat in heat. Whose idea was this karaoke shit anyway?" Maxine said, stirring her drink.

"The karaoke wasn't my idea, but having dinner tonight was. I miss hanging out with you guys on Friday," said Jamaica.

"Tell that brother you have other people in your life you have to tend to," Randy teased.

"Oh, yeah, speaking of brother, I received an invite…"

Randy interrupted Maxine, his voice intentionally loud. "Jamaica, what else has been going on with you? You and I don't talk as much like we used to."

Jamaica shot Maxine a quizzical look and was about to respond to Randy when Tillie interrupted with an announcement.

"Thank you! This next song I'd like to dedicate to my man." Tillie pointed towards Randy. "I love you, baby. You are my world—and my baby daddy."

Randy cleared his throat. He felt himself getting choked up. He smiled and blew her a kiss.

"This one is for you, baby," Tillie said, then motioned for the music. She cleared her throat and tossed her head back. Tillie belted out from deep within, *You Are My Sunshine.*

Maxine yelled, "Damn," and fell out with laughter.

Jamaica tried to suppress her desire to join Maxine, but to no avail, she fell out with laughter.

Randy kept his focus on Tillie and maintained his composure, although Maxine and Jamaica were making it awfully hard for him. "Chill out, y'all," he reprimanded. "Cut that shit out before you hurt her feelings."

Maxine was in tears. "I'm trying," she gasped, "but damn," she continued laughing out loud.

"Max, you are trifling!" he said between clenched teeth.

Maxine's laughter quickly turned to anger. "Excuse me?"

"Alright now," Jamaica interrupted. "Let's chill."

"Fuck her," Randy retorted. "I don't know why she's sitting here acting as though any of us are her friends."

"Randy, come on now," Jamaica said.

"Fuck me?" Maxine said.

"Yeah, sounds familiar, doesn't it?" he shot back.

"No, not fuck me, Randy. Fuck you!"

"You already tried, you bitch!"

"Whoa! What in the hell is going on?" asked Jamaica.

Randy turned his attention to the stage, zoning in on Tillie. She looked so beautiful to him.

"Nothing's going on," Maxine said, turning her back to them.

Jamaica looked at Randy and placed her hand on his forearm. She leaned in and whispered, "She tried to get with you, didn't she?"

Randy nodded and sipped his drink.

Jamaica leaned back in her chair, folded her arms across her chest and peered at Maxine.

Maxine felt Jamaica's gaze burning the back of her neck. She turned around and rolled her eyes. "What?"

"That's fucked up, Max. I sure hope Tillie doesn't find out."

"She won't find out," Randy said. "It would really hurt her."

"Right," Maxine said. "We don't want to cause any stress to her or the baby."

"Like you really give a fuck, Max," Randy chuckled. "You're such the actor."

"Listen, Randy, I don't know what came over me. I…well I needed someone. I felt lonely."

"You had your john, you didn't need me."

"Your what?" Jamaica said. "What john?"

"Nothing," said Maxine.

"She came to my house dressed as a trick," Randy laughed.

Maxine rolled her eyes at Randy.

"Maxine, you were…okay, you know, I don't want to know. Girl, I don't know what's gotten into you."

"Yeah, well, you better watch your man, Jamaica," Randy said, standing to his feet. "You were doing your thing, baby," he said, extending his hand to Tillie.

Maxine shot a concerned look at Jamaica.

Jamaica shook her head and turned to Tillie. "Yes, baby girl, you were awesome."

"Really?" Tillie beamed and took her seat beside Randy. She could feel the tension at the table. "Did I miss something?"

Randy leaned in and kissed her on the cheek. "No, baby, but I sure did miss you."

Maxine forced a smile and Jamaica sipped her drink.

# *16*

Driving through the city, Jamaica had imagined Derek would have a surprise waiting for her, considering the five dozen pink roses, one dozen a day, that took over her office. It was her birthday week, but she wasn't prepared for what she was about to encounter. Derek's Mercedes shined in the driveway. She pulled up behind it. She got out of the car and smoothed the palm of her hands over the fitted black dress, hugging every curve. She inhaled and patted her belly. Her birthday gift to herself would be to join a Yoga class, or any class, that would shrink that ungodly bulge. Looking up at the night's sky, she counted the stars to give her more time. She felt nervous about tonight. She couldn't understand why Derek insisted she dress in evening attire for an evening at home with movies, popcorn and conversation. She closed her car door and started toward the front door.

An instant after she rang the doorbell, as if he'd been waiting behind the door, there was Derek, smiling so broadly; she could see his back molars. His baldhead glistened under the moonlight. He glared at her for what seemed like forever before stepping to the side and allowing her entry.

"I'm sorry I'm a little late," she said, looking around the dark house, illuminated by candles. Jasmine and vanilla scents wafted through the house, providing an intimate, calming effect that had heightened her senses. She had gotten horny that fast. Must she always think about fucking him every time she sees him?

"You're not late, baby." He leaned down a bit and kissed her cheek. "You're on time."

She forced herself to look at him. The wetness between her legs was causing her thighs to stick together. "What's going on, Derek? What's with all the candles and stuff? Are you trying to make me fall in love with you?"

He chuckled and took her by the hand. He led her into the dining room. She gasped when she saw her best friends seated at the massive table decorated in purple and lavender, flanked by lilacs and lilies, her favorite flowers. The four-piece band played a familiar tune before the baritone voice crooned, *I was a lonely man with empty arms to fill.*

Derek escorted her to the middle of the floor and embraced her. They danced slowly, her eyes filled with tears. "Happy birthday," he whispered in her ear. "Are you surprised?"

"Yes," was all she could muster and her voice was faint. Her body trembled as he kissed her on the forehead.

"I'm glad," he said. "Gina really outdid herself."

"Gina?"

"My sister. I told her what I wanted and she went beyond my expectations."

Jamaica looked over his shoulder at her friends. "How did you contact the gang?"

He shrugged. "Don't know. It was all Gina's doing."

"I can't wait to thank her. This is…is…" she cried.

"Baby, don't cry. It's contagious," he sniffed. "Gina is in the kitchen, barking orders to the caterers."

Randy stood up and hovered over Tillie. He extended his hand. "May I have this dance?"

Tillie placed her hand in his and followed him to the dance floor. She smiled at Jamaica and fell into the arms of the man she loved very much. Moreover, she knew deep in her heart, he loved her, too.

Maxine felt like a third wheel. Her thoughts traveled to Frank. She wished he were here. She forced a smile at Jamaica and sipped her wine. She was envious as hell, but refused to be hurt again. Besides, she didn't need love, just an occasional fuck.

"Happy Birthday, girlfriend," said Maxine, followed by, "Your man is doing it up for you. He's definitely a keeper!"

Jamaica looked at Randy and Tillie. She was happy to see them.

She rushed over to Tillie and wrapped her arms around her neck. "Hey, baby girl, how are you?"

Tillie smiled and kissed her on the cheek. "I'm good," she said.

Randy grabbed Tillie by the hand and squeezed, as he smiled at her. "*We* are doing fine," he cosigned.

Jamaica wrapped an arm around Randy's neck and whispered in his ear. "I knew you would do the right thing." She kissed him on the cheek, and then looked toward Maxine. "Hey trick, what's going on? It's good to see you, too!"

"Oh, I can't complain. I was checking out your new boyfriend, thinking about making him my bottom bitch." They all fell out with laughter. Derek stood amazed at Maxine's comment. The message in his face – unmistakably a message – was not a very trusting one concerning Maxine. Although he didn't know what a Bottom Bitch was, he didn't like being referred to as anyone's bitch. However, this was Jamaica's night and he wasn't going to mess it up by putting Maxine out on her ass. Her comment was strike one against her.

"Nope, that's my Bottom Bitch, girl!" Jamaica exclaimed and now Derek was equally disgusted with her. It showed on his face. "Aww, baby, don't be like that. Being a bottom bitch makes you the big money maker and the king of my castle." Joy bubbled in her laugh and shone in her eyes.

Derek rolled his eyes and said, "Whatever." This was something he'd picked up from Jamaica from the first day they met.

Jamaica smiled and smacked him on the ass. He flinched, unsure he liked to be treated in such a manner in front of company. Definitely not the kind of behavior he displayed in front of people.

Being a man, Randy recognized Derek's irritation and decided to intercede. "Derek, man, I've been the bottom bitch for years," he laughed. "It only means they really like you, dog."

Derek smiled and nodded his head. He turned toward Jamaica and kissed her on the cheek. "Have I told you how exquisite you look this evening?" he said, taking her by the hand and twirling her into a circle.

Jamaica blushed. "Thank you. You're looking pretty dapper yourself."

"You do look stunning tonight, Jamaica," Tillie said, taking a sip of water. "Now I know why you've been glowing like a fly in shit." She held up her glass and looked around the massive living room.

Maxine chuckled, her eyes and smile fixated on Derek as his level of discomfort with her heightened. He cleared this throat and announced it was time for dinner.

Maxine raised her martini glass. "I'll have another."

"You've already had five of those, Max," Tillie chastised.

"Who made you the drink counter?" Max retorted.

"That's' quite all right," Derek said, sitting the pitcher of Martini in front of Maxine. "Enjoy yourselves. I have plenty of room for those who are too intoxicated to find their way home."

"I guess you'll have an overnight guest then," Tillie said smugly.

Maxine gave her the finger and rolled her eyes.

"Not tonight, guys," Jamaica said, taking her seat at the head of the table.

They feasted on lobster, fillet mignon, shrimp, crab, salmon and cheesecake topped with fresh strawberries and drizzled with sweet berry sauce. As the night ended, Maxine stumbled on her words, Tillie was annoyed, Randy was rubbing his belly and Jamaica was in a world where only Derek could enter. They sat on the sofa, in front of the blazing fireplace, intertwined in each other's arms.

"Babe, are you ready to go?" Randy asked, standing to his feet and stretching his arms above his head.

"Uh-huh," Tillie sighed in confirmation. "Come on, Maxine." Maxine shook her head and announced that she was too drunk to drive. "You rode with us, fool."

Randy extended his hand towards Derek. "Thanks for everything, man"

Jamaica watched Derek as he stood up from the sofa. He reached out and hauled her from where she sat. He grabbed Randy's hand tightly and covered the shake with the other hand. "Not a problem. Listen, we'll have to get together more often."

Jamaica slid her arm around Derek's waist. "Yes, we will. You all drive safe."

Maxine was in a drunken stupor. She stumbled over to the group and wrapped her arm around Jamaica. "Well, don't you look like the lady of the fucking house."

Jamaica leaned in and kissed her on the cheek. "I love you too, dear."

Derek and Jamaica stood in the door and watched as Tillie and Randy struggled to get Maxine's drunken ass inside the car. Jamaica waved as they backed out of the driveway.

"Nothing worse than a drunk ass woman," Jamaica said as the door closed behind them.

"She was having a good time," Derek said, pulling her from behind into a snug embrace. "Now it's time for us to have a good time." He kissed the curvature of her neck and guided her toward the bedroom. Excitement grew inside Jamaica. She'd been waiting for this moment.

Derek pulled a jogging suit from the drawer and tossed it at Jamaica.

"What's this for?"

"Put it on. It's kinda chilly out tonight."

"Yes, but I'm not sleeping outdoors."

"Just do it," he said, slipping out of his suit and into a similar jogging suit.

Reluctantly, she slipped into the clothing and looked down at her feet. "A sweat suit and high heels is not my style."

"Hmmm…that does pose a problem. Look in the closet, behind you." He was very nonchalant and somewhat smug. It began to irritate her. She had enough surprises and all she wanted to do now was snuggle up under her man and nothing else.

"For me?" she asked, pointing at the pair of petite Fila tennis shoes nestled among masculine, size thirteen shoes. "These are brand new!" she exclaimed, holding the shoes out before her. "How did you know my shoe size?"

"I have my sources. Now put them on and let's rock and roll."

An hour later, Jamaica woke as the Mercedes rounded the curb, coming to a complete stop. "Where are we?"

"Did you have a nice nap?"

"Uh-huh, where are we?"

He didn't respond. Instead, he popped open the trunk and got out of the car.

She looked around but couldn't see a thing but blackness. She jumped when Derek opened the passenger car door. "Where are we?"

"Do you always ask so many questions?"

She ignored him and got out of the car. Immediately, the high wind smacked her in the face and caused her to shiver. "It's cold."

Before he opened the car door, Derek had placed a blanket on the roof of the car. He wrapped it around her shoulders. "Is this better?" he asked. She nodded and he took her by the hand and led her into the darkness.

Jamaica had enjoyed all of the surprises for her birthday, but this was getting a little too crazy for her. Having someone else control her destiny and lead her into the unknown was a hard pill for her to swallow. She came to an abrupt halt.

"Derek, will you please tell me what is going on?"

"Do you trust me?" he asked, his back to her.

"Yes, I trust you, but…"

"Good. We only have a few more steps to go."

Jamaica squeezed his hand, turned up her senses and raised her guard. After a few more steps, she heard water, sounding like waves crashing against the shore. Derek led her to the slightly hardened rusty-colored sand. "We're at the beach?"

Derek was quiet and continued walking.

"You know, you're going to stop ignoring me, damn it."

"Stop your fussing and come on."

"What are we doing at the beach at three in the damn morning?"

"Celebrating your birthday and making all of your dreams come true," he chuckled.

"Uh-huh, my biggest dream is to be at Sandy Point in the middle of October, freezing my fucking ass off!"

Derek pulled a book of matches from his pocket, then laid out a blanket on the sand. "Have a seat and enjoy the view."

"Derek, where did this pile of wood come from?"

"You ask too many damn questions."

Jamaica sat on the blanket and gazed at the stars, then at the hundreds of headlights coming across the Chesapeake Bay Bridge. It was somewhat nice, definitely different.

"Baby, are we going to go to jail for being out here at three in the morning? State parks usually close at dusk and don't reopen until sunrise."

"I have connections," he said, striking the single match and tossing it into the pile of wood. Flames shot toward the sky causing Jamaica to fall backwards.

"Damn!" she yelled. "You trying to set my ass on fire."

"I guess he put too much lighter fluid on the wood."

"He? Who is he, Derek?"

Again, he ignored her and yelled, "We're ready," to no one in particular that Jamaica could see.

Before she could ask another question, a tall figure carrying some sort of box emerged from the darkness, startling her. She jumped to her feet.

"Relax, baby. This is my best friend, Walt. He's been my co-conspirator."

"Nice to meet you, Jamaica," Walt greeted. "I've heard a lot of wonderful things about you."

"Nice to meet you too, Walt," she smiled.

Walt sat the box in the sand and whispered in Derek's ear. "Thanks a lot, man. I owe you," Derek said.

"I hope to see you again, Jamaica." Walt waved and departed through the night.

"Let's have a drink," he said.

Jamaica sat down on the blanket and wrapped herself snugly in the blanket. "You are really something else."

"I hope that's a good thing." He popped the cork on the champagne, poured the flutes, and sat down beside her.

"So, how are you enjoying your birthday so far?"

"By far, it is the best birthday I've ever had. Thank you so much," she said, clinking her flute against his.

Derek sipped his champagne. "It's beautiful here. This is where I come to think."

"Yes, it's very peaceful, even with the traffic from the bridge."

Wrapping his arms around her shoulder, he thought of how much he enjoyed being with her. He wanted someone in his life that would bring him happiness. So far, Jamaica fit the bill. However, things seemed to be moving kind of fast and he still had unfinished business to tend to.

Jamaica rolled her pant legs up around her knees. "Let's walk toward the water."

Derek chuckled. "You're kidding, right?"

"You weren't kidding when you brought me out here," she replied, rolling his pant legs up around his knees as well.

"I'm sure the water is cold."

"No kidding, Sherlock," she said, grabbing him by the hand and dragging him toward the shore. White waves crashed against the shore as the moonlight danced around the calm bay.

"Wait! We have to take off our shoes," he yelled out to her.

Jamaica dipped her fingers in the water. "It's not too cold." She tasted her fingers. Then, she kicked off her shoes and said, "Doesn't taste too bad either."

"Ha! Now you're trippin'!"

Jamaica danced along the beach waving her arms in the air and singing *Mesmerized* by Faith Evans. She looked like a bird ready for take off. She bent down, scooped up a palm full of water and raised her hand to her mouth.

"Don't drink that," Derek yelled. "Are you nuts, woman?"

She ignored him, waited for the wave to crash against the shore again, then bent down and scooped up more water. She extended her closed hand toward him. "It's your turn," she sung.

He shook his head. "No thank you. Not thirsty."

"Oh come on. Don't be a party pooper."

He smiled and shook his head once again. "You could get sick from drinking that nasty ass water."

"Derek," she whined. "Come and get sick with me. Then we can lay up in the bed together and nurse each other back to good health."

Derek laughed aloud. For a few moments, he stared at her. She was radiant to him. Her beauty was natural. He pegged her to be a Dove girl.

Jamaica moved deeper into the water. From the corner of his eye, Derek could see an enormous wave headed toward the shore. He didn't panic. He knew it would die down before crashing against the shore, but he thought he'd warn her just the same.

The wave swirled around Jamaica, up and over her legs, wetting her pant legs. She gasped. The water was ice cold. Derek offered her his hand, but Jamaica sat her ass down on the wet sand and wiggled her toes deep into the sand.

"You are going to catch your death of cold, girl," he scolded.

Several small waves crashed against the shore before Jamaica lay down and immersed her body in the wet sand. Salty, ice cold water crashed against her. She looked like a fish out of water, flapping her fins.

"This is fun, Derek. Come on!"

"No, thanks."

"Baby, you don't know what you're missing," she laughed.

"Uh-huh, I do. I'm missing pneumonia and riding for an hour wet and cold."

Jamaica splashed at him and jumped to the side. "It's my birthday. Aren't you supposed to do what I want to do?"

"Within reason." He started back to the car.

"Where are you going?"

"To grab a blanket for you to dry off with. Had I'd known you wanted to be Mrs. Mark Spitz, I would've brought towels."

Jamaica sat up in the water and tried to see the bottom, but it was too dark. She sighed heavily, gazed up at the moon and then sprung to her feet when she felt something graze at her toes. She darted behind Derek. Her wet clothes clung to her body. It was dark and she wasn't taking any chances.

Derek could hear her fast on his heels. "What's wrong? You're about to freeze."

"No, I think I felt a shark or something!"

Derek laughed aloud.

"What's so damn funny?" she asked annoyed. "I could've been hurt. Are my toes bleeding?" She looked down and wiggled her toes.

"No, your toes aren't bleeding, but you could stand to visit a psychiatrist."

Jamaica snatched the blanket from his hand and spread it open. "Hold this for me, Funny Man."

Derek held the blanket up while Jamaica peeled out of her clothes. "I have a plastic bag you could put your clothes in."

"They may get mildewed."

"Oh, now you're concerned with your clothing?"

"Anyway," she tossed her wet panties in his face, "come wrap that blanket around me and warm me up."

Derek enveloped her inside the blanket and pulled her close into him. "Lady, you are something else."

Jamaica smiled and softly tasted his lips. His hands roamed over her face.

"Thank you for a wonderful evening," she cooed.

He smiled and whispered into her ear. "It's just beginning."

# *17*

Leslie huffed and blew air as her fingers danced across the keyboard. The air conditioning in her office had been broken for the past week and building management's response was not as quick as she'd like. The closed blinds on the open window across from her desk flapped in the gusting, swirling breeze that swept up sporadically from 15th Street NW, three floors below.

"Damn, it's hot in here," she mumbled, reaching for the ringing phone. "Thank you for calling Metropolitan Construction. This is Leslie. How may I help you?"

"Mr. Braxton please," came from a woman's voice.

Something in the woman's voice gave Leslie a gut wrenching feeling. She hesitated. "Mr. Braxton is out of the office," she lied. She could hear him rumbling through his desk drawer in the adjacent office. "Is there something I could help you with?"

"No thank you."

"Would you care to leave a message? I'll see that he gets it."

"Uh, yes, that will be fine. Could you please let Mr. Braxton know that Jamaica Kingston called and I will be able to meet him for lunch?"

A knot rose in Leslie's throat. She almost choked on her words. She swallowed Jamaica's words hard and cleared her throat. "Does he have your number?"

"Yes, he does," Jamaica replied.

"I'm sure he is going to ask if I took down your number," she said, not giving up easy. "He always does."

" No, trust me, he has my number programmed in his phone. But just in case, my number is (202) 555-7869."

A disapproving frown crept across Leslie's lips. She didn't like the confidence in the woman's voice. Who did Miss Jamaica Kingston think she was? Leslie leaned back in her chair and stared at the wall, as if she had Superman's x-ray vision. She contemplated her next move. There was no way in hell Mr. Derek Braxton was going to get away with this bullshit. He was going to pay and pay royally.

Leslie had the run of Metropolitan Construction Company and had been running it quite well for two years, long enough to survive Derek's initial close scrutiny of her work, her short battle with complacency and eventually won his wholehearted trust. She had a slight inkling Derek was messing around, so she started the ball rolling months ago. It had been little things at first: ordering extra office supplies for her friends to sell at corner vending stands; small checks written to fictitious vendors, that somehow ended up in fictitious accounts, which she created. The "never bite the hand that feeds you" rule of life was blown out the window when he decided she wasn't enough for him.

She thought back to when she first met Derek in the park, among the boxes, shopping bags and rags she wore on her back. He was the most beautiful creature she'd ever seen. She spoke to him as he walked by. The spark in her eyes stopped him in his tracks. He looked at her and wondered how long she'd been down on her luck. Something about her impelled him to offer assistance.

"Hi," he said. "You don't have any family?"

Leslie told him of how she'd lost her job and apartment, all in the same day. She had too much pride to ask for help from the family she had broken ties with years earlier. The park had been her home for six months.

He handed her one hundred dollars. "If you want to work," he said, shoving his business card in her face, "I have a job for you."

That following week, Leslie was answering telephones for Metropolitan Construction Company. Within two months, her cardboard boxes turned into a plush apartment in Prince George's County, a candy apple red Mercedes Benz, a promotion to office manager, overseeing two offices, and four hundred employees, and what she believed to be a fulfilling relationship with her boss.

Leslie strategically wove through the people between her and her target. Target…already, she was thinking of him in this way—what he unknowingly transformed into the moment she saw him seated in Legal Seafood with another woman. Her pace quickened to beat the light to cross Connecticut Avenue NW. She was directly on his heels, enough to smell the Curve cologne she had given him last Christmas.

As her target approached DuPont Circle NW, he stopped abruptly and waved at something or someone she couldn't make out. A tall, wide burly man had obstructed her view. When she stepped to the side, her target had disappeared.

"Fuck!" she blurted. The elderly woman beside her looked at her with a turned up face. "What are you looking at?" she snapped at the woman.

Looking up, down and across the street, and around corners, she spotted her target entering Burberry's. She jetted down the street and stopped at the store's window, trying to see inside. She frowned at what she saw. Confirmation. "Dirty bastard," she mumbled under her breath.

She crossed the street and stood inside the Metro, where she had a perfect view inside of Burberry's. She cringed when the target wrapped his arms around the waist of the woman who occupied his time.

"Son of a bitch," she mumbled. "Fucking with my feelings as you please. You've fucked with the wrong bitch."

She lit a cigarette and waited for her target to exit. She wanted a good look at the woman who had stolen her meal ticket.

The sun reflected in the tinted lenses of her sunglasses as Leslie glared at the back of the woman's head that was occupying her man's time. "The bitch probably wears a weave," she fussed, blowing cigarette smoke through her nostrils.

Leslie tailed them for most of the afternoon and well into the evening. Her Mercedes pulled behind her target at the intersection of Military Road NW and Wisconsin Avenue NW, in the direction of Bethesda-Chevy Chase. She lowered her sunglasses on the bridge of her nose and caught a glimpse of him leaning over into the passenger side. It looked like they were kissing.

Enraged, Leslie slapped the gearshift into reverse and skidded several feet back up the street, barely missing the thirty-something woman crossing the street.

The woman leapt over the safety zone symbolized by the curb. "Hey!" the woman yelled. "Watch it!"

Leslie rolled down her window, raised an angry finger at the woman, followed by "kiss my ass, bitch!" and peeled down Western Avenue NW, unaware she could have sent the woman limb-flipping, spine-cracking across the road.

Leslie removed her sunglasses and dried the puddle that had formed in her eyes. The pain she felt was undeniable. She loved him and thought he loved her, too. However, she realized all she was to him was a piece of ass when he got horny and someone to run his business while he played with his new toy. He had fucked her for two years and it was time for him to be fucked.

# *18*

Maxine stood behind Tillie as she sat at the bar and sucked on a chicken wing. Martini's was busting at the seams. The thirty and over crowd was out in full force. The music throbbing from the carefully situated speakers in each corner blared sounds that were coupled with contemporary rhythm and blues and old school. It left the body with no option except to translate into motion.

Tillie looked over her shoulder and spoke to Maxine. "It's like a meat market in here tonight," she said.

"Yeah and it's only a quarter past ten. It's still early." She held her glass to her lips and tilted it back, then dismissed it to the bar. She ran her tongue over her lips, absorbing the gloss of moisture the glass had left behind. She danced in place, hips swaying to the rhythm as her fingers snapped in unison.

He looked no more than twenty-three years old. Invisible traces of breast milk still lingered. Maxine watched him from the corner of her eye. She stopped dancing. He stared her up and down, taking in every inch of her. A smile crept on his lips. He took a step closer and shook his head.

Maxine faced him and released a slight chuckle. "How old are you?" she asked.

Tillie overheard her question and turned around in her seat. "He looks pretty young," Tillie said.

"Old enough," he replied with a smirk at both of them.

Tillie smiled and said, "Well, I guess he told us."

Maxine shook her head. "Yeah, I bet you do think you're old enough."

"What's that suppose to mean?"

"Nothing," she said and turned to face the dance floor.

He looked in the direction of her glare. "Want to dance?"

She took his hand and led him away from the bar. "I hope you know what you're getting into," she smiled, feeling friskier than she'd felt in quite some time. In addition, she was overly flattered that a young man appeared to have been turned on by her. He obviously wanted to play with grown folks and she intended to teach him the objective of the game.

With his hand grasped firmly in hers, she took the lad into a neglected corner of the dance floor that looked as if it had been designed for intimacy. The lights, which swept the rest of the dance floor, somehow missed the small area. It was a blind spot, an escape route highlighted by its lack of lighting.

He stood for a moment and observed the relaxation of her face. "What's your name?"

"Maxine and you?"

"Malcolm."

Maxine looked around at the shifting limbs, torsos and heads, shuddering, swaying, gyrating, and pumping in sexual simulation.

When he began to dance, everything about him was fluid. She took second place to him, kept her steps to an instinctive interpretation of the sounds that filled the room, leaving the limelight to him alone in this dim corner of the dance floor.

Several songs later, the tempo of the music descended to something more intimate. She placed her hands softly on his arms, feeling his muscle tense. Without trouble, she ran her hands over his biceps and elbow, eventually settling with a knitting of her fingers between his. He enjoyed her torso pressed against his, gently swaying. Pleasure overwhelmed him, slightly tenting the front of his pants. They moved tightly, cemented together, dancing cheek to cheek. Her hand stroked up and down his back, eventually making way to his waist and around to the front of his pants. Easing an inch away from him, she unzipped his pants and thrust a rummaging hand inside. He pulled her into him and eased his hand down her back, resting on her ass. He grew in the grasp of her hand.

"What are you trying to do?" he asked.

She said nothing, enjoying the thrill she was giving the youngster.

When the next song died, she separated them. "Shall we leave?" she asked. "I'm ready to move to level two, if you are."

He nodded and fumbled with his pants. He followed her towards the bar. She whispered in Tillie's ear and headed toward the door.

"Do you drive?" she asked.

"Yeah."

"Good. You're driving."

Malcolm leaned against the wall and eyed Maxine's apartment. "You have a nice place," he said, fidgeting with his ear.

Maxine looked at him and smirked. "I know you're not getting scared on me now. Are you?"

He dropped his hand to his side, the other shoved deep inside his pant pocket. "No, not at all."

She nodded towards the sofa. "Rest yourself."

He sat on the sofa and rubbed the palm of his hands against his pants.

Maxine stood before him and closed her eyes. She swung her hips from side to side, in motion with the music playing in her head.

Malcolm anxiously adjusted himself on the sofa and tugged at his crotch.

Maxine slowly turned around, her back facing him and bent over as slow as she could, until her fingertips touched the floor. She looked around at him. "Kiss my ass," she instructed.

Malcolm's brow raised in doubt. Then, he figured, what the hell, go with the flow. He knelt down before her, his face inches away from her ass.

"Kiss it," she said softly, slowly moving her hips.

Malcolm puckered his lips and kissed her on the left cheek.

"Kiss the other one," she cooed.

He kissed her right cheek.

"Kiss the crack."

Now she was going too far. Malcolm's frowned up face eventually turned into a smile, knowing he would have his opportunity to be in control. For now, he'll let her play her game. He planted his lips against the seam of her pants and turned up his nose. He leaned back and pressed his finger up into her crotch. He withdrew his finger and sniffed it. He grabbed her around the waist.

"Hey, baby, listen," he said pulling himself to his feet, "I've been dancing and sweating, and whatnot. Let's take a shower."

She rose up and turned to face him. "Okay," she smiled then giving him an open-mouth kiss. Their tongues fluttered and danced, as kissing sounds escaped and aroused them more, as his hands explored her ass and her hands searched for his dick to ensure he was worth her time. She took him by the hand and led him to the bathroom.

# *19*

Too many Long Island Iced Teas had Tillie fumbling to get her key in the door, before it fell to the ground. "Shit!" She bent down to pick up the key. The front door flew open.

"Where have you been?" Randy snapped angrily.

Tillie stood erect and looked him square in the eyes. "How did you get in my house?" Her speech was thick and slurred.

"You gave me a key. Remember?"

"Oh," she said, closing the door behind her. "I was out with Max."

"Where is out?"

"You ain't my damn daddy!"

"No," he pointed to her belly. "But I am the daddy to the baby you're carrying."

"Uh-huh," she said, tossing her left hand lazily in the air. "I don't see no ring on this finger." She walked toward him.

He quietly studied her. "You're drunk," he declared.

"Duh," she laughed. "You're not as dumb as people think you are."

"Tillie, you can't be drinking with the baby!"

"Oh, so now you give a shit about the baby."

"That's not fair. I've always cared about the baby…and you."

She pursed her lips together and then spoke between clinched teeth. "Was this before or after you wanted to kill our baby?"

Randy stood frozen. Her words stung deep and sent chills throughout him.

"Get the fuck out of my house," she said, walking toward the kitchen. "And leave my damn key. You don't pay rent here."

Randy slammed his fist against the wall. "Damn it, Tillie."

Tillie whipped around, stunned at Randy's outburst.

"Why are you doing this?"

"What? Tell me what it is I'm doing, Randy?"

"Why are you endangering the baby?"

"I am not endangering the baby. Why are you overreacting?"

"You're drinking and doing God only knows what else."

"What are you insinuating, Randy?"

Randy looked away from her. "Nothing."

"Oh, yes, you're insinuating something."

"Fine! You're hanging out with Max and we both know she's a big time trick."

Her eyes closed as she inhaled deeply. "Don't bring Max into this. This isn't about her. This is about you not taking care of your responsibility and trying to run my goddamn life. It's about you," she yelled, her voice almost an octave above a high pitch. "Take responsibility for your actions, Randy."

"What do you want me to do, Tillie?"

She approached him, standing close enough to feel the air blowing from his nostrils. "I want you to step up to the plate and be the man I fell in love with." She caressed his face. "Why is having this baby so bad?"

He shook his head. "I've accepted the baby and my responsibility. What I can't accept is your behavior. Baby, you can't drink and party while you're pregnant. You just can't. I don't know what I'd do if something happened to you or the baby."

His words shocked her, throwing her into a whirlwind of emotions.

"Tillie, I want you to take care of yourself...of our baby."

She offered him a forgiving smile. She did not want to admit, deep down inside, she was overwhelmed by his concern. "I will take better care of myself. Nevertheless, I am a grown ass woman. You will not dictate my life, unless I see a ring. And even then, you won't rule me."

# 20

Leslie was losing count. It was his second, third, maybe even fourth time he'd greedily snorted his line of cocaine. She wondered if he had a limit as to how often he could do this.

"I wish you wouldn't do that shit around me," she said.

He wiped up the residue with his finger and wiped it across his teeth. "You don't know what you're missing, baby girl,"

Leslie thought for a minute, wondering if she shouldn't say no. So far, she'd declined everything that had come her way. "No thanks. I'm on a natural high," she smirked. "But you on the other hand…how are you going to do what I need you to do if your nose is full of that shit?"

"Hey, I can still do my job."

She stood over the huge man, who sat with a broken mirror dusted with cocaine residue in front of him. "Do you remember what your job is?"

"Uh-huh," he grunted in affirmation. "Yeah, I remember."

"Tell me one more time. Just to be certain."

"Don't speak," he recited as he formed three new rows of cocaine on the mirror. "Nod only." He leaned down and lowered his head toward the freshly cut lines. "Don't smile." He snorted hard, throwing his head back. "But don't speak," he said, with this mouth opened, allowing his passageway to open for the cocaine to run its course, down the back of his throat.

She raised her eyebrows over the frames of her sunglasses, accentuating their plucked curves into taut arches.

"At the rate you're going," she said, looking up his nose as he tilted his head back, "you're going to burn the last bit of brain cells you have left. That's a damn shame," she nodded in discord.

He cut his eyes at her and returned his attention to the mirror on the table.

She kicked him on the ankle. "What else?"

He rolled his eyes around the room. "Er...?" Swallowed alive, his sentence disappeared. His eyes glazed over. It was the same glazed look he had when they met three years ago in the park, his box nestled next to hers.

"Gloves, you idiot," she huffed. "No fingerprints on anything."

He grunted. "Yeah, gotcha!"

"Don't fuck this up, Robert! I mean it."

"I won't, don't worry about it."

"If you fuck this up, you could ruin everything for us."

"I wont' fuck it up, a'ight?"

She snatched her purse from the end table and stormed towards the door. "You better not!" The door slammed behind her and Robert returned to his favorite pastime, one more line.

# 21

Her heart rate spiked, and it wasn't due to his smooth chocolate skin or his full lips that curved into a sexy Colgate smile. It was all she knew and had yet to discover, that blew love through her like a sand storm through the Sahara Desert. She was in love, a stranger she thought would never knock at her door.

"I have something to tell you," she whispered, walking toward him, unbuttoning her blouse.

He smiled. Although she didn't have the body of a model or a video vixen, she still turned him on. She was sexy in her own right.

She leaned into him and whispered into his ear. "Actually," she moaned, "I have two things to tell you." She nibbled his lobe and blew into his ear. It sent chills down his spine. He shivered.

She straddled his lap and looked him in the eye. "The first thing I have to tell you is," she hesitated, then kissed his eyelid, making her way down to his cheek. "I want to taste you," she cooed.

His dick got hard. He nestled his head in her chest.

"The second thing I want to tell you," she said, pulling up his chin. "I'm so in love with you," she declared as she gazed into his eyes.

His smile was forced. "Uh…" He moved her off his lap and paced the floor. "Uh."

"What's wrong?"

He propped his hands on his hips and stared down at the floor.

"Derek?" She stared at him dumbfounded.

"Baby, those are powerful words. They aren't words you can just go tossing around freely."

"No, I don't know what you mean."

"They are words I take very seriously."

"So do I."

"Listen, baby, I like you and all. I like you a lot," he hesitated. "I'm not sure I'm ready for a relationship. I mean, you know…"

"What are you saying to me, Derek? Are you telling me that these past three months didn't mean shit to you?"

"Baby, these have been the best three months of my life."

"Then I don't understand."

He sat on the sofa, intertwined his fingers, and twirled his thumbs. "I don't want to feel rushed."

"Oh, I see." She buttoned up her blouse. "I thought we were on the same page."

"We are, baby, but I'm not feeling the whole love thing."

She slipped on her shoes. "Uh-huh, well, I am. So, it looks like we have a problem here." She tossed her shawl around her shoulders and wrapped it around her neck. "I never learn," she said, walking toward the front door. "I always open myself up for a let down."

Derek shook his head, but said nothing. He didn't know what to say. His thoughts dashed to Leslie. He's been down this road before with her.

"Don't leave, Jamaica."

With her hand affixed to the doorknob, she lowered her head and cried. "I'm not going to put myself through this anymore. I'm sick of putting my all into a man who doesn't give his all in return."

He approached her from behind. "There's so much you don't know about me. I think we should take it slow."

"How can you say you don't love me," she sobbed.

"I never said that, Jamaica." He turned her around. "I didn't say that I don't love you. I said I care about you a lot." He wiped away her tears. "Baby, give me time. Let's not rush it."

She pressed her face against his chest and sobbed. Her tears shook her so she bounced in his arms. Her tears dampened the front of his shirt.

He lifted up her chin, smiled in her face and wiped away her tears. "You're cute when you cry," he lightly chuckled.

She closed her eyes, took a long deep sigh and wrapped her arms around his waist.

"I want to take my time loving you," he said, kissing her softly on the nose. "I want to fall so deep in love with you that I won't know my left from my right." He kissed her cheek. "I want to smother you with love, baby," he said, kissing her eyelid. "But in my own time. Okay?"

She nodded as their lips met. "I'm a patient woman."

## *22*

The pounding on the door did not jar him from his white lines leading to wonderland.

"Open the goddamn door, Robert!"

Robert pulled himself from the sofa and trudged to the front door. "Who is it?" he yelled, leaning against the door.

"Open this fucking door, Robert!"

He recognized the voice and cracked a smile. "Promise to be good," he teased, speaking through the door and looking through the peephole.

"I'm not promising you shit. Open the goddamn door before I kick this bitch in!"

"Who pissed in your corn flakes?" he asked, as the door flung open. "You have a nasty mouth, lady."

Leslie stormed through the opened door. "Don't play with me. Why weren't you at my house?"

The door quickly closed shut and she flipped around on her heels.

"Could you keep it down?"

"Robert," she said between clenched teeth. "You were supposed to have been…" She hesitated, noticing the white residue around the edges of his nose. "Damn, are you fuckin' high, again?"

Robert smiled and lazily walked over to the chair and plopped down in front of the small table that held his cracked mirror and white lines.

"You ain't worth a good goddamn. You know that?"

He shooed her and said, "Leave me be, woman. Get someone else to do your bullshit work. Just face it. The nigger doesn't want your ass."

Leslie stood behind him and calmly said, "If you want something done, then you must do it yourself," and bashed him on the back of the head with the lamp she retrieved from the side table.

Robert's head jerked back and then forward as he tumbled over the table and crashed to the floor.

She headed toward the door. "I told that motherfucker not to fuck with me," she said as the door slammed behind her.

A few more minutes and she would've missed her.

Parked at the corner of 16th Street and Connecticut Avenue, Leslie slipped on her sunglasses and slid down in the seat behind the steering wheel, and watched as Jamaica exited Southland Apartments and strolled up 16th Street, towards the Metro bus stop.

Leslie reached in the backseat, retrieved a plastic shopping bag and slipped out of the car. She looked both ways, her eyes still peeled on Jamaica, and jogged across the street. When her foot touched the curb, she gathered her composure and tried to act as naturally as she could. Truth be told, and despite her bad bitch demeanor, she was terrified. However, it was something she had to do.

Jamaica sat on the bench, under the glass-encased shelter, reading the November 2005 issue of *Black Enterprise*. As she thumbed through the pages, she was oblivious to her surroundings, which was unheard of in the nation's capital.

As she approached the shelter, Leslie slowed her pace and slipped on the black knit skullcap, pulling it down over her face. Her eyes and lips were exposed. She was not feeling so good. She could not decipher if it was nerves, fear or she was coming down with something. Either way, she was going to teach Jamaica a very good lesson and worry about feeling better later.

Leslie stood before Jamaica, smiled and yelled, "Stay away from Derek!"

The connection between Leslie's fist and Jamaica's jaw was powerful enough to knock Jamaica clean over. She fell on the ground and landed on her face.

Leslie bent over her and snarled. "Be careful, tramp. The next time you won't get off so easily." She reached into the shopping bag, pulled out a urine-filled jar with floating feces, and poured it on to the back of Jamaica's head.

Leslie looked around and sprinted up the street. When she reached her car, she felt much better.

# *23*

"Uh-huh, someone is in love."

"Who me? Nope, not in this lifetime," Derek said, with his feet propped up on the desk.

Gina stood in the doorway of Derek's home office. "Does Leslie know about your new found love?"

"Leslie is my employee. She doesn't need to know my business."

"I can remember when you two were a hot item."

"That was in the past."

Gina took a seat in the wingback chair positioned in the corner of his office. "You better be careful, brother dear. Something about that woman I never liked. There is something sneaky and conniving about her."

"I have no concerns when it comes to Leslie."

Gina raised a brow. "No? Seems mighty funny you're working out of your home office more than the office you're paying monthly…" she stopped when Derek raised his hand to silence her.

"Everything is cool, sis. I have no worries and you shouldn't have any either."

"Okay then, don't say I didn't warn you." She stood to her feet. "Oh, by the way, you have a package that arrived this morning."

Gina retrieved the securely wrapped box from her desk and placed it in front of Derek. "This thing stinks, too," she said walking out of his office.

Derek smiled and began opening the package. With precision, he cut the string from around the package and opened each end . "You're right," he yelled to Gina, "this does stink." He checked the package for a return address. "Hey, Gina, do you know who this came from?"

"What does it say on the return address?" she yelled back.

"There is no return address."

"Well, Derek, I don't have ESP. How am I supposed to know? Check out the postmark."

He rolled his eyes and peeked at the postmark. "It says Virginia."

Gina stood in the doorway, with her arms folded across her chest. "Derek?"

Not looking up, he said, "Huh?"

"Open the damn package and then burn that damn box!"

Derek turned up his nose and proceeded with removing the brown shipping paper from the box. Using scissors, he cut the tape from each side of the box. He removed the top. What came next was jaw dropping.

"What in the fuck is this?" Derek said, jumping to his feet.

"Oh my God!" Gina jumped from the doorway, backwards to her desk. "What in the world... Derek?"

"This is sick!" Derek yelled. "Why would anyone send me some shit like this?"

"I don't know, but get it out of here!" Gina cried. "Please, Derek, take it out of here."

"Okay, okay...it won't hurt you." Derek slowly returned the top to the box, covering the partially decomposed rodent. As he picked up the box, his stomach began churning from the overwhelming stench in the air. "This is disgusting," he said, walking toward the doorway. "Oh my God," he said. "There are some sick people in this world."

Gina stood in the corner, pinching her nose closed. In the back of her mind, she knew the degenerate who sent this disgusting package. She wondered what message she was trying to send. She also wondered how long her brother would keep his blinders on.

"Damn, G, it's dead!"

"Never mind me, get that crap out of here. Now I have to call in to have the place fumigated!"

# 24

"Jamaica, baby, it's me Maxine."

"Is she in a coma?" Randy asked, staring down at Jamaica as she lay motionless. "Hell, is she breathing? I don't see her chest moving up and down."

"Shut the hell up, you fool. Of course she's breathing," Tillie chimed in.

"Hey, I'm not going to be too many fools, damn it."

"Hush, y'all. Damn!" Maxine retorted. "Stop all that bullshit."

"I wish you all would shut the hell up," Jamaica said, looking up at them. "Damn, can a girl get some rest?"

They all took a sigh of relief.

"Girl, what happened?" asked Tillie.

"I don't know. I was sitting at the bus stop and someone approached me."

"Did you see who it was?" Randy asked.

"No, she was wearing one of those knit caps that come down over your face."

"How do you know it was a she?" Maxine asked.

"She's not stupid," Tillie said, rolling her eyes at Maxine.

Maxine sucked her teeth and said, "Go ahead, Jamaica."

"I could hear her voice and it sounded familiar. Like I've heard it before."

"What else happened?" Randy asked, anxious and annoyed with Maxine and Tillie asking so many questions and not allowing Jamaica to finish.

"She approached me and hit me hard enough to knock me to the ground. I wasn't completely out cold, because I heard her voice and I heard her say, "Stay away from…" She stopped and turned her head to the side.

"What?" they all said in unison.

As much as she wanted to tell them, she decided against it. The last thing she wanted to hear was them saying, "I told you so," and "I knew he wasn't worth a damn."

"Nothing," she said. "I don't want to talk about it anymore."

"Where is your man?" Randy asked.

"I haven't," she hesitated, "called him yet."

"Why not? I'm sure he's worried about you," Tillie smiled, rubbing Jamaica's covered foot.

She forced a smile. "I don't want him to worry about me."

Maxine rolled her eyes and sucked her teeth. "What's the number, Jam?"

"I'll call him when I get home," Jamaica said.

"Man, if it were my woman, I'd want to know. That's for damn sure," Randy said.

Tillie smiled at Randy and said, "I agree, honey," and walked over to the closet. "He needs to know."

"Tillie, please. I'll tell him when I'm ready."

"Grab her purse, Tillie," said Maxine. "You're being silly, Jamaica."

"Got it," Tillie said, digging inside Jamaica's purse.

Jamaica sighed and Randy said, "You know you're fighting a losing battle with those two." Jamaica nodded and closed her eyes.

"What's the number?" Tillie asked.

"Check the directory, Tillie, damn," Maxine huffed.

"Max, will you please calm down?" Tillie said, looking through the cell phone's directory. "It's ringing."

"Tillie please don't call him," Jamaica pleaded one last time.

"Hi, Derek, this is Tillie. Jamaica wants to talk to you." She extended the phone towards Jamaica.

Jamaica turned her head.

"Girl, give me that damn phone," Maxine said, taking the phone from Tillie. "Derek, this is Maxine. Jamaica was attacked and she's in the hospital. She's at Washington Hospital Center. She didn't want to tell you, but we thought you should know." Maxine ended the call. "He's on his way," she announced.

"Goddamn it, Maxine!" Jamaica blurted. "Do you ever mind your business?" Tears streamed down her cheek.

"It wasn't totally her fault," Tillie said. "I called him."

Jamaica looked at Tillie. "You need to mind your damn business, too!"

"Cool, I'm out," said Maxine.

"Bye!" Jamaica grunted.

"I'll see y'all later," Maxine said to Randy and Tillie before storming out of the room.

Tillie sat on the side of the bed. "Honey, we were wrong. I'm sorry."

Jamaica took her hand and gently squeezed it. "It's okay."

Randy leaned in and kissed Jamaica on the cheek. "We're going to let you get some rest. Besides, your boy is on his way."

Jamaica nodded and closed her eyes.

An hour later, Jamaica was startled by a tug at her toe. When she opened her eyes, Derek was smiling down at her.

"Hey, beautiful," he said.

Jamaica swallowed hard. "Could you get me some water, baby?"

"Sure." He picked up the plastic cup that sat on the movable tray at the foot of the bed. "You should've told me you wanted to take a vacation," he chuckled.

"This is hardly a vacation," she smiled.

Derek returned to the bedside with the cup of water. He held the cup to her lips as she held her head up and sipped. "Well, it's not the Bahamas, that's for sure."

Jamaica looked into his eyes. "I didn't want you to worry. That's why I didn't call you."

"Oh, baby," he said, gently stroking the large bruise on her cheekbone. "What happened?"

"Nothing really. Some crazy woman attacked me."

"For no reason. Just out of the blue?"

Jamaica smiled, but Derek could tell it wasn't genuine.

"Baby, you're not telling me something," he said.

Jamaica sat up in the bed. "Can you please find out when they are letting me out of here? I'm feeling fine and I have to go to work tomorrow."

"Let me see what I can find out and you're not going to work tomorrow. You'll stay at my place until you're feeling better."

"I'm feeling…"

"I won't take no for an answer."

"Derek, I do have bills to pay," she snapped, getting annoyed at everyone wanting to tell her what to do. First Maxine and now Derek.

"Not on my watch."

"Derek, look…"

"I love you, babe, and I don't know what I'd do if something were to happen to you," he gasped at the words that escaped his mouth.

Jamaica sat up in the bed. "What did you say?"

Derek smiled. "I said I love you."

Jamaica smiled and Derek loved the way it sounded, too.

## 25

"Change the station," Tillie said, as they drove up Georgia Avenue. "I'm sick of hearing all that bee bop stuff."

"It's not bee bop, its R& B," Randy chuckled.

"Whatever it is, I don't want to hear it. It's giving me a headache."

"John Legend is giving you a headache."

"Damn it, Randy, just do what I ask!"

"Okay, you don't have to bite my head off."

Tillie settled into her seat and huffed. "Sorry."

"It's okay. I know you're dealing with raging hormones."

"Not in the mood for jokes, Randy."

"What's wrong, babe?"

"Maxine. What is wrong with her? Why is she so damn rude?"

Randy remained quiet, his opinions of Maxine bordered on worthless.

"She acts so envious of people…of us. She doesn't have to be. We are best of friends."

Randy nodded his head and grunted.

"What?" Tillie asked. "You have something on your mind. I can tell."

Randy shook his head. "I'm cool."

"No you're not. How can I be fucking someone on the regular and not know when something is on their mind?"

"True that. I'll just say that your girl is raggedy. She doesn't have your best interest at heart, that's for sure."

Tillie shook her head. "No, I have to disagree with you there, babe. She's very concerned with all our well-being."

"You keep on thinking that and see where it'll get you," Randy retorted and turned up the radio.

Tillie turned the radio off. "And what does that mean?" she snapped in a defensive tone.

"I don't want to get into an argument over Max," he paused. "The tramp ain't worth it," he mumbled.

"What the fuck did you just say?"

"Nothing," he said.

"No, you called my best friend a tramp. Who the fuck are you to call anyone names, Randy?"

"I call them as I see them."

"Oh, yeah? Well, how long have you been seeing her this way because you used to be crazy about her at one time?"

"Leave it alone, Tillie. Don't get yourself worked up."

"To hell with that!"

"Fine. Your girl tried to fuck your man. Okay?"

Tillie's jaw dropped in her lap.

"I told you to leave it alone," Randy said.

Tillie closed her mouth and stared out of the passenger window. Every murderous thought flew through her mind. She cleared her dry throat. "Suppose I were to believe you. And I *said* suppose. When did this, supposedly, take place."

Randy shot an angry look at her and swerved the car off the road, running into the curb. "You think I'm lying to you?" He turned around in the seat to face her. "Huh?" He slammed his hand on the dashboard. "Answer me, damn it!"

"I don't know what to believe."

"You know, Tillie. I believe that baby you're carrying is mine. I never doubted you for a second."

Tillie snapped her head to face him. "What are you trying to say? You think I fucked around on you?"

"Like you," he said, his stare cold and distant, "I don't know what to believe."

# *26*

Maxine sat on the side of the bed smoking one cigarette after another, a habit she kept well hidden. The smoke lingered around the ceiling like rain clouds. She opened the window she had cleaned hours before, and right away a breeze came through. She put a hand to the wind, enjoying the coolness, and one thing came to her: she was alone.

The telephone blared throughout her apartment. She looked at the charger and cursed. "Where is the damn phone," she huffed, walking through the apartment, trying to determine the phone's location. She reached the sofa and snatched up the phone. "Hello?"

"Hello, Maxine."

She looked at the caller ID on the handset. It was an unfamiliar area code. Her heart raced.

"Hi," she meekly said. She sat down on the sofa, a million questions running through her head. "How are you, Frank?"

"Good, and you?"

"I'm good." Her voice was distant.

"Did you get my letter?"

Unable to speak, she nodded her head instead.

"I wanted to call you long before now, but you know how it goes," he said. "Not knowing where I'm going to be from one minute to the next."

"Uh-huh, sure…"

"Maxine, I'll be in DC next week and I would love to see you."

"Okay."

"Great. I'll give you a call the day before I arrive."

"I thought you were dead," she managed to say. "I received word from your sister saying you were dying."

He cleared his throat and said, "I'll explain it all when I see you."

Maxine stood to her feet and paced the floor. "I would like for you to explain it to me now."

"Maxine, this isn't a good time, sweetie."

"Why not?"

"Because I can't really talk right now."

"Why would you call me when you can't talk?"

"Max, let's talk about this next week. We'll have dinner…you choose the place and I'll put everything out on the table."

"Frank, are you married?"

"What? Of course I'm not married," he chuckled.

"I cried for you," she yelled into the phone. "I thought you were dying. I cried day and night for your ass!"

He was silent.

Her pacing turned to brisk walking from room to room, trying to make sense of what she was feeling. "It's been a year, Frank. How could you do this to me?"

"Maxine, I promise to explain it all to you next week. Unless you don't want to see me."

She came to an abrupt halt. "I want to see you," she said, without hesitation. "I do want to see you, Frank," she hesitated. "But I don't know. I'm a big ball of confusion and emotions. I don't know how to feel…"

"About what, Maxine?"

"About this…you…seeing you."

"Maxine, I never meant to hurt you. Listen, I can't talk right now. I need to get back…"

"Get back to what?" she asked.

"I'm in a training session," he said in a whisper. "Can you pick me up from the airport?"

"What day are you coming in?"

"Next Thursday," he answered, his voice was deep and smooth, with sexual overtones. Every time he spoke, tiny hairs on her arm raised, giving her chills. "I'll call you on Wednesday with my flight information."

"I never stopped loving you," she said, feeling it was something she needed to say in case this was the last time she spoke with him.

"Thank you," he said. "I'll talk to you Wednesday."

*Thank you*, she thought. *What about I never stopped loving you either?*

"Max?"

She snapped out of her trance. "Yes, I'm here. Okay, I'll talk to you Wednesday."

"Take care of yourself, Max."

"You, too."

She wanted to be pissed, but the excitement she felt wouldn't allow her to do so.

# *27*

"I really can stay at my place," Jamaica said as Derek's Mercedes sped down Military Road, making a left onto Wisconsin. Jamaica gazed at Saks Fifth Avenue, Lord & Taylor, and Mazza Gallery, thinking how long it's been since she had been shopping. "I know you can, but I want to take care of my baby," he said taking her hand and kissing her knuckles.

"Derek, all of my things are there."

"We'll buy new things."

"And I have to go to work."

Derek shook his head. "I'll take care of it. I'll have Gina call your job…"

"No! You can't have Gina call my job. Are you crazy?"

"What? She's very professional. She'll know exactly what to say."

"Derek," she whined, tossing her hands around. "You're going to get me fired."

"Then I'll hire you."

Jamaica lowered her head and shook it in defeat.

"I won't let you fall," he said. " I have your back."

She raised her head and looked at him. His side view was beautiful, with a strong bone structure. "No one has ever said that to me before."

He squeezed her knee and smiled. "I'm going to take off some time from the…hey, you know what we need?"

"Hmm," she said.

"A vacation. Where do you want to go?"

"You are so silly," she chuckled. "I thought I needed rest, supposed to be taking it easy."

"Yeah, but you can do that anywhere."

"This is true."

"I'll have Gina make arrangements for us."

"Where are we going?" she asked, unable to hide the excitement in her voice.

He pulled into the driveway, pulled up the handbrake and turned off the car. He stretched his fingers around the wood-grained steering wheel. "Italy."

Jamaica looked at him and blinked several times. "Italy?"

"I've always wanted to go and there's no better time than now."

"Well, then, Italy it is."

# *28*

Tillie lay nestled amongst the ocean of pillows that covered the top portion of her bed, wiggling her toes and watching a rerun of *Sex and the City*.

"She's a slut," she said to Randy as he stood in the bathroom, door slightly cracked, shaving.

"Who?"

"Maxine. I can't believe she tried to make a move on you. What kind of shit is that?"

"I don't know, babe. I really didn't want to tell you, not wanting to mess up your friendship and all."

"You didn't mess it up. She did when she tried to bed you."

Randy stood in the door, towel wrapped around his cream coffee muscular build and tiny waist.

"Turn around," said Tillie. "I like your butt."

Randy smiled and asked, "With or without the towel?"

Tillie chuckled. "Trust me. If you take off the towel, we're fucking for sure."

Randy removed the towel, his penis was slightly erect, but rising from a nest of soft curly hair between his toned thighs. Tillie could not stop herself from looking at him.

As he came nearer, she stroked her tongue across her lips and spread her legs. He crawled on top of her and gazed into her eyes as he slowly entered her semi-moist pussy.

She cried out. Her head dug back into the mound of pillows as his hardness drove deep inside her orifice.

Randy's thrusts were slow and gentle, concentrating on the small knot at the roof of her vagina. He released deep guttural moans as she clamped down on his driving force.

He pulled out. She turned over and tooted her ass in the air. He inserted his finger into her sopping wetness and stroked up toward her rectum, repeating this several times until there was enough moisture for insertion.

His finger stroking her clitoris relaxed her as the tip of his head slowly inched into her rectum. She knew the pain would be excruciating, but she wanted him badly.

As he continued inching inside her with ease, she didn't feel the throbbing pain of her rectum stretching, but the flood of juices dripping from her and a new moan escaped from her as she opened herself to him.

He spread her cheeks apart and ease in deeper. She cried. He continued until he was halfway inside her. He stroked gently, as if her hole was fragile crystal that might crack if he moved too fast.

Still stroking her clitoris, he bent down on her back and kissed the back of her neck, sending chills throughout her. Her moans were deep and indescribable. Like nothing he'd ever heard before.

"You okay, baby?" he asked.

She nodded her head and pushed herself, ever so gently, into him.

"Wooooooooweee," she squealed.

"Does it hurt?"

"Uh huh, but it's that good kinda hurt," she managed through pants.

He continued kissing and licking her neck, and stroking her clitoris, sending waves of ecstasy washing through her body.

"Oooo, shit, motherfucker!" She hunched up her shoulders. Her quivering thighs closed tighter as she tightened her rectum around his dick. "Ooooooooooooooooooooooh!" Her body shook as she buried her face in the mound of pillows.

Randy removed his erectness from her rectum and stroked his manhood until his seed shot on her back and in her hair.

"I love you, baby," he said as he laid her down on the bed and drew up beside her, spooning her and nestling his face in her neck.

"I love you, too, boo."

"Babe, you know I hate that word, *boo*."

"And we hate it when you call us Ma, but do we say anything?"

"Do you think what we just did will hurt the baby?"

"Naw, your son is protected by lots of placenta and padding."

"Son? How do you know it's a boy?"

"I don't really. I'm hoping, just as you are."

Tillie pulled the cover up over them and nestled her butt into his abdomen, causing his nature to rise again. "Damn, Randy."

"What did I do now?"

"You're getting hard again."

"I can't help it. Shoot, you make my dick hard, so it's your fault," he chuckled. "I'll let you rest."

"Thank you," she giggled. "I want us to be a family, Randy."

"We are a family."

"Man and wife, fool."

"Babe, you have perfect timing for everything you want to discuss."

"Randy, this is your baby."

"I know it is."

"Then why did you say what you said? I haven't messed around on you."

"I know it, babe, and I was only saying it to get back at you. That's all."

Tillie inched away from him and snatched the bedcovers, leaving his naked ass exposed.

"Cute, Tillie," he said, pulling enough bedcover to his side to cover his behind.

# *29*

On the walls of Leslie's bedroom were photographs of Derek and their trips to Cancun, the Orient and Hedonism. She picked up the portrait of them that was taken six months ago at the Earth, Wind & Fire concert at Constitution Hall.

The knock at the door startled her. The building she lived in was secured. All guests must be buzzed in. She wasn't expecting anyone. Immediately, excitement flashed through her, thinking it could be Derek. It had to be him, he was the only one with the pass code.

"Coming," she yelled. "Just a minute!" She slipped out of her jeans and into something more comfortable. "I'm coming," she sung skipping towards the door. She smoothed her hand over her hair, which was pulled back into a ponytail. She pressed her lips together and entered into sexy diva mode. She flung open the door. "Hey ba—" Her draw dropped open. She noted his set face, clamped mouth and fixed eyes. This was no casual visit.

Quickly, the door flew open wider and banged against the wall, the doorknob leaving an impression.

Leslie stammered toward the kitchen, almost tripping over her full-length satin nightgown.

Nervously, she licked her lips and looked into the eyes of a demon, ready to massacre her. One corner of his mouth was pulled into a wicked smile. "I had to get stitches," he said, calm and cool as a cucumber. "That wasn't nice what you did."

For the first time in her life, she felt afraid, fearing for her life. "It was an accident," she said, her voice trembling, her eyes roaming the room looking for anything to strike with.

His face took on an unpleasant twist. "I should fuck your ass up. You know that?"

"Robert, I didn't mean anything by it. You know Derek has my mind all messed up," she cried. "I don't know what I was…"

He raised his hand in the air, his arm swung down and swiped the side of her face, like an axe connecting with wood. Saliva flew from her mouth and across the room, as she fell back onto the kitchen floor.

Leslie touched the back of her hand against her mouth. Her lips were slightly swollen and throbbing, traces of blood were on the back of her hand as she gently wiped her lips.

"I usually don't like putting my hands on a woman like that," he said, extending his hand to assist her to her feet. "But karma is a motherfucker."

She took his hand and remained silent as he pulled her to her feet.

A dishtowel sat on the kitchen counter. He reached into the freezer and grabbed a handful of ice cubes, wrapping them inside the dishtowel.

"Here, put this on your mouth. It'll take the swelling down."

She took the ice pack and gently pressed it against her lips. She flinched and hissed at the stinging pain.

Her reactions seemed to amuse him. "I'm really sorry about that," he said. He took her by the elbow and escorted her to the bed in her bedroom.

She looked up at him, stunned. Actually, she had a new found respect for him. He does have a backbone after all.

Looking at the photographs on the wall of Derek and Leslie, Robert asked, "Why don't you get rid of them?" while sniffing and wiping at his nose.

Quiet as it is kept, her loss of Derek was beyond tears. She wanted to cry, but she couldn't bring herself to doing so. Her voice broke miserably. "I can't just throw him away."

"He did it to you."

She dropped her lashes quickly to hide the hurt.

He continued, "All that you're doing," he paused, hoping he could talk some sense into her. "That nigger ain't worth it. You think you're hurting them, when you ain't hurting nobody but yourself."

She didn't want to hear a word he was saying. She knew it was the truth, but she couldn't give up that easily. She had to at least try to get Derek back. That way, she would know in her heart that she did all she could do, regardless of who was affected or hurt.

He leaned forward and rested his elbows on his scrawny thighs. "Let that man alone. What is it with women anyway? Why can't you all just accept it when the man has moved on?"

She didn't like his question nor did she like being categorized. In her mind, she wasn't like other women. Derek rescuing her when she was at the lowest point in her life was a distant thought. So distant, it was like it never happened. She was about to say something nasty, but the throbbing in her mouth made her think twice. However, she really wanted to talk to someone. And since friends were scarce, she would use Robert instead.

"Can I get you a drink or something?" she asked him.

"Uh," he said in disbelief. She was treating him like a guest for a change. "What do you have?"

"Jack, Grey Goose, pretty much a stocked bar."

"Heineken?"

She shook her head no and said, "Corona."

"I'll have one."

When she retuned with the drinks, Robert had moved to the living room and was sitting on the sofa. Leslie sat in the loveseat across from him and crossed her legs. Her bare foot pointed toward him. Her toes didn't look scruffy. As a matter of fact, they were freshly manicured and the bottoms of her feet were smooth as a baby's butt. Robert salivated.

"I like pretty feet," he smiled.

She uncrossed her legs, folding her feet beneath her. "Let's talk honestly, shall we. I love hearing the assholes of the opposite sex."

He chuckled. She chuckled, too, knowing he had no clue what she was talking about. Despite the presence of his new backbone, she considered him to be the biggest idiot this side of creation. When it came to smarts, the empty light was eternal.

"Okay, tell me something," he said, lifting the mouth of the Corona to his. He tilted his head back and allowed the cold beverage to flow down his throat, his Adam's apple moved with each deep swallow. "Why try to hold on to someone who doesn't want you?"

His question was one she'd asked herself over and over, but chose to ignore. She turned her head to the side and sighed heavily. "You just don't understand."

"You're right, I don't understand. If a bitch didn't want me, I sure as hell wouldn't want her ass."

Bitch. The number one most hated word by women. "Why does she have to be a bitch?" she asked in disgust.

"If she ain't my woman, then she's a bitch. Hell, you a bitch, too."

Leslie's typical reaction would be to curse him a new asshole, but she decided against that too, considering the previous series of events.

"He loves me and I'm not giving up without a fight," she said, sipping apple juice through tender, puffy lips. "Ouch," she hissed.

"I'm really sorry about that, but you know what they say. A hard head makes for a soft ass."

She ignored him. She wasn't in the mood to be big and bad. "He just needs a little persuasion."

"Your boy seems pretty convinced to me."

She smiled and stared him in the face. "I need to get her out of the picture."

Robert sat the bottle on the table and raised his hands to surrender. "I ain't going to jail for nobody."

"Neither am I. What I have in mind is harmless."

"Woman, nothing you do is harmless." He rubbed his chin. "Let me hear it."

"All you have to do is make a delivery. Can you manage it?"

He nodded. "How much are you paying?"

"The same as before."

He stood up and paced around the room. "No, it has to be more. I definitely deserve more," he said, his voice raising an octave. "Shit, you got me fucking around with dead rats and shit." Robert cringed. He felt nauseous thinking about the rat he killed and delivered to Derek in a wrapped box.

"I can't afford more than what I'm paying you," she said, her nerve resurfacing. "Take it or leave it."

He thought about being low on blow. He forced a smile, nodded and poked out his bottom lip. "It's all good." He held out his hand. "I need my cash upfront."

"I'll pay you the way I've always paid you."

"You will pay me now or forget about it."

"Fine," she said, in a huff. "I don't have any cash." She wrote out a check, signed it Cherry Lou and folded it in half.

She prayed he wouldn't look at the check. "You can cash it tomorrow."

Her prayers were answered. Without looking at the check, he stuffed it in his back pocket and said, "I don't accept checks. I'll hold on to this until you give me the cash. At least with this, I have your bank account number." He smiled an evil wicked grin.

Leslie plopped back down on the sofa; a soft tendril fell into her eye. She smiled wickedly. "You handle Ms. Jamaica and I'll take care of Derek."

He clasped his hands and rubbed them together. "Finally, I can get down and dirty."

She wagged her head. "No, nothing like that. Just need you to make a delivery."

Disappointment flashed across his face. "When do I make this delivery?"

"Tomorrow. Meet me here around noon."

# *30*

Maxine thumbed through *Sister2Sister* magazine as she waited the arrival of Frank's flight. Despite what she kept telling herself, she was nervous as hell and couldn't understand why she was waiting to meet someone who had betrayed her. Part of her wanted to get up and walk away. The other part wanted to hear what he had to say. She knew it had to be good.

She knew his plane had touched down at least ten minutes ago. Already feeling the stress of the situation, she prayed a silent prayer. "God, please give me the strength to have an open heart."

She stood patiently and watched as women with children, businessmen and casual travelers walked through the security area. She doesn't know how many people had traveled through security area, but thus far, no Frank. Or did he? Truth be told, she didn't know what he looked like. She'd never seen him before. Even though they had chatted regularly using Web cams, she really wouldn't know him from a hole in the wall. She became impatient and tossed the straps of her purse over her shoulder.

"This is ridiculous," she blurted out before walking off. "Maxine," she heard, his voice was courteous and gentle. She faced him. "Frank?" she said with quiet emphasis.

"Where are you going?" he asked, with a hearty chuckle. "You're just going to leave a brother?"

She spoke in a broken whisper. "I was sure…"

He walked towards her, his powerful well-muscled body moved with easy grace, carrying himself with a commanding air of self-confidence. He stood before her and opened his arms, welcoming her into an embrace.

"It is so good to finally meet you," he said.

She was conscious of his tall, athletic physique, as his muscular arms encircled her small-boned petite build. "It's good to see you, too," she whispered into his shoulder.

"You feel wonderful," he smiled, breaking the embrace. He stared at her, pleased with the sight before him. She was quite happy as well.

"So," she said, not knowing how to react. "How was your flight?"

"Rough."

"Are you hungry?"

"Starving."

"Great. Well, would you like to go to your hotel first?"

"No, I have guaranteed late arrival, so we can eat first."

"Baggage pickup up this way," she said, walking away from him.

"I packed lightly," he said holding up the small travel bag.

The walk to the car consisted of small talk, nervous giggles and then, "I see you're in good health." As they approached the car, Maxine used the key remote to open the trunk.

He tossed the bag into the trunk. "We have to discuss this now?"

"Yes indeed." She climbed into the car and closed the door. This was going to be a long ride. When he got into the car and closed the door, her head snapped toward him. "Why, Frank? Why did you have to make up a story like that?"

"Maxine, I didn't know what else to do."

"When in doubt, try the truth."

"Things were getting too…" he paused.

"Yes?"

"Maxine, you were moving too fast."

"Excuse me?"

"Yes. You wanted something I wasn't in the position to give you."

"Would it have been so bad for you to love me, Frank?"

"At that time, yes. Max, there was so much that I could not tell you...the places, people, locations...a time in my life where there was no room for me to open my heart."

"Instead, you hurt my heart by lying," she cried. "My God, do you even have a sister?"

"Yes."

"Does she know you used her to fake your death?"

He reached for her hand. She snatched it away.

"The reason I came here is to tell you that I do love you. My life is different now."

"You don't lie to the one you love," she said.

"You do if you don't know of any other way not to hurt them." He took her by the chin and leaned in close. "I'm sorry, Maxine. Hurting you was never my intention. Please understand." He softly grazed her lips. "Please understand," he whispered, kissing her again, his tongue broke through, tasting the sweetness of her breath. She succumbed.

His hand left his lap and ventured to the buttons on her jacket. He slowly unbuttoned her jacket and slipped his hand inside, palming her left breast. She released a soft cry as his hand left her breast and wandered down her belly towards her pants.

She gently shook her head no.

He mouthed yes.

She closed her eyes tighter, not believing this was happening to her. The man she had been in love with for five years was taking her breath away.

Maxine felt his fingers wiggle beneath the waistband and down toward her crotch. Her breath became uneven, feeling the moisture between her legs as though a grape had been squeezed there. She softly moaned and sucked on his tongue.

His fingers felt the moisture between her thighs, playing with her pubic lips, smoothing his fingers through the pubic hair, and finally catching a lock of it to pull and tease idly.

She spread her legs slightly, scooted down a notch and raised her hips, allowing him passage. "Sweet baby," she whispered in his ear. "I've missed you so much." Her back arched when his finger entered her, bringing her to a near explosion. She tilted her head to the side as he sucked around her neck and up to her earlobe.

She shivered as he stroked his tongue up and down her neck. "Oooh, Frank. Baby…ah yes," she cooed, experiencing the best orgasm ever.

# 31

Once she set her mind to something, she never backed off until she was completely satisfied.

Leslie shuffled through the papers on her desk, searching for the company's checkbook. A noise startled her. She froze. Her eyes rolled around, intently listening for the source. She shrugged it off and continued searching for the checkbook.

"Where in the hell did I put it?" she mumbled, opening drawers and then slamming them shut. "Damn it!"

She leaned back in her chair and gazed out the window. The sky was cloudy and unusually dark for nine-thirty in the morning. It looked like it may snow, giving her an eerie feeling. She hated driving in the snow and Washington, DC was not known for having the best drivers.

She faced the wall, a petition separating her office from Derek's. She pushed away from the desk and slowly stood up. She slowly walked to the door and opened it, looking right then left. She proceeded to Derek's office, closing the door behind her. She could hear voices in the hallway, so she froze where she stood and waited for the voices to disappear.

She looked around the office and on his desk, before going through the drawers. She looked behind his desk and spotted the checkbook on the credenza beneath the window. "Bingo!" she whispered.

She tucked the checkbook inside her suit jacket and rushed to her office. She closed the door and locked it. She smiled widely as she reached for her favorite pen.

Standing in the foyer of 1stTrust Bank, Leslie was the vision of a late thirties actress with sunglasses and scarf draped over her head and tied around her chin. She had watched enough Joan Collins' movies to play the part perfectly. Her ruby red painted lips protruded as she approached the counter. Not removing her glasses, she handed the blonde teller a check.

"I'd like large bills please."

The teller looked at the check, then at Leslie and back down at the check. "Excuse me, please." She walked from behind the counter and into a private inside office.

Leslie glanced in the direction of the teller and caught the eye of the bank's manager, who rose from his seat and approached Leslie.

"Good morning," he paused, looking down at the check. "Ms. L'Enfant."

Leslie smiled and responded, "Yes," to the alias.

"Do you have an account with us?" he asked, staring at his reflection through the lenses of her sunglasses.

"No, I don't. Is there a problem?"

"Since you do not have an account with our bank, we will have to get authorization to cash a check over fifty thousand dollars."

"Oh, I see."

"However, if you would like to open an account with us…"

"No thank you." She reached for the check. "I'll take it to my bank and make the deposit."

"Very well," he said handing her the check. "Is there anything else we can do for you today?"

She shook her head no, turned on her heels and sashayed to the door, while the bank manager admired the sway in her ass. The bank teller cleared her throat.

"Uh," he said, gathering himself. "Did you get her full name?"

She nodded and replied, "Lynette L'Enfant."

"I think I'll give Mr. Braxton a call. Something about that check doesn't sit right with me. He's never written a check that big before."

# 32

Gina had slipped into her coat and was easing her fingers into her gloves when Derek's private line rung. She started not to answer it, but thought against it.

"Derek Braxton's office," she answered, scooping her keeps from her purse.

"Hello, Gina. This is Cliff Skaggs from 1stTrust Bank."

"Hi, Cliff, how are you?"

"I could complain, but what good would it do?"

"None at all," she chuckled. "What can I do for you?"

"I'd like to speak with Derek."

"He's taking a mini vacation until next week."

"I suppose this could wait, but…"

"Is it something I could assist you with?"

"Well, a Lynette L'Enfant tried to cash a seventy-five thousand dollar check drawn on Metropolitan Construction's account."

Gina gasped. "What? Who is Lynette L'Enfant?"

"The amount raised a red flag. How long has Derek been on vacation?"

"Since yesterday…"

"The check was dated for today's date."

"I'm glad you pay attention to your red flags. As long as I've been working for my brother, I've never seen him write a check that large. All of our vendors are small-time."

"I don't have a good feeling about this one, Gina. The check was signed by Derek."

"You didn't cash it, did you?"

"No, we didn't cash it. When we told her we need to call and get authorization to cash a check over fifty thousand, she declined, took the check and left."

"Can we stop payment on the check?"

"Sure. I made a copy of the check before I gave it back to her."

"Can you fax me a copy?'

"It's on the way."

"Cliff, thank you so much. I'll contact Derek and let him know about this."

"It's my pleasure."

"Oh, by the way, can you describe this woman?"

"Not really. Except she was a sister wearing dark shades and a scarf."

"Thank you, Cliff. You have a great day."


Derek had just stepped out of the shower when the phone rung. He wrapped the towel around his waist. Wet footprints on the marble floor followed him to the opposite side of the master suite bathroom. "Hello," he answered, wiping his hand over his face.

"We have a problem," Gina said. "Are you alone?"

"Yeah, Jamaica went home to pack. What's up?"

"Does a Lynette L'Enfant ring a bell?"

"Who?"

"My sentiments exactly."

"Gina, what are you talking about and who is this Lynette person?"

"Derek, I know you didn't, but I have to ask you."

"Damn it, Gina!" he yelled, annoyed and frustrated, wanting her to get to the point before he exploded.

"Did you write a seventy-five thousand dollar check out to one Lynette L'Enfant?"

"Hell no!"

"I didn't think so. I received a call from Cliff a few minutes ago. He says this woman came in and tried to cash a check, drawn on Met Construction."

"Well, did she cash it and who the hell wrote her that check?"

"It had your signature…

"Was it cashed?" he spoke through clenched teeth, his blood was now at its highest boiling point. He had no proof, as of yet, but he knew exactly who was behind it all.

"No, it wasn't cashed. He told her he had to get authorization to cash such a large check."

Derek took a sigh of relief.

"Derek, you know who is behind this, right?"

"I think I do."

"Uh huh, she sent the dead rat, too."

"We don't know that for sure, Gina."

"Derek, will you please pull your head out of Jamaica's ass for one minute and smell the sunshine? You know damn well Leslie is not happy with the way you just cut things off with her. And I'm sure she knows about Jamaica, too," she paused. "I don't trust her Derek."

Derek was silent, sorting through his thoughts.

"How is Jamaica doing, by the way?"

"She's fine, a little bruised up."

"What happened to her anyway? You never told me."

He grunted. "Good question. I don't know myself."

"Was she attacked, raped, what?"

"I'll let you know when I find out, sis."

"This shit has Leslie Wilson written all over it," she stated. "I'm going to the office tonight."

"For what?"

"Just call me Ms. Columbo."

He chuckled. "Okay, Ms. Columbo."

"Derek, this bitch might be taking you to the cleaners and you don't even know it. I told you about trusting people with your business and your finances."

"I never gave Leslie authority to write checks on my behalf. She processes invoices and submits them to accounting."

"Uh huh, she's not a dumb bitch, by far."

"Gina, you know I hate that word…bitch."

"I call it as I see it. I'll call you tonight to let you know what I find out."

Derek lowered his head. After a long minute, he looked into the mirror. His face frowned and his brows drew together. "Fuck! I should've left her ass where I found her—in a raggedy ass box in the park."

# 33

Jamaica stood in front of her closet. What do you pack for Italy? She'd never been out of the country and didn't know the first thing to pack. She counted on her fingers the number of outfits she may need. She didn't need to pack a lot of underwear. Derek didn't like her wearing underwear to bed. When he pulled her close, he wanted to feel the warmth of her flesh, not a pair of cotton underwear.

She couldn't stop thinking about him. She'd been in love before, but it never felt quite like this. This was different than the others. Derek was different.

Jamaica pulled the suitcase from the closet. The phone rang just as she unzipped the zipper.

As the phone rang for the fifth time, she opened the suitcase and picked up the phone. "Hello."

"Hi honey. Are you busy?"

"Hey, you! Yes, I'm quite busy. I'm packing!" she yelled with laughter. "Derek, I'm so excited I don't know what to do."

"That's good, babe. Can you give me a few minutes of your time?"

Jamaica could hear the concern in his voice. "Sure, babe, what's up?"

"You never told me how you ended up in the hospital."

Jamaica's eyes widened and her mouth fell open. "I…I…didn't want to concern you. Everything will be alright though."

"Concern me," he demanded.

"What?"

"Jamaica, something's going on and I don't know what it is, but…"

"Derek, nothing's going on. I didn't do anything. I was mugged and that's all it is to it."

"I wouldn't be mad," he said.

"You shouldn't be mad," she snapped.

"Jamaica, do you love me?"

"That's not a fair question, Derek."

"If you love me, then you'll tell me."

"There's nothing to tell, damn it," she cried. "Why can't you just leave it alone?"

"Anything that affects you, affects me, honey," he consoled.

"Alright, Derek. About an hour after you left, I felt like going shopping. I didn't feel like taking a cab, so I walked to the bus stop. The woman approached me, dressed in black from head to toe, with a ski mask.

"She stood in front of me and yelled for me to stay away from you. Then, she knocked me to the ground. She hit me so hard and fast, I never saw it coming.

Derek's stomach knotted. "Why didn't you tell me this earlier?"

"Because…I don't know, Derek."

"You're staying with me tonight."

"I have so much to pack before we leave in the morning," she whined.

"Pack what you can. If you forget something, we'll go shopping. But I'd feel better if you were here tonight, where I can protect you."

Jamaica sighed. "Tillie and Maxine are coming over to help me pack."

"You call me when you're ready and I'll pick you up. No matter the time. Okay?"

"Okay. Goodbye, Derek."

# *34*

Leslie had gotten over the pop in the lip and she was back to her old self, as she rapidly pounded on the door. "Shit! Robert, open the damn door."

The door flung open, causing her to slightly fall forward.

He yelled, "I'm sick of you banging on my goddamn door."

"What in the fuck happened to you?" she yelled, her arms waving about. She marched into the kitchen. "I've been calling and calling," she said, dropping her handbag on the table. "You are fucking everything up, you asshole!"

"Look, watch your mouth and I forgot. A'ight?"

"No, it ain't *a'ight*, you dumb ass!"

"I ain't gonna be too many fucking names, Leslie. No wonder that motherfucker don't want to be bothered with your ass, banging on my door like you done lost your damn mind." He reached into the refrigerator and pulled out a jug of ice tea. If it weren't for her supporting his habit, he wouldn't be putting up with her bullshit. He still had a headache from the lamp she crashed against his head several days ago. "Want some tea?"

"No thank you." She hopped up on the wooden stool and crossed her arms across her chest.

He reached into the cupboard and grabbed the bottle of aspirin. "I still have a damn headache, no thanks to you," he said.

Leslie watched him open the bottle and pop four aspirins, before drinking the tea from the jug. "Why are you taking so many aspirins?"

He looked at her and rolled his eyes. "I don't know why I put up with your shit," he snapped. He returned the jug of tea to the refrigerator. "All this work, I should at least get some ass out of it."

"I already apologized once and you put up with me because you have a habit and I help you maintain it."

He sniffed and used the back of his hand to wipe his nose. "You know what? Naw, fuck this shit. Keep your money and get the fuck out of my house."

Leslie didn't budge. After all, she'd witnessed his temper tantrums on more than one occasion.

He asked, "Why are you still sitting there?"

"Fifty thousand dollars."

His eyes bulged out and his mouth fell open.

"I knew that would change your mind," she smiled. "Just imagine all the blow you could shove up your nose with fifty big ones."

He stretched his arms out on the kitchen counter and lowered his head. He was fed up with feeling as if she had him by the balls at every turn because of his habit. Fifty thousand dollars was a whole lot of money though. Moreover, she was right, he could party for months on that kind of loot. He could become a businessman, sell his own supply and one day, buy that A-frame house, which sat on the Chesapeake Bay in Annapolis. The house he fell in love with over the summer.

He faced her. "Where are you going to get fifty thousand dollars?"

"Easy. I write you a check for one hundred thousand dollars. You deposit it into your bank account. We wait for it to clear and you write me a check for fifty grand. Simple as A, B, C."

"In other words, you want me to launder money for you."

"Well, I wasn't really thinking about it in that way, but I suppose you could call it that."

"I thought you were smart," he chuckled. "That would be some serious jail time if we got caught."

"But we won't and Derek has millions. He's not going to miss a measly hundred thousand."

"You keep on thinking that man has no sense. He didn't get this far being an idiot." He folded his arms across his chest, contemplating her proposition. "You know, since I would have the biggest risk, with my name being on the account and all, I should get at least eighty percent."

She fell over with laughter. "I don't think so, honey."

"I'm the one chancing jail time."

"Hmmm," she said, the wheels spinning faster than a hamster running on a wheel. "You have a point there. But you seem to forget something."

"Which is…"

"I would be facing jail time, too. I could give a shit if you go to jail or not. This was all my idea. So, you're lucky I'm offering you half."

He chuckled and shook his head. "You are truly a heartless bitch."

"Heartless is cool, but why must I be a bitch?"

"Because it fits you to a tee." He walked out of the kitchen. "You know your way out."

"You know you need me, Robert; I don't know why you're frontin' like you don't!"

He slowly walked back into the kitchen and stood in the doorway, his hands shoved down the waistband of his sweat pants. He stared at her. His disgust quickly changed to pity.

"Leslie, how many times do you have to meet karma face-to-face before you realize it's time to quit?"

She looked at him like he was crazy.

He continued, "Yeah," he smiled. "That karma ain't no joke. You better watch your back." He turned up his nose. "You smell that?"

"How can you smell anything?"

"There's this foul stench in the air. It has exactly thirty seconds to vacate before I eliminate it."

"Crazy motherfucker," she mumbled, snatching her purse and exiting stage left.

# *35*

"You couldn't have chosen a better spot," Frank said, eating a spinach salad with mushrooms, cherry tomatoes, bacon bits and crumbled feta cheese. He spooned the mushrooms off the plate and on the table, scooting them under his plate.

Maxine thought his table manners left a lot to be desired, but wasn't anything she couldn't correct, in time.

"I love this spot. I don't get to come here often."

"Why not?" he asked, chewing with his mouth open.

Maxine frowned at the sight of seeing food dance around in his mouth. She turned her head and said, "I'm on a strict budget. I cant' afford this as much as I would like."

"Now you can."

"What do you mean?"

"I'm relocating here and you will have someone to help you afford your wants."

"Oh please, man," she chuckled.

"Now see, a man try and do right by a sister…"

"Not telling me that bold face lie would've been sufficient"

"I see you're still holding it against me."

"Forgive me if it takes me a minute to have trust in you."

Frank dropped his fork in his plate. "Damn, Max, what do you want me to do? Beg for your forgiveness every fucking day?"

"That would be nice."

"Fuck that, I'm not about to humiliate myself for a piece of ass."

Maxine followed suit, except her fork flew across the table, just missing his cheek. "A piece of ass?"

He said nothing.

She said, "This is one piece of ass you won't get, motherfucker." Maxine rose from her seat, pushing it back with the backs of her legs, almost turning over the chair. Every bowed head in the restaurant was now focused on her. "To think I was going to give you the benefit of the doubt."

"I think you're overreacting," he said, wiping his mouth with the white linen napkin.

She turned to him and said, "You made up the story about dying and now all of a sudden, you're back in my life. No, I'm not overreacting. You can kiss my pretty black ass and that's putting it mildly." She left him sitting there. Alone. The ultimate embarrassment. "Jive time turkey," she yelled as the door closed behind her.

Frank felt like an idiot. All eyes were on him. The women sucked their teeth and rolled their eyes and the men mumbled, "Go get your woman, man."

He was hot on her heels, as she marched down Wisconsin Avenue with fire blazing beneath her feet.

"He called out, "Maxine!" He called out again, "Maxine! Hold up."

Maxine raised her arm above her head and extended her middle finger. "Fuck you, motherfucker," she yelled, causing people to stop in their tracks. The snooty residents of Georgetown weren't used to such behavior."

"Damn it, Maxine, just stop!"

She stopped with her back to him.

He approached her from behind, out of breath. "I'm sorry. Okay?"

"Yeah, you're sorry alright." She whipped around and said, "You are one sorry ass…"

"Max!" he cut her off and asked, "How long are you going to punish me?"

"As long as it takes," she said.

"And how long is that?"

"Might be your lifetime. Don't quite know."

He pulled her into him and palmed her face. "I love you, woman. Always have loved you."

Maxine showed no expression on her face. She'd heard those exact words before. She said, "Love don't live here no more." She stepped out of his embrace. "Besides, I'm only a piece of ass. Remember?"

"Maxine, I don't know what else you want me to say or do. You know my line of work."

"Any line of work that causes you to be untruthful to someone you *supposedly* love, isn't a job I would apply for."

He stepped back and raised his hands in the air. "I'm waving the white flag."

Maxine slouched her shoulders and relaxed the muscles in her face. She really did love him, despite it all. For the first time since her failed marriage, she wanted to let her shield down and feel complete. Feel loved.

"You can stay at my place," she said.

He pulled her into him and covered her mouth, their tongues frolicking. He sucked her tongue. She sucked his. After a long minute, he raised his head and cupped her face with one hand, while the other pressed firmly into her lower back, pulling her closer into him.

She looked up at him and smiled. "I'm glad you're here. And, I'm sorry. I do love you, Frank." She wrapped her arms around his neck, closed her eyes and exhaled. Her shield was down and it felt wonderful.

"Let's go," he said, releasing his hold on her.

# *36*

The front door slammed behind her as she tossed the brown bag on the kitchen counter and rushed to the bathroom. She sat on the toilet and peed. Before flushing the soiled toilet paper, she wiped her hands with it, cringing at her action, but quickly got over it.

In the kitchen, she stood in the middle of the floor, looking around and then at her hands. She did not want to touch any of her things with her contaminated hands.

"Fuck it," she said. "I can call Molly Maids tomorrow," and tore through the cupboards for the cake pan, measuring cup and mixer.

She opened the refrigerator and pulled out the carton of eggs, milk and butter, and preheated the oven to 350 degrees. A wicked smile slowly formed on her face as she poured the contents of the brown paper bag onto the kitchen counter: chocolate Duncan Hines cake mix and four packs of chocolate flavored laxatives, better known as Ex-Lax.

She mixed the batter with her hands, while trying her best to cough up a lung, making sure her germs floating from her insides into the cake batter.

Leslie did not want to kill Jamaica. Her intention was to make her miserable for a while. To feel the pain she was feeling.

Tears welled in her eyes and streamed down her face. "You motherfucker!" she cried. Her salty tears dripped into the batter. "I gave you the best years of my fucking life!" Jamaica had replaced her and she had to pay.

Jamaica definitely wasn't going to Italy with Derek, not if she had anything to do with it. She learned of the intended trip when Derek's travel agent called the office, instead of his private home office.

Leslie was of only one opinion. There was only one woman for Derek and she was the one. "I'm the one who should be going to Italy, not that troll bitch," she fussed as she turned on the hot water faucet and reached under the sink for the dishwashing liquid. She squeezed a dime-sized drop of Palmolive into the palm of her hand and rubbed her hands together, vigorously.

She looked at the batter and turned up her face. There was one last ingredient she needed to add. She pressed her index finger on the side of her right nostril, inhaled deeply and quickly blew out a wad of green mucus into the batter. She stirred the batter and then gently placed the cake mixture into the oven.

She reached into the refrigerator, pulled out a Heineken, grabbed the bag of potato chips and headed for the living room, where she plopped down on the sofa, grabbed the remote and turned on the television. Maury Povich was consoling a woman who found out the man she thought was her baby's daddy wasn't her baby's daddy.

It amazed her how people would go to great lengths to act like fools, airing their dirty laundry for the world to see. "The dumb ass should keep her legs closed," she huffed, shoving chips into her mouth followed by a gulp of ice cold Heineken.

In public, Leslie thought herself to be the ultimate diva. Men found it hard to ignore her. Her skin was the color of raisins you'd find in moist oatmeal cookies. Her body was slender, her hips slim with piercing eyes—eyes she always kept hidden behind dark shades, her way of keeping people from looking into her soul, seeing her true self. She wasn't petite nor was she stocky. At five feet three, her medium build fell slightly in between.

She looked at her watch, everything's on schedule. She had called the courier during her drive from the grocery store. The balloons and a dozen of roses were in her car. Leslie knew she needed a foolproof plan to make this work and keep her anonymity. Yeah, Robert had let her down, but she called a courier service and used a fictitious credit card. The courier was going to pick up the cake and balloons on the porch of a house she had chosen. She had exactly one hour and thirty minutes to drop off Jamaica's goodies to the house around the corner. She chose that house because the owner had been out of the country for months.

She set the alarm on her cell, closed her eyes and dreamed of Jamaica held up in the bathroom. She giggled at the idea. She'll be known as *little shitty* from now on.

Exactly an hour and a half later, Leslie sat across the street and watched as the late eighties Ford Escort pulled up in front of the empty house. She watched as he carried the dozen roses, balloons and boxed chocolate cake from the front porch to the Escort, placing them in the back seat.

Leslie fell over with laughter as the Escort pulled away from the curb and sped up the street. Her laughter ceased as her thoughts turned to Derek. She wondered what he was doing. She missed him. She missed his touch. A heat of anger rose inside her as she visualized his lips caressing Jamaica's body, his dick swimming inside her.

Her cell rung and the caller ID show Derek's private number. She smiled and answered. "Hello, Baby."

He huffed in disgust at her greeting. "We need to talk," he snapped.

"Oooh, and how are you today?" she chuckled, obviously annoying him.

"Leslie, you and I need to have a one-on-one," he said, trying to remain calm.

"You know where I live," she said. "Or have you forgotten that, too?"

"I remember," he said coldly.

She ignored the hostility in his voice. "You hungry? I can have dinner waiting…"

"No thank you," he said sharply.

"Oh." The disappointment resounded in her voice. "Okay then. Well, I can't wait to see you. It's been a long time since we've…"

"I'll see you in an hour." He hung up in her ear.

# 37

"This is home," she said closing the door behind him. "Make yourself at home."

He dropped his bags to the floor and pulled her into him. He embraced her lips with a warm, soft kiss.

"Oooh," she cooed.

He kissed her cheek, moving down to her neck, settling behind her ear.

"Ahh." She panted, "Oh, Frank."

With ease he removed her leather jacket and tossed it over the chair. His fingertips roamed her body, down her arms and round her elbows, sending chills through her.

He sucked her neck vigorously, causing her to wiggle and squirm about in his arms. "That tickles," she said. She loved having her neck sucked.

Remembering their many conversations over the 'net, he was primed to do the things to her that she enjoyed—that made her stimulated. He continued sucking as he unbuttoned her cotton denim shirt and eased it off her shoulders. It billowed to the floor. His hands maneuvered her bra, unsnapping it, sliding it down her arms and letting it fall to the floor.

They hungered for each other. She groped his dick and he fondled her vagina. "Get out of those jeans," he whispered.

She quickly unbuttoned the fly of her jeans and wiggled, easing them over her curvaceous hips and down her toned thighs and bulging calf muscles. She stepped out of them and kicked them across the room.

He tore out of his smothering clothing and tossed them on the sofa. He knelt down before and looked up, gazing at her beauty. "You are beautiful," he said.

She blushed. "I could stand to lose a few pounds."

"Don't do that. You're perfect."

"You're blind," she said.

"I see very well and so does my heart," he said, pulling her down to the floor, lying her flat on her back. He slowly pulled her lilac panties over her hips, down her thighs and legs and over her painted red toes. He held them up to his nose and inhaled.

"You smell sweet," he said, spreading her legs open.

She covered her held in stomach and abdomen, hiding her slightly protruding belly.

He smiled and said, "I want to see all of you."

She slowly moved her hands and placed them flat on the floor beside her.

His fingers roamed up her legs toward her thighs and resting in her fiery bush. She softly moaned and slightly arched her back. He eased his finger into her wetness, outlining the lips of her pussy, poking and prodding, becoming familiar with her. It had been over a year since they talked over the 'net, but his mind was fresh with her likes.

The growing longing in his dick was unbearable. He needed to feel her. He needed to join with the woman he'd yearned so many years for. But, he had waited this long, he could wait a few more minutes longer.

His tongue found its way to her love. He sucked her clitoris, then her pussy lips, down around her anus and back to her clitoris, where he focused under the hood. He could feel her bud swelling between his lips.

She arched her back and wiggled her hips into his face, fucking his mouth. "Ahh, don't stop," she moaned heavily.

"That's it, baby, right there." She grabbed the back of his head and held on for the ride. "Oooh, shit, motherfucker, don't you stop eating this pussy," she demanded. "Ahh shit, here it comes," she yelled. She wrapped her legs around his neck, holding him in-place, making sure he didn't move from the spot.

Her body gyrated, her legs shot straight over his head, her hands and fingers grabbed at the carpet. She was nearing climax.

He stopped sucking and quickly inserted his dick into her pool of juices. He grunted from deep with in. "Damn, you've got some good ass pussy," he announced, as if she wasn't aware that she could tame the wildest of the wild with her sweet pussy.

She contorted her body into different positions, making his thrusts even deeper until she screamed loudly, scaring him, "No, it's okay, it's pleasure, not pain. More, more." Tracing the lumpy texture of her vaginal walls with the probing tip of his dick, he could feel the sweat pouring down his forehead onto her cheeks, his tongue embedded in her mouth, his dick growing harder inside her orifice, with every forward movement, her insides melting around his dick, pleasure mounting. He arched his back and pulled up inside her, deeper and deeper, pounding the bottom.

She yelped several times, wrapping her arms around his waist, pushing him deeper. She enjoyed the pain of pleasure he inflicted. She wrapped her legs around his waist. "Fuck me, damn it," she cried. "Fuck me hard, Frank. Fuck me!"

Frank's thrusts grew faster and harder. His face distorted, his climax building. She could feel the veins on his dick growing, about to explode inside her.

"Fuck your pussy!" she yelled.

With one last powerful thrust inside her, he yelled. She yelled. He yelled again. She yelled again. Her eyes rolled back in her head. His back arched and he continued thrusting.

"Grrrrr," came from him, sounding like a wounded animal. "Grrrrrrr!"

She opened her eyes. And looked into his. He laughed.

"What's so funny?" she smiled, panting, trying to slow her breathing.

He relaxed on top of her. "I think I broke my dick," he said into her neck.

She hugged and fell out with laughter. "And I think you knocked the bottom out of my ass, too!"

## 38

"I want us to live together," she said, flipping through the baby section of the *JC Penny Catalog*. "Since we're having a baby, and you're practically over here day and night, we should at least live like a family."

Randy lowered *The Washington Post* and peered at Tillie over the paper. "I'm not ready to play house. I told you that already."

"Children play house."

"And so do adults. I'm not feeling that at all."

"You have a key and you're over here more than you are at your place. Why pay to stay at two places."

"I don't pay rent here," he said, raising the paper up to finish reading the sports section.

Tillie closed the catalog and stared at the paper, becoming more and more annoyed at him. She headed to the kitchen to begin preparing dinner. "I don't see what the big deal is," she shouted. "I mean, we are going to get married anyway."

Randy lowered the paper. "We are?"

"Yes, we are. I'm not raising my baby without a father."

"What are you talking about, woman, that baby has a father," he snapped, irritated with having to revisit the topic he loathed. He didn't like being pressured into something he wasn't ready to handle.

The pots and pans clanged and the water faucet ran as Tillie bumped around in the kitchen. "You know what I mean, baby." She peeked around the corner from the kitchen. "Baby,

I don't want to argue about this. I'm only expressing my concerns."

"You're trying to make me do something I don't want to do," he said, tossing the paper to the side. "This topic of discussion is getting old. I'm not ready for marriage and I'm not ready to play house. Hell," he stood to his feet, "I ain't ready for no damn baby, but I don't have a choice in the matter. But with that other shit, I have a choice and my mind is made up. So you can just stop talking about it, 'cause I'm through."

Tillie stood in the doorway of the kitchen. "You didn't have a choice?"

He stood in the middle of the floor and looked at her, with his hands propped on his hips. "You didn't ask me if I wanted to be a father."

"If you didn't want to be a father, you should have covered up your dick."

"You trapped me!" he yelled, the veins in his neck pulsating.

"I did what?" Tillie laughed. "I trapped you? Nigger, it takes two to fuck."

"I thought you were on the pill. You're supposed to protect yourself. If you didn't, then you were trying to get pregnant."

Tillie couldn't control her laughter. "You sound like a goddamn fool."

"I don't like that word, Tillie."

"What?"

"It ain't right, you using God's name in vein like that."

"Nigger, please. God is probably pissed off your ass anyway."

Randy tilted his head to the side, a questionable look on his face. "What do you mean?"

"His creation turned out to be a sorry ass motherfucker. That's what I mean." She grabbed her purse and keys and headed for the door.

"Where are you going?" he asked, ready to bash her head through the wall with her last comment. If he were to ever hit a woman, she'd be the first because of her damn mouth.

"Going to mind my *goddamn* business," she said, the door slamming behind her.

# 39

"Sounds like an old married couple to me," Jamaica chuckled, trying to fit twenty outfits into one garment bag.

"You have entirely too much shit in that bag," Tillie said, lying on her stomach across the bed and inhaling the sheets. Jamaica always sprayed her sheets with Jasmine and Sandalwood scents. Earthy scents, blending with her earthy nature.

"Derek said to only bring one garment bag and a carry on bag. He doesn't like to check luggage."

"What am I going to do about Randy?" she whined.

"Respect his wishes," Jamaica said, pulling the suitcase from under the bed.

"I thought he said one garment bag and a carry on bag."

"I ain't thinking about Derek. I ain't shoving all my clothes into this one bag."

"Girl, you better ball that shit up and iron it when you get there," Tillie chuckled, her legs rose in the air, swaying from side to side.

"Don't lie on your stomach, Tillie. You may hurt the baby."

Tillie frowned, huffed and rolled over onto her back. She crossed her feet at the ankles.

"I don't want to raise my child up fatherless."

"It won't be fatherless."

She frowned. "My child is not an *it*, Jamaica."

"Sorry. You know what I mean. Don't go getting serious on me now, hormones about to start raging, I'm sure."

"So I should respect his wishes and let him neglect his responsibility?"

"Randy is a grown ass man. If he doesn't take care of his responsibility, then you do what every other woman does. Take his ass to court for child support."

The doorbell rang. "I'll get it," Tillie said, rolling off the bed and toward the door. "You expecting company?"

"Nope, only you and Max show up unannounced."

Tillie closed the door and yelled down the hall. "That man is in love with your ass, girl."

"Wow," Jamaica said, coming down the short hallway to the living room. "How do you know they are from Derek?" She propped her hands on her hips. "Girl, did you read my card before I could?"

"Nope, just an assumption."

Jamaica read the card silently.

"What does it say?" Tillie asked, being nosey, which wasn't unusual.

"It says, *'Roses are red, violets are blue, I love you and I think you love me too.'* " She smiled widely.

"Well, do you love him?"

"Girl, yes!"

"You sure it ain't lust?"

Jamaica rolled her eyes and focused on the box. "I wonder what's in here."

"Open it," Tillie said, anxious to get a glimpse. "Probably a diamond or something."

Jamaica chuckled. "Oh, Tillie, not in this big box. Besides, I would think he would give me a diamond in person."

Jamaica removed the deep lavender ribbon from around the soft pink box and neatly folded it. "I'm going to start up a keepsake book for me and Derek. This will be the first to go in it."

Tillie faked a yawn and said, "Will you please open the fucking box already?"

"Okay, okay." Jamaica opened the box and admired the beautifully iced chocolate cake.

"Now that looks good. Let's cut it!"

"Damn, could I please admire my gift for a minute before you devour it with your greedy behind."

"Girl, it ain't me. It's Tillie, Jr. She's hungry."

Jamaica's smile broadened in approval. "Okay, get a knife," she said, as Tillie rushed to the kitchen and back like the speed of light. "Cut it for me, Tillie. I have to pee."

"TMI, just TMI, Jamaica," she said, slicing the sharp knife through the moist, delicate cake. She pinched off a piece and tasted it. "Umm, it's good," she yelled.

"I want a big piece," Jamaica yelled from the bathroom.

"Uh-huh, wash your hands before you leave out of there!"

"Yes, Mama," she said, smiling and trotting down the hall. "I'll grab the bottle of wine."

"Sounds good!"

"And I'll grab the sparkling cider for you," Jamaica teased.

"Whatever."

They stretched out on the floor, eating cake and drinking Riesling and sparking cider. "I'm going to ask Maxine about her hitting on Randy," Tillie said, inhaling her second slice of cake.

"I hate it when there is dissension among us."

"She betrayed me, as far as I'm concerned. She knows Randy is my man. Why would she try and fuck him?"

Jamaica sliced her third piece of cake and poured her fourth glass of wine. "You know Max hasn't been right since her marriage ended. You know it really fucked her up, finding out her man was cheating on her. She has problems trusting."

"What does that have to do with her trying to fuck Randy?"

Jamaica was silent. She noticed the stress lines hardening in Tillie's face. "Did he fuck her?"

"No, so he says."

"Then don't worry about it."

"She betrayed our friendship, Jamaica. How can you tell me not to worry about it? If the bitch will try it once, she'll definitely try it a second, third and fourth time."

"He handled it. He turned her down. Let it be. You have other things to worry about, like godparents for the baby and picking names.

"Maxine is our friend, but a woman just the same. Watch her closely and handle her with a wooden spoon."

"You mean a ten-foot-pole."

"No, I mean a wooden spoon. Keep her close, but at a distance."

Tillie sat her plate on the floor and grabbed her stomach. Her stomach grumbled.

"Damn, I could hear your stomach all the way over here."

"Yeah, I'm not feeling so good. I have cramps."

"Is that normal during pregnancy, to have cramps?"

"I don't know, but these cramps are different." She bent over.

"Are you okay, girl?"

Tillie shook her head no. "I need to use your bathroom."

"Go ahead." Jamaica rose to help Tillie off the floor. "Are you sure you're going to be alright?"

Tillie nodded. "Uh-huh, I'm sure it's just gas."

Tillie pulled down her trousers and sat on the toilet. "I'll be fine. You don't have to stay in here with me."

"I don't like the way you're looking. You look pale, like you're about to pass out."

"I feel like I need to throw up."

Jamaica put the trashcan between Tillie's legs and dampened a washcloth with cold water. "Throw up in the trashcan and put this wash cloth on your forehead. It'll make you feel better."

Tillie grabbed her stomach and leaned over. "Oh God, this hurts."

"Don't hold it, let it out, Tillie."

Tillie pushed one time before letting out a massive fart, making way for a badly needed bowel movement.

The smell overwhelmed Jamaica. She pinched her nose closed. "Ooh, girl, you stink!"

Tillie pulled the trashcan up to her chin and regurgitated. Tillie was unstopped at both ends.

Jamaica heaved, "Oh Lord, let me get out of here," and ran out the bathroom and into the kitchen. She leaned against the refrigerator and bent over down to her knees. She grabbed her now rumbling stomach. She felt dizzy. She couldn't hold it. She ran to the bathroom. "Tillie, are you finished? I have to go, too."

"I can't move," Tillie said. "I'm sorry, but I'm still shittin'. I feel like shit, girl."

In a one-bedroom apartment, Tillie was occupying the only bathroom. She rushed to the kitchen and frantically turned in circles, hunched over, like a dog chasing its tail. She grabbed the large crab pot from underneath the sink and sat it on the floor. She quickly pulled down her pants and sat on the pot and let out a sigh of relief.

Feeling queasy, she reached into the refrigerator and grabbed a bottle of water from the door. She took big gulps of water. Within seconds, the water would find its way from her stomach, up through her throat and on the kitchen floor, with chunks of chocolate cake.

"Tillie," she yelled. "Tillie!"

In a weak voice, Tillie yelled, "I'm okay. You okay?"

"What in the fuck was in that cake?"

"Don't know, but what ever it was gave us a good colon cleansing."

"We can't tell anyone about this," Tillie managed to chuckle. "We'll never hear the end of it."

Jamaica's thighs were going numb sitting on the edge of the crab pot. "Uh-huh, nobody but Derek. He's going to know this cake made us sick as dogs, shittin' out of every orifice of our body."

"Can I take a shower? I feel like, like, shit!"

They both laughed.

"Yeah, me, too!

"By the way," Tillie said, unable to control her laughter. "What did you use to shit in?"

"My best crab pot I paid sixty-five dollars for."

"Remind me to never eat crabs over here again!

# 40

It was after seven when Derek arrived at Leslie's apartment. He didn't have to be buzzed in. He knew the pass code. After all, his name was on the lease. The door opened before he could knock.

"Hi baby," she squealed, jumping into his arms and wrapping her arms around his neck. "I've missed you," she said, kissing him on the cheek.

Roughly, he thrust her away from him and entered the apartment. She lost her balance and fell to the floor. Her silk robe wrapped tightly around her waist, not allowing for movement. She slipped out of the robe and stood to her feet. The matching silk gown hugged every curve, accentuating her firm breasts, like two ripe melons.

Looking around, he noticed not much had changed. Every piece of furniture he purchased was in its rightful place. Prior to Leslie starting work at Metropolitan Construction, Derek was living in the Lake Arbor Towers in Mitchellville, Maryland. Three months after their relationship began, he purchased his current home in Foxhall Estates. He allowed her to stay so she would not end up on the streets, where he found her.

She walked around him, eyeing him, wondering if he knew about what she did to Jamaica. "Want a drink, baby?" she asked, standing behind the glass-encased bar, filling a snifter with ice cubes.

"No thank you." His words were harsh. He took a seat on the Italian leather sofa, sitting back and resting his leg over his knee.

"Oh, okay, well, what do you want to talk about?" The diva bitch had turned into a meek, innocent being. A role she could flip flop at the drop of a hat.

"Would you mind telling me why you were trying to cash a seventy-five thousand dollar check at my bank?"

She nervously chuckled. "Excuse me? I have no clue…"

"Cut the bullshit!" he yelled, now leaning forward. "You entered my bank with a check you forged my name on."

"I did no such thing. And I don't appreciate your accusations."

"It is fact," he said, reaching inside his left breast jacket pocket. "I have proof and your ass is going to jail." He tossed the checkbook on the coffee table. "I just want to know why. Everything I've done for you. Took your ass off the streets and put you in a home. I gave you a job and trusted you with my business." His face was set, his clamped mouth and fixed eyes struck a chord and put a little fear in her heart.

"Derek, baby, there must be some misunderstanding. And, believe me, I do appreciate all you've done for me. I would never do anything…"

"No lies tonight, please. I'm not in the mood."

She sat down in the chair and said, "I know about her."

His eyebrows rose inquisitively and a muscle quivered in his jaw.

She continued, "I know all about her. I know where she lives, too," she taunted, releasing a wicked soft chuckle. Her plan was working. She was pissing him off. "Your little girlfriend is probably full of shit by now, and I don't mean that in the literal sense either."

He continued to stare at her, but remained silent. In many ways he was seeing her for the first time. She had problems, she had issues. She was *walking drama* and he felt foolish, because he had been bamboozled. Unfortunately, he felt he had bamboozled himself. Trying to do the right thing doesn't always result in the desired outcome.

She walked over to him, close up in his face. He could smell the Alize on her breath. "I saw you in Burberry's, Legal Seafood and now you *think* you're going to Italy?" she said, walking circles around him.

In one fell swoop, he grabbed her by the throat, his fingers wrapping around her neck, adding pressure with each spoken word. "You are fucking with the wrong one."

Tears of fear streamed down her cheeks and down her mouth. "My body still craves for you," she managed to utter, as the life was being squeezed from her.

He released his grip and took several steps backward, not taking his eyes off of her.

She coughed and rubbed around her throat. "I thought you loved me," she cried. "How could you dance around in her? Why, Derek?"

"Where is the check?" he asked.

"I don't know what you're talking about," she lied.

She wiped away the tears with the back of her hand. She forced a smile and tossed her head back, releasing a sexy chuckle. She slipped each strap from her shoulders and the gown billowed to the floor, nestled around her feet.

"For old time's sake," she said, running her moist tongue across her full lips.

He turned his head.

She sat on the sofa and opened her legs wide. "Come on, Derek. You know you can't deny me. You were never capable of denying me, always wanting me."

Her fingers started at her belly button and worked its way to her wet forest, gliding in and out of her cave. "One last time and you'll never have to worry about me again."

"You disgust me," he said, reaching for the doorknob. "Your services are no longer needed at Metropolitan Construction, effectively immediately." He turned his back on her. "I've canceled the lease as well. You have until the end of the month to vacate."

She jumped to her feet. "It's that bitch, isn't it? Well, you let me tell you something, you black motherfucker. For five motherfucking years, I was your whore. I did what you wanted, when you wanted and how you wanted it. You fucked me whenever and wherever you wanted. I let you do it because I loved you and I thought you loved me, too.

"I gave you the best fucking years of my life and you cheat on me with your new cunt!"

"I did not cheat on you," he belted. "You and I were over a long time ago. Why do you think I stopped working out of the office?"

"Because you are a coward!"

"Because I didn't want to see you hurt, day in and day out."

She dropped to her knees. "Please, Derek, I am all that you need. Hell, you are all that I need. I can't function without you. Please, baby, don't do this to me."

"You've done it to yourself. I want you out of my life, Leslie."

"To hell with you then!" she yelled, hurling her shoe at his head.

He quickly moved to the side, avoiding a smack in the face.

"It's your loss, you bastard!"

"If you so much as look at Jamaica, I will have your ass arrested for embezzlement." He growled down at her and twisted up his face. "Believe me, bitch, you're getting off easy."

As he walked down the hall towards the elevator, he heard her call him every name other than a child of God.

# 41

"Get that for me please, sweetie," Jamaica yelled from the shower.

"Okay," Tillie said, running to catch the phone before the answering machine picked up. "Kingston's residence."

"Hey Tillie, it's Max."

"Oh, hi."

"What are you doing there? No one told me there was going to be a get together."

Tillie gritted her teeth and refrained from lashing into Maxine's ass. "Jamaica is packing for Italy."

"Italy! That wench didn't tell me she was going to…"

"It was last minute. Hold on." Tillie walked to the bedroom where Jamaica was getting dressed and tossed the handset on the bed. It's your friend," she snarled.

Jamaica motioned for her to chill out. "Hey girl, what's going on?" she asked Maxine.

"Nothing much. What's going on with Tillie? She sounds like she has an attitude or something."

"No, it's cool. She's tired. You know how it is when you're pregnant. The hormones get to running and whoever is in your path, watch out!" she chuckled, but Tillie wasn't finding any of it the least bit funny.

"Ask her why she tried to fuck my man," Tillie whispered to Jamaica. "Friend my ass."

Jamaica covered the mouthpiece and shushed Tillie. "Will you please stop?"

Tillie sucked her teeth and said, "Bitch," under her breath.

Maxine continued, "Let me find out your ass is going to Italy! Girl, I hear Italian men love some black women."

"I won't get to find that out. I'm going with Derek."

"Really? Oh, how nice. I'm so happy for you, Jamaica."

Jamaica held the phone an arm's length away. She couldn't believe her ears.

"What?" Tillie said.

"She says she's happy for me," Jamaica said, still not sure she heard Maxine right.

Tillie grunted. "She wanna fuck your man."

"What was that?" Maxine said through the phone. "I wanna do what? I heard that shit Tillie."

"Maxine, you heard wrong," Jamaica said.

"No, I didn't either," Maxine said.

"Tillie, damn, I asked you to let it go," Jamaica scolded.

"Let what go?" Maxine asked.

Tillie ran in the kitchen and picked up the wall phone. "Maxine, did you or did you not attempt to fuck Randy?"

Maxine gasped. "No, I would never do that."

"You're a lying ass bitch, Max! Randy told me everything."

" He…he…he lied to you," she stuttered.

"Maxine, how could you?" Jamaica asked. "Randy is our friend."

"Hell, she fucked him behind our backs," Maxine retorted. "Why can't one of us fuck him, too?"

"You are a slut," Tillie declared. "Just like you took that little boy home from the club. You didn't know him from Adam and you fucked him."

Jamaica gasped, not believing her ears. She knew Maxine was capable of many things, but she always felt she was discreet and reserved when it came to sharing her body.

"You are nothing but a cheap piece of ass," Tillie continued. "I hope your ass catches something before you catch my foot up your ass!"

"Tillie!" Jamaica scolded. "Let's not go there."

"Bitch, I'll fucking kick you in your stomach. You trapped him any damn way. You know he didn't want a fucking kid. Who is the whore? You're the trick ass that's prego," Maxine teased, laughing psychotically. "You want a piece of me. You know where I live!"

"I'm on my way, bitch," Tillie said, slamming down the phone and storming toward the door.

"Tillie, stop it! Don't you leave this apartment," Jamaica warned, but it was too late. The door slammed behind Tillie.

Jamaica dropped the phone and ran into the hallway of her apartment building. She could hear Tillie's shoes pounding on the steps. "Tillie, goddamn it!"

"What?" Tillie yelled. "I'm going to whip that bitch's ass. Calling herself my fucking friend and trying to fuck my man all in the same breath!

Jamaica tore down the steps behind Tillie.

Tillie hopped down four steps and stormed out the door, tripping over the welcome mat and falling down three concrete steps.

"Oh my God, Tillie!" Jamaica rushed to her side. "Are you alright."

Tillie cried, "I don't know. I feel something wet between my legs."

"Don't move. I'm going to call 911."

Tillie slipped her hand down her pants, pulled her hand out and screamed. Her fingers were covered in bright red blood.

# 42

"It's all my fault," Maxine cried on Frank's shoulder. "She was mad at me and that is why she fell."

"You didn't push her down the steps," Frank said, consoling her.

Jamaica cut her eyes in the direction of Maxine and Frank and chuckled. "Can you believe her?" she said to Derek.

Randy paced the floor, asking every nurse that crossed his path about his lady. "Please, is she alright?" he asked the nurse sitting behind the desk. "Is our baby alright?"

"Sir, the doctor will be out to speak with you shortly."

"I need to see her!" he yelled. "That's my wife back there!"

"When did they become married?" Maxine asked Jamaica.

Jamaica ignored her. She was thoroughly disgusted with Maxine and didn't trust what might escape from her mouth.

The double doors opened, leading to the emergency room. A tall, cream-colored man walked through the door, donning a white medical coat.

"Excuse me, are you a doctor?" Randy asked.

"Yes, I am. I'm looking for Randy Smith."

"Yeah, that's me. Is Tillie going to be okay?"

They all gathered around and listened to what the doctor had to say.

"She's going to be fine. We had to give her a transfusion. She lost a lot of blood."

"A transfusion? We don't want her having any transfusion. She could get AIDS that way," Maxine said.

"Don't be a foolish ignoramus, Maxine," Jamaica snapped and Maxine glared at her in shock. "Doctor, how is the baby?"

He looked at Randy. "I'm sorry, Mr. Smith."

Randy fell down to his knees and cried like a baby. Derek dropped down beside him, consoling him.

"Oh my God," Jamaica cried. "Does she know?"

The doctor shook his head. "She's resting now. I thought it would be better if it came from Mr. Smith."

"When can we see her?" Maxine asked.

"In about an hour. We want to keep her overnight, for observation. We usually don't allow more than two visitors in the Emergency Room, but I'll make an exception tonight.

"Thank you, Doctor," Jamaica said, kneeling down beside a crying Randy. "Baby, come on. It's going to be all right. You two can have more babies."

"Not what they really need right now, Jamaica," Maxine said.

Jamaica snapped her head toward Maxine and said, between clinched teeth, "May I speak with you outside please?" Jamaica turned on her heels and Maxine quickly followed.

Outside, Jamaica pulled her collar up around her neck. Gusty winds blew through her like she was onion paper.

"I'm going to make this brief and…"

"Listen, Jamaica…"

"No! You listen to me for a change. All you ever do is talk, talk and talk about not a damn thing. You're always scolding people and trying to be everybody's mama and you are the most fucked up person I know."

Maxine's jaw dropped open, the cold air chilling her front teeth, sending chills throughout her body.

"Can you *please* tell me what in the hell possessed you to try and bed Randy?"

Maxine closed her mouth and shoved her hands inside her jacket pocket. She sat on the bench against the building, lowering her head in thought.

Jamaica sat beside her and looked straight ahead. "Maxine, why?"

"Honestly, Jamaica, I don't know what came over me. I was going through an emotional roller coaster, wanting someone to be with, if only for a hot minute. I envy Randy and Tillie's relationship. I want that kind of love." She chuckled. "Truth be told," she paused. "I envy you, too. You lucked up and found a wonderful guy in Derek."

Jamaica wrapped her arms around her, pulling her into her. "You have to have patience, baby girl. And, you have to tear down that wall you have up. How do you expect anyone to break through that wall?"

Maxine wiped the tears from her eyes. "Do you remember they guy I was having an online relationship with, Frank?"

"Yep, I remember. You took his passing pretty hard. We were all worried about you, too."

Maxine chuckled. "He's not dead."

Jamaica looked at Maxine and pouted. "What you talking about, Willis?"

Maxine laughed again.

"It's good to see you smiling," Jamaica said. "You've had such an ugly frowning face for so long."

"Frank is in the waiting room."

Jamaica shoved Maxine in the arm. "Get out of here!" Jamaica looked around. "You mean that fine ass man in there is Frank?"

"Yep."

"How…"

"It's a long story."

"You better tell me later, damn it!"

"I will."

"How long has he been here? You didn't tell me he was coming to DC."

"I didn't want to get my hopes up. You know how I do. I get excited and make all kinds of plans for nothing but a big let down."

"How long is he staying?"

"Not sure and I don't care. All I want to do is relish in the moment. Enjoy each day with him as if it were my last. You know what I mean?"

"Yeah, I know." Jamaica kissed her on the cheek. "I love you, girl."

Maxine smiled. "I love you, too, girl."

"I'm glad Tillie is out of the woods, considering the shitting spell earlier."

"Huh?"

"I'll tell you later."

# *43*

It was a busy night at the Washington Hospital Center's Emergency Room. The yellow, red and blue lights from the ambulances and police cruisers lit up the night, carting in those ailing from gunshot wounds, spousal abuse, pneumonia, bronchitis, asthma and other symptoms that weren't considered life threatening, causing you to wish you had kept your ass at home, because it would be a minimum of three hours before you would be seen by a doctor.

The sliding doors connecting the Emergency Room to the chilled night air opened wide for Derek. "Hi, Honey," he said to Jamaica. He sat down beside her. "Hi, Maxine, how are you feeling?" he asked, rubbing Jamaica's back and shoulders.

"Tired, but doing good. Thanks for asking, Derek," Maxine said, fiddling through her pockets. "Damn, I wish I had a cigarette."

Jamaica playfully shoved her. "Girl, you don't smoke."

"Well, not anymore," she chuckled. "Girl, I hid that nasty habit from y'all for several years. I couldn't wait to get home so I could get my smoke on."

Jamaica asked Derek, "How is Randy holding up?"

"As well as could be expected, considering…" he paused.

"I guess you two won't be going to Italy now, huh?" Maxine asked.

Jamaica said, "Why wouldn't we go?"

"Duh," Maxine said, chuckling. "Because of Tillie."

"Tillie is out of danger."

"Wait a damn minute," Maxine said, standing to her feet. "When you were knocked upside the head last week, Tillie was at your bedside. I think it is only right you pay her the same respect.

Maxine paced in front of Jamaica and Derek. She continued. "You know something, Jamaica. You're the main one preaching about how we are all friends and the rest of that bullshit, and you're ready to leave Tillie high and dry. Something she would never do to you."

"Babe, Maxine has a point," Derek interjected.

"That's all fine and good," Jamaica said, eyeing Maxine. "But no one dictates where I can or can't go or what I can and can't do. Are you feeling me, Maxine?"

Maxine faced her and snarled. "No, I can't say that I do," and walked through the sliding glass doors and into the waiting room with Frank.

"Damn it, she gets on my damn nerves!"

Derek pulled her into an embrace. "I know she does, but she does have a point. Italy will always be there and we can go any time you want."

Jamaica pouted and whined, "I know you're right, but I want to go now."

Derek smiled and kissed her on the lips. "You know what I want?"

She giggled. "What do you want?"

"I want some pussy!" he blurted out.

She quickly covered his mouth with her hand. "Hush up, man. Why are you so loud?"

"No one is out here but us," he said.

"You never know who is lurking around corners."

"Good point, but I still want me some pussy."

They both fell out with laughter.

"Where are we going to do it, in the bushes?"

He raised his brow. "That's not a bad idea."

"Shit, I know you're crazy now," she laughed. "How about the car?"

"My two-seater and your long legs?"

"Good point…"

"The bathroom," he said with excitement.

"No, I don't want to do it in the bathroom."

"It's the hospital. You know the bathrooms are well sanitized."

She said, "You're not joking, are you?"

He shook his head no.

The thought of him loving her jump started the throbbing between her legs. "Lead the way, stud muffin."

Derek locked the door to the bathroom and turned off the lights. "I can't see," Jamaica said, her arms stretched out before her, feeling for something, anything.

"I can feel you."

"What? I don't feel you touching me," she said.

"No, I mean I can feel your energy."

"Ouch!" Jamaica cried, bumping into something. "I think I found the sink," she said, feeling the spigot.

"Okay, stay put."

"Damn, you would think we were in a bathroom that was three thousand square feet," she laughed.

"There you are," he said, his hand resting on her arm. He moved in closer and found her lips. He started rising and her pussy was dripping from the anticipation and thrill of possibly getting caught fucking in the bathroom.

"Take off your pants and underwear," he instructed.

"Okay, done. Now what?" she chuckled, getting a kick out of it all. She felt like a teenager sneaking sex in her parents' house.

"Kind of prop your ass up on the sink so I can slide my dick inside you. Once I'm in, wrap your legs around my ass and hold on."

She hopped up on the sink, wrapped her legs around his ass and helped to guide him inside her. "Oooh," she moaned, her head falling back as he thrust deep inside her.

"Not so loud, baby."

"Hurry up and come, Derek."

"I can't. Don't have a condom."

"You didn't put on a condom?"

Her line of questioning broke his concentration. He slipped out of her and deflated. "No, I don't carry condoms around with me," he snapped.

"Well, if you're going to insist on doing spur of the moment activities, then you need to keep a few in your wallet," she instructed.

She hopped down from the sink. "Can you turn on the light, please, so I can see?"

Derek zipped up his pants, unlocked the door, flipped on the light switch and left the bathroom, without a word.

"Well fuck you, too," Jamaica yelled at the closed door.

Within seconds, Derek had opened the door and entered the bathroom, locking the door behind him. "What was that all about, Jamaica?"

"I'm just giving back to you what you gave to me."

"Huh?"

"You left me in here alone, without a word. It's like you said, 'fuck you' to me in silence."

"That's ridiculous."

"Oh, it is?"

"Yes it is. Now I know you're going through some kind of emotional trip because of Tillie and that's cool. I'm here for you, in whatever capacity. But I will never tell you 'fuck you' nor will my actions tell you that. So, I would very much appreciate you not saying those words to me. It is disrespectful and quite honestly, I don't take kindly to people telling me to kiss their ass."

"I didn't tell you to kiss my ass, Derek."

"It's all the same thing to me." He leaned over and kissed her lips. "I love you. Hurry up and get out of this toilet."

## *44*

Derek convinced Jamaica she needed to stay in DC, instead of Italy, in case Tillie's condition worsened.

"She needs you and as I said before, we can do Italy any time."

"You're right," she smiled at him, feeling blessed to have such a caring and loving man in her life. "Oh, baby, I forgot to thank you for the roses and cake. The roses were absolutely beautiful, but the cake…well, let's just say I'm thoroughly cleansed," she chuckled.

He frowned at her. "What roses and cake?" Derek was clueless. He didn't know what to think. Was someone else trying to push up on his lady or was there something more sinister going on?

"Okay, you need to stock up on Ginkogoloba," she teased. She studied his facial expression. He truly did not know what she was rambling about. "Honey, you sent me roses and a cake, with lots of color—"

Derek shook his head. "No, babe, it wasn't me."

"Honey, yes it was. I have the card." She pulled the card from her purse and showed it to him. "See? It has your name on it."

Derek look dumbfounded. "I don't know what's going on, but I didn't send them."

"Well, maybe Gina sent them on your behalf." She crossed her fingers, hoping this was the case.

Derek shrugged. "It's possible. She's known for doing stuff like that, but she would've told me."

Concern overtook Jamaica and flowed through her like fire, as she was having her on private summer near the sun. "Derek, please call Gina and ask her if she sent the roses and the cake."

He grabbed his cell from his jacket and dialed Gina's number.

"We ate that cake and got sick," she mumbled, thinking back to her attacker's words, *Stay away from Derek.* Jamaica may have been many things, but a stupid woman was not one of them. She watched enough movies and read enough books to know when a woman whipped your ass over another man, she had been scorned to the highest level. She was also a firm believer of what was done in the dark shall come to light or it'll come out in the wash or karma was a motherfucker.

"Hey, sis, it's me. Question for you, did you send a bouquet and a cake to Jamaica from me?" Derek's eyebrows drew together, his lips turned up. "Uh huh, I see," he said, rubbing his chin. "No, not at all. Thanks. Bye."

He frowned up his face. The veins in his neck bulged out. He looked at Jamaica and saw the fear in her eyes. He, too, knew she was not a dumb woman.

He pulled her into him and embraced her tightly. He kissed her earlobe and whispered, "We need to talk."

She patted him on the back. "I was waiting until you were ready," she said, breaking the embrace. "Let's sit over here, where it's quiet."

She led him to two empty chairs in the far corner of the waiting room. Of course, eagle eye, nosey ass Maxine had them in plain view, totally ignoring Frank, who was leaned over, his head resting on her shoulder, with spurts of snoring occasionally annoying her.

"Who is she?" she asked, situating herself in her chair, her arms folded across her chest, eyes plastered on his face. She did not want to miss any of his expressions. She had gotten good at reading him and his thoughts before he expressed them.

Derek leaned over, resting his elbows on his thighs and clasping his hands together, intertwining his fingers. He closed his eyes, deep in thought, trying to get it together.

He inhaled and then sighed heavily before opening his eyes and staring down at the floor. "Her name is Leslie. She works for me...*used* to work for me, as my office manager. I fired her last night." He paused.

Jamaica remained quiet.

"I met her in a park, living out of a box. She was homeless. I gave her a job. One thing led to another—"

"You fucked your employee?" Her words cut deep. "Don't you have any damn dick control?"

"It wasn't like that, baby. We dated—"

"Dating an employee is worse, Derek." Her voice raised an octave.

Derek looked across the room at Maxine. Her eyes were glued on them. "Can we please keep this between us?"

Jamaica looked toward Maxine. She dropped her arms and huffed. "Excuse me one minute, baby." Jamaica approached Maxine and smiled.

Sometimes it's hard to explain the temperament of strained relationships, especially when one party doesn't realize the relationship is strained. They say there is a thin line between love and hate. Friendship has always pushed that line.

"What's going on, girl," Maxine whispered, not wanting to awake Frank.

Jamaica swiftly smacked Maxine across the mouth. "Find some damn business of your own," she yelled.

Frank stirred from his nap and looked at up Jamaica, and then at Maxine, who was holding the side of her face, in shock.

"You bitch!" Maxine yelled, charging at Jamaica. They both fell to the floor.

"Get off of me!" Jamaica yelled, grabbing a handful of Maxine's hair .

"Get off my hair, bitch!" Maxine shouted.

Derek could not believe his eyes. His feet were planted in concrete. He could not move.

Jamaica and Maxine rolled over and over until Jamaica ended up on top, swinging and landing powerful blows to the side of Maxine's head.

"Cut it out, y'all," Frank laughed, reached down and grabbed hold of Jamaica's neck.

Derek sprinted towards Frank and punched him in the face. "Motherfucker, you don't put your hands on my woman!" Derek stated to Frank, who landed hard on the floor.

"What in the hell is going on out here?" Randy yelled, walking through double doors from another hallway. "Why are y'all acting like fucking hoodlums?

Derek pulled on Jamaica. "Baby, it's over."

"I am sick and tired of this bitch," Jamaica cried. "Always in somebody else's business, trying to have what someone else has." Jamaica stood to her feet, with Derek's help. "Get your own fucking life, bitch," she snarled, kicking Maxine in the back.

Hospital security entered the waiting room in a huff. "What's going on in here? Y'all are going to have to take this mess outside," he barked.

"Everything's cool," Derek said.

"This is a hospital, not a damn playground," the security guard belted.

Frank pulled his wallet from his back pants pocket and opened it. "Everything is cool, officer," he said, flipping open his wallet and displaying a gold badge.

All eyes fell on Frank, except for Maxine's, who was stretched out on the floor, crying, unable to grasp what just took place between her and her best friend.

The security guard nodded at Frank, smiled, and shook his hand. "It's a pleasure, man. Just try and keep it down," he said, exiting the waiting room.

Derek pulled Jamaica into him. "It's over, baby. Chill out, please."

"Yeah, it's over," Jamaica cried. "Our friendship is over, you tramp, before you try and take my fucking man!"

Frank's ears perked up. "Huh? What do you mean by that?"

"Nothing," Randy interjected. "It's all good. They're always having their little spats—"

"No," Frank said. "This is no little spat."

"Frank, if I were you," Jamaica began. "I would leave that tramp alone. Her *so called* best friend just lost her baby because of that bitch."

"Baby, let it go," Derek pleaded.

Maxine remained on the floor in a fetal position, still crying.

Jamaica looked down at her. "You tried to fuck Randy."

Derek nudged her. "Baby, please. That's not necessary."

"You call yourself a damn friend. I saw how you were looking at Derek at my birthday party. You would've tried to bed him that night if Tillie and Randy hadn't insisted on driving your drunken ass home!" Jamaica faced Frank. "If you want that shit, it's all yours!" She leaned into Derek's neck. "I'm ready to go home. I'll come back and check on Tillie in the morning."

Randy was still trying to figure out how to pick his jaw up off the floor. "Damn," was all he could muster, stopping Jamaica in her tracks.

"Randy, that trash on the floor is why Tillie is in here and why your baby is dead."

Randy looked dumbfounded. He felt his ears heating up. "What are you saying, Jamaica?"

"Tillie fell down those stairs because she was rushing over to Maxine's house to whip her ass because of you."

Randy fell back into the chair behind him, placed his head in his hands, and cried like a baby. "Oh my God," he cried.

Frank tossed his hands in the air. "I'm out, folks."

"You're just going to leave her like that?" Derek asked Frank.

"Too much drama for me, man. In my line of business, I can't have it." He reached down to help Maxine get up off the floor.

She jerked away from him. "Get the fuck off me. I knew you weren't about shit," she cried.

He chuckled and placed his hands on his hips. "That's funny…pot calling the kettle black. It was nice meeting you good folks," he said, before walking toward the exit. He stopped and turned around. "This shit should be in a damn book," he laughed and walked out of the hospital and into the street.

Randy regained his composure and did the gentlemanly thing. He helped Maxine off the floor.

"Thank you, Randy," Maxine cried. "I am so sorry."

Randy shook his head. "It's all good because I don't expect to see or hear from you after tonight. Don't bother contacting Tillie either."

Maxine sat down in the chair and licked her wounds.

Derek wrapped his arm around Jamaica and they headed toward the exit. "Remind me not to pick a fight with you," he whispered into her ear.

She laughed and kissed him on the cheek. "I love you," she cooed.

"I love you too, babe."

"We still have to talk when we get home," she reminded him.

"Yes, I know."

# 45

Maxine's tear-filled eyes watched as Jamaica and Derek left through the Emergency Room doors. She wrapped her arms around her and hugged herself tightly. She was all she had. She was the only one who loved her. Now, the pity party began.

Randy stood at the nurse's station, waiting to hear news about Tillie. It had been over three hours and he had taken all he could and was ready to explode.

Maxine wiped away her tears and walked over to Randy in hopes of…well, she really did not know what she was hoping to gain.

She placed her hand on his shoulder. "Randy," she whimpered.

His body stiffened, his jaw flinched.

"I know I've fucked up and I don't blame you for not wanting to ever speak to me again, but—"

He twirled around. "But what Max?"

She jumped nervously and cried. "I don't want everyone to hate me."

The lines in his face softened, his shoulders relaxed. He shoved his hands in his pockets. "I can't speak for everyone else, but I don't hate you. I feel sorry for you. It takes a miserable person, someone who doesn't want to see someone else happy, to treat people the way you do."

She lowered her head in silence. She felt shameful for her actions, and she could not take them back. Life did not allow for such a thing.

"What happened to your boy?"

"He's gone," she mumbled. "Good riddance to his ass too."

"You don't have anyone's life left to destroy, do you?"

His words were sharp, cutting her deep below the surface. "Damn," she sighed.

"Sorry, but you brought it all on yourself, Maxine."

She nodded. "I know. I know."

"Just keep your distance for a while. I know that Jamaica and Tillie love your life."

"Do you?"

He smiled and said, "Just give them some breathing room."

"Thank you, Randy," she faintly smiled.

"No problem."

She lunged toward him and wrapped her arms around his neck. "You're still the best bottom bitch in the world," she whispered.

He chuckled and patted her on the back. "Go home and get some rest. I'll call you when Tillie wakes up."

She nodded and walked away, looking back one last time.

He smiled and waved.

Maxine slowly trotted back toward Randy when she saw the doctor approaching him. "Is she okay?" Maxine asked the doctor, her voice an octave higher than normal, but not quite yelling. "My friend, is she okay?"

"Yes, she's going to be just fine. We are going to keep her overnight, for observation. She's awake and hungry."

Maxine chuckled. "She stays hungry."

"She'll be headed to her room in just a few minutes. You can meet her there, if you'd like to."

Maxine's eyes widened with hope of seeing Tillie, until Randy shot her a look of disappointment. "Go home and get some rest, Max. I'll call you in the morning."

Maxine's eyes watered. She wiped them with the back of her hand. "I suppose you're right," she said, shifting her weight from one leg to the other.

When the nurse on duty returned to her station, Maxine looked at her and fell over with laughter, her smooth yellow complexion turned crimson. She laughed so hard, she sounded like a hyena.

"Uh, Maxine, what's so funny?" Randy asked, with a look of embarrassment on his face.

"She…she," she stuttered, trying not to choke on her words. "She looks like—" she paused, bending over holding her stomach. "Oh my God, she looks like Fiona!"

The doctor cleared his throat as a smile slowly crept across his face and Randy looked around the room, trying not to look at the nurse.

"I'm sorry, but you look just like Fiona, Shrek's wife," she blurted out.

Randy grabbed her by the arm and escorted her out of the building. "Go home with your crazy ass!" he yelled.

"Okay," she said, trying to gather herself. "You'll call me tomorrow?"

"Bye, Max!"

Maxine crawled under the heavy duvet cover, curled into a fetal position and stared into the blackness of the room. She closed her eyes and winced at the pain in her left eye. *Jamaica packs a serious punch*, she concluded, followed by a soft chuckle. Truth be told, it wasn't the pain in her eye, but the aching throb in her heart. Once again, she was alone and lonely. She and Jamaica have been friends since college. Randy was right. She knew what they needed was time away from each other. She and Jamaica have had their spats, but it was never this bad or to this magnitude. Despite the brewed anger, she loved Jamaica and always will. She was the sister she'd never had. She would give her as much time as she needed. After all, she knew that Jamaica loved her too.

Maxine was about to count her last sheep before the doorbell rung. She slowly opened her eyes, blinked a couple of times and looked at the clock. She couldn't think of who could be ringing her doorbell at three in the morning. Unless it was Jamaica. At the thought of it possibly being her best girlfriend in the world, she shot straight up, slid out of bed, her bare feet slightly chilled against the wood floor, she trotted to the door and flung it open. "Hey, girl—"

"Did I wake you?"

Maxine flung the door to close, but Frank stopped it with the palm of his hand.

"What do you want?" she scowled.

"I came to apologize."

"Aw hell, go fuck yourself, you bastard!" She flung the door to close again, this time catching his foot.

"Ouch!"

"My bad. I thought you were *out* folks," she mimicked.

"Maxine, listen, I was wrong. I shouldn't have left you there." He entered the apartment, closed the door and followed her into the kitchen. "You have to understand. I can't have any drama in my life. Not with my line of work."

She swiftly turned to face him. "You didn't have to leave me." The huskiness from a deep sleep lingered in her throat. "Do you know how that shit made me feel?"

"Max—" he paused, his voice was tender, almost a murmur.

"Speak up, I can't hear you. Don't be fucking timid now, Mr. Deserter." Her voice was filled with heavy sarcasm. She was pissed and rightfully so. As far as she was concerned, he showed weakness and there was no room in her life for a weak ass man.

"Sweetie—"

"Don't you fucking *sweetie* me! How dare you show your fucking face here? You are so full of apologies. Well, take your pathetic ass on somewhere, 'cause I don't wanna hear it!" She turned her back on him.

He lowered his head and reached out to her. "Maxine," he said calmly. "I was wrong. A real man can admit when he's wrong."

She wrapped her arms around her and lowered her head. She whimpered.

He continued. "Please believe I would never do anything to hurt you. Please understand that you mean a lot to me—"

"Where were all those damn feelings at the hospital? Why didn't you help me out? Why would you let someone pounce on me like that?"

"Like I said before, my job—"

"Frank, please leave."

He pulled her into him. "No, I'm not leaving you again."

"Please, Frank," she cried. "Please. I can't take any more pain in my life. I just can't take it. I'm not as strong as you think I am."

He kissed her cheek.

She continued. "This is too much for me," she cried.

He shushed her and kissed her lips. "It won't happen again. I promise you. I'll never leave your side." He kissed her neck, down around her throat and then planted soft kisses on her chest.

"Oh, Frank—"

"Shhh," he said, pulling up her night gown.

"Oh, God," she moaned, stretching her arms above her head.

He got on his knees and pulled her panties to the side. His tongue slithered its way between her hairy bush and teased her clitoris.

She parted her legs and her hands began to roam freely over her silk covered breast, finding herself short of breath. "Oh, yes," she cooed. "Hmm, Frank," she sweetly whispered his name.

"Yes, baby," he responded, bringing her down to the floor, spreading her legs wide. He masturbated her clitoris with his left hand, while he pulled a condom from his pocket with his right. With the condom packet between his teeth, he ripped open the pack, spat the wrapper onto the floor and, using one hand, rolled the condom over his hardness. "This is all yours, baby," he said, lowering himself on top of her. "Ahhh," he moaned, as his hard dick swam around inside her wetness.

She raised her legs, resting them on his shoulders, her hips raised as his love throbbed deep inside of her, consistent long deep strokes sent her over the edge, into a pool of orgasm. As her body shook, he stroked faster, harder. His thrusts turned to rapid pumps, her full breasts danced about her chest. She grabbed them, holding them together. This turned him on more.

"Oh, fuck!" His face distorted. He growled. "Yeah, yeah, yeah," he said, with each slowing thrust.

Panting heavily, he looked into her eyes. "I'm scared," he said.

She blew air through her lips. "Of what?"

"Relationships. They scare me. I always end up getting hurt." He rolled off of her and onto the floor, lying beside her.

She rolled over, lay her head on his chest and nibbled on her finger. "Me too."

"One step at a time," he said.

She nodded yes and closed her eyes.

The next morning, Maxine woke up on the floor, covered with the duvet from her bed and no Frank. She sat up, pulled her knees into her chest and rested her chin on her knee. "I knew it was all too good to be true," she said, looking around for any sign of him. He was gone.

She pulled herself up from the floor and walked toward the bedroom. She stopped in the doorway at the sound of keys unlocking her door. No one, except Jamaica, had keys to her place. And even still, Jamaica never used them unless she knew Maxine was out of town and she was there to water her plants.

Maxine could not see the door from where she was standing, so she remained still and quiet.

The door opened and closed. "Honey, I'm home!" Maxine smiled at the sound of Frank's voice. "I picked up coffee and donuts from Dunkin' Donuts!"

Maxine walked back down the hall toward Frank, frowning. "I'm not a coffee drinker, but I'll take a donut."

Frank smiled widely. "I know, which is why I got you Vanilla Chai instead."

"My favorite!"

"Yep, believe it or not—"

She interrupted him. "You do pay attention."

# 46

Derek showered while Jamaica lay in bed under a mound of Italian imported silk duvet covers and sheets. Jamaica painfully stared at the ceiling, listening to Derek's version of Prince's *Purple Rain*. She flipped over and covered her head with the queen-sized pillow. It was torture. While she loved Derek dearly, his singing left a lot to be desired.

As she cringed each time he belted, *Purple Rain*, she thought about her Emergency Room brawl with Maxine. Her heart began to ache, thinking about all of the nasty words she spewed at her best friend. She regretted acting on her yearning to bash her head in. She and Maxine had had their fallouts before, but this one was different. As far as she was concerned, there were two things you did not do when it came to your best friend — have sex with their man and cause them harm. Even though Maxine's attempt to bed Randy did not work, her taunting and teasing Tillie, causing her to miscarry deserved the ultimate ass kicking.

Her thoughts turned to Randy, whom she felt was very unbelievable. She could not believe how patient he was with Maxine. Granted, no man should put his hands on a woman, but in this case, him tossing her around a bit would've been justifiable. But then again, when Jamaica's fist connected with her eye, justice was done.

It was getting hot under the pillow. She tossed it to the floor and sighed heavily, her eyes focused on her cell phone. She reached for it and pressed five, the direct dial number for

Randy's cell phone. Derek's singing was annoying the hell out of her.

On the third ring, Randy answered. "What's up, Champ?"

"Real funny. How are you doing?"

"I'm doing good, just tired."

"How's my girl?"

"She's going to be okay, a little out of it though. The doctor sedated her after she found out we had lost the baby."

"Oh, Randy, I am so sorry. I wish there was something I could do."

"She took it pretty hard." His voice broke.

Jamaica felt a heaviness in her heart. She could hardly lift her voice above a whisper. "Oh, sweetie—"

Randy cleared his throat and chuckled. "So, how's your fist?"

Jamaica laughed. "You're so silly. Did you tell Tillie what happened?"

"You mean, did I tell her that you whipped Maxine's ass?" he chuckled. "No, I didn't tell her. She doesn't need to hear about that right now."

"Yes, you're right."

"I really like Derek," he said, speaking freely about what he was thinking. "And I can tell he really does care about you."

Jamaica sat up in the bed and glanced at the bathroom door. The shower was still running. Derek did not believe in taking military showers, short and sweet. Long, hot and relaxing was his motto.

Randy broke her silence. "What's on your mind, Jamaica?"

Jamaica pulled the covers off of her and swung her legs over the side of the bed. "Why do you think something is wrong?" She lowered her voice, being purposely mysterious.

"I can hear it in your voice," he whispered. She could hear the smile in his voice.

Her feet pressed against the cold wood floor as she stood up; her panties the only clothing she had on. "I am curious to know why you didn't whip Maxine's ass," she said, her feet sticking to the floor and her breasts bouncing, as she trotted from the bedroom, down the stairs to the kitchen. "I mean, if it were me—"

"What would that have proven?" Randy interrupted.

"That you were pissed at what she did, that's what," she snapped in a hushed tone.

"I won't lie, I *was* very pissed. I felt like wrapping my fingers around her throat, until she lost oxygen." His voice was cold and exact, which scared Jamaica.

"Wow," she said below a whisper.

"I know my limits. I chose to remain cool. If I didn't, I would be in *The Man's* jail now, calling folks to bail me out. Besides," he chuckled, "Champ Kingston took care of her"

Jamaica laughed out loud. "Will you cut that out?" She looked around the kitchen and listened intently up the stairs. Derek was still in the shower. "May I ask you a question, Randy?"

"Uh-huh."

"Well, it's not really a question, more like I need your advice."

"Shoot. What is it?"

"There was something I didn't tell you all that happened to me that day I was attacked," she hesitated, again listening intently up the stairs for any movement out of Derek. He was still in the shower, on marathon mode.

"Uh-huh, I'm listening."

"Well, the woman who attacked me said something to me. She told me to stay away from Derek."

"Word? What did Derek do about it?"

"He doesn't know."

"You need to tell him, so he can take are of that shit."

"Do you think I should stay with him, since he lied to me?"

"How did he lie?"

"He didn't tell me about her, so to me it's the same as lying."

"You want my advice?"

"Yes, I do."

"Don't fuck it up. He's a good guy, Jamaica. Better than those other useless niggers you used to fuck with. Listen, men don't volunteer information. If you never ask, then you'll never know. Simple as that. If you didn't ask, then that's on you. What you need to do is talk to him, tell him everything about the attack and work it out. He loves you, girl. Don't fuck it up!"

She remained silent, contemplating Randy's words. She surely did not agree with that don't ask, don't tell policy. The bottom line was she wanted a fulfilling and trusting relationship. She no longer felt she could trust Derek. She felt betrayed. She felt hurt. But Randy was her friend and as a man, he knew about the "men codes." What makes them tick and act so damn stupid, strange and weird. Maybe it was true, women are from Venus and men are from Mars or some other strange planet.

"Hey lady, you there?" Randy asked, breaking through the thick silence.

"Yeah, I'm here and I heard everything you said."

"Don't let another trick come between you and Derek. You've got a good thing. Trust me, I know what I'm talking about."

She inhaled deeply, exhaling slowly. "Yeah, okay. Let me chat with Tillie for a minute."

"She's sleeping. She's pretty much out of it right now."

"Are you going to be there all day?"

"Yep."

"Randy, you have to get some rest."

"I will just as soon as my baby gets home."

Jamaica smiled. Who would've thought that Randy and Tillie would be an item, considering how ignorant they always acted toward each other while they all attended Howard University.

"Have Tillie call me when she wakes up."

"I will and you talk to your man. Don't let the lines of communication break down because you're being stubborn. I know you, Jamaica. Don't fuck it up."

"I love you too, bye!"

Jamaica trotted up the stairs, toward the bedroom. Derek was still in the shower, singing *Purple Rain*.

She sat on the bed and stared at the door. Randy's words played over in her mind and it all made sense. But when it came to relationships, trust had always been a big issue for her. It seemed as though every man she dated had a trust issue. She couldn't trust them as far she could see them.

# *47*

Derek finally switched artists and Smokey Robinson's *Oooh, Baby, Baby* ended his mini concert as stepped out of the shower, his body glistened as beads of water dripped over his muscular toned body. "Hmmm, hmmmm, hmmmm—" he hummed because he didn't know the rest of the lyrics.

"You've been in that damn shower for close to forty-five minutes," she said, standing at the door, speaking through the crack. "Can I come in? I have to pee."

Derek opened the door, allowing her to enter.

"Thank you." She raised the toilet seat and pulled down her panties. "Whew, I've been holding it for a while now."

"Why would you do that? There are five bathrooms in this house."

"Oh, I guess I wasn't thinking."

Derek stood in the mirror and turned his face from side to side, looking at his chin. "I need a shave," he said, reaching for the electric razor.

"No, don't shave. I like your five o'clock shadow, that rough rider look you've got going on. It's hot."

His image stared back at him. "Yeah, it does look nice, doesn't it?"

Jamaica wiped, flushed the toilet and sang, *You're so vain,* and chuckled.

"Oh, hush," he said, swinging at her behind, missing.

She stood behind him and folded her arms across her chest. "So, finish telling me about the employee you fucked."

"Damn, babe, do you have to be so harsh?" Derek squeezed toothpaste onto his toothbrush.

"Sorry." She pulled down the toilet lid and took a seat. "I'm listening."

"There's nothing to tell, really. She worked for me, we had a thing—"

"You mean a relationship."

"I wouldn't call it a relationship. Although, I'm sure she would've definitely labeled it as being one."

"Babe, one thing led to another. I gave her a job, a place to live and now she's biting the hand that fed her. Typical of a bitch."

"Wow," Jamaica said, crossing her legs. "That's kind of harsh."

"You think so?"

"Yes I do. I never liked that word," she said.

Derek fell out with laughter. "You're shittin' me, right?"

She looked at him with a smirk. "No, I'm not."

"For someone who didn't like the word, you sure did say it enough last night to Maxine."

Jamaica smiled and nodded. "Yeah, you've got me."

"I hope you will resolve whatever it is that has ruined your friends—"

"Uh, don't even go there yet. You're not done."

Derek shoved the toothbrush in his mouth. He talked while brushing his teeth. "I did find out one thing though."

"What's that?"

"She was the one who attacked you."

Jamaica jumped to her feet. "What?"

"Not to worry though," he said, spitting in the sink. "She won't bother you anymore."

"Well, what did she say? How did she tell you?"

"I don't remember, babe. All I know is that it took all I had not to pimp slap her ass."

"Aww babe, you would've done that for me?" Jamaica smiled, resting her chin on his shoulder.

"Nope, not even for you. I don't believe in hitting a woman."

"That's my baby," she said, kissing his shoulder. "I bet you she sent me that fucking cake too, had me and Tillie shittin' all over my place. I had to go so bad, I had to use a—" she stopped.

"What?"

"Nothing," she said.

"I'm sure she did. Gina seems to think she did too."

"Really?"

"Yeah, well, Gina never liked her anyway."

Jamaica frowned. "But I don't understand. How would she have gotten my address?"

Derek kissed her lips and walked out the bathroom and into the bedroom. "Nothing is private anymore. Hell, you can find out anything you want to find out about anybody on the Internet."

"Damn," she said in amazement. Jamaica knew very little about the Internet or its capabilities. She walked into the bedroom and climbed into the bed, nestling herself beneath the covers. "I sure would love to pay her back for that cake shit."

"I say just leave it be. Don't pay her the attention she's craving."

She shook her head and poked out her bottom lip. "No can do and you're going to help me."

"Why would I want to do that?" he chuckled.

"For one, you lied to me."

"Wrong again, Sherlock. I did not lie to you. As a matter of fact, I've shared more with you than I've ever shared with anyone."

"You lied because you didn't tell me about Leslie."

"I didn't lie, babe, I just didn't tell you."

"Same goddamn thing!"

"Would it have made any difference if I had told you?"

She rolled her eyes and sucked her teeth.

"Oh, here we go," he said. "I see you're bringing out Sha Na Na—"

"Fuck you, Derek!"

"Oh my goodness! Such strong words," he chuckled.

"I am so glad you think this shit is funny. I had my fucking face bashed in because you showed no restraints in keeping your fucking dick inside your fucking pants!"

" Whoa now, Jamaica. I think you should slow your roll baby—"

"I don't need to slow—"

Derek quickly interrupted and pointed at her in anger. "Jamaica, you need to calm down. I don't appreciate being talked to in this manner. I don't speak to you this way and I won't have it."

Jamaica straightened up her posture and folded her arms across her bare chest. "Ahhh, now I see," she said, slowly walking circles around him. "You're no different than the rest of the dogs, letting your—"

Derek grabbed her by the arm and yanked her toward him, startling her. Her heart jumped in her chest, beating rapidly. "Letting my what?"

"Ouch, you're hurting me. Let me go!"

The unwelcome tension stretched tighter between them. "Letting my what?" He leaned in closer and peered into her eyes, as if holding his raw emotion in check. "Letting my what?"

She breathed in shallow, quick gasps as tears streamed down her face. "You're hurting me, Derek," she cried.

The tense lines on his face relaxed as his tight grip loosened. "The only thing I'm doing is letting my heart love you, which is something I rarely do. I don't deserve this, babe."

She jerked away from him, swallowed with difficulty and found her voice. "If you want your life, you'll never put your fucking hands on me again."

His expression darkened with an unreadable emotion.

She walked toward the bathroom, glancing uneasily over her shoulder, and closed the door behind her.

Derek fell back onto the bed and stretched his arms above his head. He blinked repeatedly, trying to make sense of what had just happened. He was in love with Jamaica, but he wasn't in love to the point where he would be disrespected in his own home. However, he didn't want to imagine his life without her. He had to right the serious wrong he had just done. His mother had raised him better.

The door to the bathroom slowly opened. Jamaica stood in the doorway, draped in Derek's oversized terrycloth robe.

He pulled himself up, sat on the edge of the bed and looked at her. He smiled. She looked like an angel being swallowed in his robe. Her presence gave him joy.

He reached out his hand to her. "Come here, babe," he whispered to her.

She slowly walked to him and grabbed his hand, squeezing tightly.

His head lowered, moving from side to side. "I don't know what came over me. I should have never put my hands on you in that manner. It will never happen again. I promise you." He pulled her closer into him, taking her around the hips, smothering his face in her belly.

She rubbed his head and looked down at the man she was growing to love more than anything.

"I should have told you," he said into her belly.

She was not sure, but it sounded like he was whimpering. She remained silent.

"I don't—" His words lodged in his throat. "Want this to come between us."

*Oh my God*, she thought in amazement. *This man is crying*.

"Babe," he continued. "I don't have vengeance in my heart for anyone."

She closed her eyes and stroked the top of his smoothly shaven head.

He unwrapped the belt from around her waist.

She tilted her head back and licked her lips. She knew what she had to do, but her love for him would not allow her to do it. She could not end their relationship. For once, she was going to listen to Randy. She leaned down and kissed the top of his head. "I love you," she whispered.

"I am so sorry," he cried. "I'm so sorry, babe."

She knelt down before him. "It's okay, honey." She kissed his lips. "We'll get through this." She kissed each eye.

He slowly opened the robe, exposing her breasts, with silver dollar size areolas and erect nipples.

She sighed heavily and cooed with the stroke of his fingers against her soft skin.

He leaned forward and took her left nipple inside his mouth and nibbled, ever so gently, sending excitement throughout her body. The right nipple did not go neglected for long, as he held it in the palm of his hand and gently squeezed.

She reached under his towel grabbing his erectness, stroking briskly, concentrating on the head.

He softly moaned as his tongue outlined her areola. "I love you, babe," he whispered.

"And I love you," she said, opening his towel. Her glare never left his as she lowered her head into his abdomen, taking him inside the warmth and moisture of her mouth. She could hear his uneven breathing as he grabbed the back of her head, pushing himself deeper inside, touching the flesh at the back of her throat.

She closed her eyes, trying not to heave, opening her throat as wide as possible to accommodate his girth.

"Oh shit!" he yelled, from deep within. "Oh yeah, babe!" He fell back on the bed and stretched his arms high above his head. "Oooh, babe, yes! Damn you suck a mean dick."

Her head bobbed up and down, faster and faster and for the first time in her life—she swallowed.

## 48

It was after six in the morning. The world was lighting up and the birds had begun to chirp. Randy stretched and rolled his head from side to side, working out the kinks from sleeping for hours in a chair beside Tillie's hospital bed. He stood up and walked over toward the window, looking down at the nurses and colorful scrubs and doctors hurrying across the campus of Washington Hospital Center.

"Good morning."

Randy twirled around at the voice of his angel. "Hey, you. How are you feeling?"

"A little groggy, but I'm okay. You were here all night?"

"Didn't leave and won't leave your side for a minute," he smiled, kissing her on the forehead. "Hungry?"

"Yeah, I could eat something, but not this hospital food. The dinner last night wasn't good at all."

"You could have fooled me, the way you inhaled it."

"Oh, hush, I was hungry. Anything is good when you haven't eaten all damn day." She pressed her hand against her abdomen.

"Are you feeling any pain?"

She shook her head no. "Only the pain in my heart."

Randy felt awful. He did not know what to say or how to console his woman. He wanted to take her into his arms and make all of her worries disappear.

"Oh, well, it was God's will," she said.

"We can have another baby," he blurted out, before he realized what he said.

"Really?" Her smile brightened up the room and warmed his heart.

His large hand took her face and held it gently. "Really."

The mere touch of his hand sent a warm shiver through her. "You really mean it?"

He kissed her on the nose. "Let's get married."

Her eyes widened. She couldn't believe her ears. "What did you just say?"

"I can't believe I said it either," he mumbled. He hesitated for a long while and disappointment danced across her face. He couldn't stand to see her that way, so he said, "Tillie, will you marry me?"

She blushed but remained silent.

A momentary look of discomfort crossed his face. "Well?"

Tillie laughed out loud. "Don't be asking me no dumb ass questions. You know I will!" She wrapped her arms tightly around his neck. "I love you so much!"

The peanut gallery stood inside the door and applauded. "It's about damn time," Jamaica said, walking toward the bed, with Derek fast on her heels.

"Congratulations, man," Derek said, shaking Randy's hand.

"You guys are next," Tillie announced.

Jamaica glanced at Derek.

Derek looked away.

"Oh, he makes me sick," Jamaica chuckled.

Tillie tilted her head to the side and stared at Jamaica's face. "What happened to you?"

"Nothing, why?"

Tillie threw Derek a nasty look. "Did you put your damn hands on her?"

"No, baby," Randy interjected. "Uh—"

"Then why is there a bruise on the side of her face?" Tillie inquired.

Jamaica remained silent.

Derek didn't utter one word.

Randy was laughing out loud.

"What it so damn funny, Randy?"

Randy gathered himself and told Tillie of how Jamaica and Maxine showed their behinds in the emergency room the night before. "You should've seen those two," he laughed. "It was a sight to see, for real."

Tillie laid there, with her mouth wide open. "Jamaica, you and Maxine."

Jamaica nodded her head.

"Tillie, my baby got a good lick in too," Derek chimed in, proud of his Laila Ali impersonator.

Though Jamaica never uttered a word, her face spoke volumes.

"Jamaica Kingston. I can't believe you were acting like an alley cat in the Emergency Room." she hesitated. "Did you get in a good lick for me too?" she chuckled.

# *49*

"Are you sure you want to do this?" Frank asked Maxine as they sat in the parking lot of the Washington Hospital Center.

She nodded.

"It's not going to be pretty, Max. Your friends are holding a lot of animosity toward you right now and—"

"It's not the first time and it surely won't be the last."

"Well then, let's go." He climbed out of the car and walked around to the passenger side, opening the door for her. "I'm by your side," he said, clutching her hand in his.

She smiled, stepped out the car and searched her purse for her shades, before she sashayed, the way only Maxine can do—diva style, hand in hand with Frank, toward the entrance.

Not knowing what to expect, Maxine was terrified. She'd fallen out with her friends before, but never on this level, never this serious. She had to admit one thing to herself. She was wrong for making a pass at Randy. But worse, she knew she was wrong for not correcting her behavior or changing her ways after he rejected her.

Frank leaned against the Information Desk, with his back turned toward the receptionist, while Maxine inquired about Tillie's room number.

"You should stop at the Gift Shop," he suggested. "Take her a gift, some flowers, something."

Frank knew Maxine wasn't a bed of roses, but he was willing to work with her. As it is the norm with the world, he figured he could change her, turn her into a caring, refined woman. He also knew his garden of roses didn't smell so well either. He was fighting with commitment issues himself, and knew he was wrong for leaving Maxine stranded at the Emergency Room, not being there for her after her best friend beat her like she stole something. Maybe Maxine's self-indulgence and lack of concern for other people's feelings, was just what the doctor ordered to help Frank face his demons. A true match made in heaven, in a sarcastic kind of way.

Maxine thanked the receptionist and headed toward the Gift Shop, as Frank suggested. She browsed the quaint shop filled to the brim with greeting cards, get well wishes, balloons, teddy bears, silk floral arrangements, night gowns, slippers, snacks, drinks, and a variety of many other things. You name it, they had it. It was all quite overwhelming for Maxine. She was unable to locate to anything Tillie might like. Besides, it was going to take a lot more than silk flowers and a teddy bear to gain Tillie's forgiveness.

"I don't see anything in here. Too much shit in here," she said to Frank, as he pulled a Coke from the antique-looking Coca Cola vending case.

"Something to drink?" he asked, holding up the Coke bottle.

"No thank you," she sighed. "I'll pick her up something later. Right now, I just want to get it over with," she said, approaching the counter.

"It's going to be fine," he said, handing the cashier a five dollar bill. "As long as you are honest with yourself and then, right the wrong, all will work out."

"Yeah, I guess so," she mumbled. "I'll meet you at the elevators." An overabundance of nervous energy was built up inside of her. She decided to walk it off before it completely overwhelmed her. She no longer liked the woman she'd become — bitter and self-absorbed. She always thought she put her friends first in her life. To her, they were her only family. After her parents died in a fatal car accident when she was one month shy of graduating from Howard University, she clung to Jamaica, Tillie and Randy, making them the only family she needed.

All that was missing was the black dress and veil, Maxine walked as if she was in a funeral procession, her mood somber and her eyes welling with tears; afraid of what she was going to encounter.

As they stood outside the doors of Tillie's hospital room, Maxine looked at Frank with a quizzical look.

"What's wrong?" he asked, looking from her to the door. "It's going to be okay."

"No, that's not it. I just realized something."

Frank extended his neck and popped out his eyes. "Yeah—"

"Last night, you entered my apartment with a key." She folded her arms across her chest. "It just dawned on me. I was so distraught, I didn't realize it, I was just happy to see you—" she paused. She held out her hand. "Give me the key."

"What key?" he chuckled, like a kid with his hand caught in the candy bowl.

Maxine nodded toward the small waiting area down the hall.

Frank followed on her heels, looking like the cat that ate the canary. "I'm innocent," he laughed.

Maxine did an about face. "I'm not laughing, Frank. If we are going to do this, you can't be doing shit behind my back. Give me the extra key you had made to my apartment."

The devilish smile left his face. He jammed his hands inside his pant pockets. "I did not make an extra key. When and where would I have had the time to do such a thing?"

"Then you explain to me how you walked into my apartment, without me having to open the door for you."

He shrugged his shoulders. "I tried the doorknob and it was unlocked. I didn't think you would mind—"

"I may have been labeled as being many things, but a dumb ass isn't one of them."

"You've got me pegged all wrong—"

"The next time you walk into my place, like you're paying rent and shit, I'm shoot your ass."

Lines of annoyance appeared on his face.

She continued. "You're in law enforcement. You know you can shoot intruders."

Frank lowered his head and shook it in disgust. "I don't take kindly to threats, especially idle ones." He turned to walk away, but thought against it. He faced her. "What in the hell is wrong with you, woman? What happened to the Maxine I adored so much? The Maxine who laughed like a school girl at my corny jokes over the phone. The Maxine who danced for me on the Web cam. The Maxine whom I thought was caring, compassionate and loving. Where in the fuck is she? Was that all a farce?"

"Well, ain't this about a blip, the pot calling the kettle black. This Maxine changed when you decided to fake your own death and take me through a roller coaster of painful tears and emotions. Why don't you go and fuck yourself? Leave me alone. Do not call me anymore. Do not instant message or e-mail me. Eliminate all sources of communications with me." She walked off down the hall.

"What about my things at your place?"

She turned around and snarled. "You don't have shit at my place, and remember what I said about being an intruder."

"No wonder your friends don't give a shit about you. I hope they disown your bitch ass for good!" he angrily snapped, before taking off down the hall, never to be heard from again.

Maxine stood in front of the door to Tillie's room. She took a couple of deep breaths and squared her shoulders. *Fuck you too*, she said to herself. The only people she needed stood on the other side of that door and she was willing to do whatever she needed to do to regain their trust and love.

# 50

When the elevator doors opened, Jamaica's stomach dropped as she peered at the back of Maxine's head. She blew air of disgust through her lips and stepped off the elevator. She stood perfectly still as the doors closed behind her.

Maxine had the uneasy feeling of being watched. She glanced over her shoulder and saw Jamaica. Her heart sank. It was her best friend, with a bruised bottom lip.

"What are you doing here?" Jamaica asked, her feet planted firmly to the floor. That familiar hospital stench of urine and disinfectant was making her a tad bit queasy.

Maxine faced her best friend. It took all she had not to respond with an offhanded smart ass comment. Instead, she said, "I'm here to see Tillie."

Maxine's response seemed to have amused her. A flash of humor crossed her face. "I doubt if Tillie wants to see you—"

"Let Tillie make that decision."

Jamaica shook her head in dismay and walked toward Maxine. "You are really a piece of work," she said, stopping in front of her. "Why don't you let well enough alone, Maxine?"

"I don't want my best friends in the world to hate me."

Jamaica shrugged her shoulders. "Was Randy your best friend when you—"

Maxine stopped her with a raised hand. "Okay, Jamaica, you don't have to keep throwing it up in my face. I know I fucked up. Damn!"

"I'm glad you are *finally* taking responsibility for your actions."

"Right, I deserved that," Maxine said, stepping to the side. "Even if you don't want to hear my apology, I'm sure Randy and Tillie will."

"Ha! Girl, you're better off slitting your wrist if you think those two will give you the time of day." Jamaica stepped in closer, Maxine's breath heavy on her face. "If it weren't for you, Tillie wouldn't have lost the baby," she said between clinched teeth.

Ouch! Jamaica's words cut deeper than a razor could ever cut. And, as much as Maxine tried, the emotional flood gate opened wide, flushing a dam of tears.

"I didn't push her," she cried.

"Not physically, but it was because of you that she lost the baby!" Jamaica's voice had raised an octave, while Maxine couldn't hold back her loud cries.

"I would never do anything to harm Tillie and you know that, Jamaica."

The door flung open and a hand, massive and strong, spun Maxine around. "Get in here and stop all that damn yelling," Randy said, yanking Maxine by the arm into the room. "Jamaica, don't you think you've caused enough commotion in this damn hospital?"

Jamaica held her head up and strutted past Randy. "She started it."

"I don't care who started it," he said, closing the door. "Why must you two be so damn ghetto?"

Tillie raised her head up from her pillow, straining to see what was going on. Jamaica rushed to her side, adjusted her pillows, making her comfortable.

"Hi, sweetie," Jamaica greeted Tillie. "Feeling better?"

"You two are embarrassing," Tillie snapped.

"How are you, Tillie?" Maxine looked timid, afraid to take a step. "I am so sorry about—"

Tillie stopped her with a raised hand. "I'm really not in the mood for this shit today."

Randy waved his hand in a gesture of dismissal. "Yes, Tillie is right. You two should leave."

Tillie rolled her eyes. "That is not what I said, Randy. Don't go putting words into my mouth."

"Baby, you need your rest—"

Tillie made a dismissing gesture toward Randy. "What I need is to talk to my girls. How about you go to the cafeteria and grab yourself some lunch. We'll be fine."

Randy rubbed the back of his neck. He looked at Maxine, then to Jamaica, and back at Maxine. "I don't know—"

"Out of here," Tillie said.

"I'll be back in ten minutes," he said.

Tillie smiled and said, "Make it thirty." She watched the door close behind Randy and then asked Jamaica for a glass of water. "The air in this place is so dry, but the food is drier." She made a funny face, as though she had swallowed something bitter.

Tillie reached for the plastic cup of water and sipped from it, her eyes plastered on Maxine. She swallowed hard and briefly sat in silence. She placed the plastic cup on the night stand and turned her gaze to Jamaica.

"We are too old for this shit," she huffed. She rubbed her belly. "I've already lost my baby. I'm sure as hell not going to lose my best friends."

Maxine leaned back on her elbows against the widow's ledge. "I never wanted any of this to happen."

"Look at your eye, Max," Tillie said, falling out with laughter. "I'm...I'm sorry. I shouldn't be laughing at that big ass black eye you have."

Jamaica smiled, proud of her handiwork.

"And, Jamaica, get a load of that fat lip of yours."

Jamaica pressed her fingers against her lips. She flinched at the pain.

"Okay, I am going to end this right here and now. Jamaica, you were wrong."

"How was I wrong?"

"You shouldn't have put your hands on Max," Tillie responded.

"She put her hands on me first, trying to show off for that no good nigger."

Maxine shot Jamaica a sharp look. "You approached me, being big and bad, talking about my being all up in your business."

"You were in my damn business," Jamaica yelled.

"Keep your voices down. You are in a hospital, not a damn alley."

Maxine stood motionless in the middle of the room, silent as a mouse.

"You wouldn't be in here if it weren't for Maxine."

Tillie pulled the covers off of her and swung her legs over the edge.

"What are you doing?" Maxine asked. "Should you be getting out of the bed?"

"I miscarried, I'm not dying. Besides, I have to go to the bathroom." Tillie reached out for Jamaica. "Give me a hand, please."

Jamaica shuffled to her side and helped her to the bathroom. As Tillie sat on the toilet, she insisted the door stay open so she could keep her eye on both Maxine and Jamaica, ensuring there will not be a re-enactment of last night.

"You really could close the door," Jamaica chuckled. "We'll behave."

"Whatever," Tillie said.

Maxine approached Jamaica from behind and embraced her. "I am so sorry, Jamaica. You know I would never intentionally do anything to hurt you, Tillie or Randy.

With a deliberately casual movement, Jamaica turned and faced Maxine. She gently touched her eye. "Did I do that?" They all fell out with laughter. "I'm sorry too, Max. You know you're my girl, but there are times when you push me to the edge, and last night you pushed me a little too much."

"I know I can be a bitch at times—"

"Ha! Try *all* the time," Tillie chuckled.

"And, Tillie, I'm really sorry about. . .well making a move on Randy. Honestly, I don't know what I was thinking. I was going through some shit and I guess. . .I don't know. It will never, ever happen again. Believe me, I do feel awful about my actions." Maxine lowered her head and kicked at the floor, kicking up imaginary dirt. "I would hug you, but you're sitting on the toilet," she laughed.

"Yeah, speaking of toilets," Tillie said. "Did you ever get a chance to tell her, Jamaica?"

Jamaica shook her head. "Nope, but we can tell her now." Her smile was as bright as rays of sunshine.

"Wait, let me get back into bed first."

"Wash your hands," Maxine joked.

Tillie rolled her eyes and said, "By the way, Maxine. My miscarriage is not your fault. It's mine."

"What are you saying, Tillie," Jamaica chimed in, instead of keeping her mouth shut.

"If I weren't so headstrong about getting to Maxine," she chuckled, "wanting to *tap* that ass, I wouldn't have taken that fall." Tillie crawled into the bed and crossed her legs at the ankles. "We are too old to be acting like this and we are the best of friends. Maxine, I am sorry I wasn't there for you to help you sort out whatever it was you were going through."

"I never shared it, Tillie, so it's okay," Maxine replied.

"True, but we are friends. Very close friends and if we can't recognize when one is in need, then we're going to have problems. You know what I mean?"

Jamaica and Maxine responded in unison. "Yeah, I know," they said.

"I have to apologize to Randy. I'm sure he hates me."

"Don't you worry about him," Tillie smiled. "I have Randy wrapped around my finger, only he don't know it." They all laughed out loud because they knew, better than anyone, that Tillie was telling the truth.

"Okay, so tell me about whatever it is you were going to tell me about," said Maxine, pulling a chair up to the foot of the bed and taking a seat.

Jamaica sat on the side of the bed and told her girls the story of Leslie and Derek. They remained quiet through Jamaica's re-cap of her conversation with Derek. When she got to the part about the chocolate cake and how she and Tillie had the runs, and how Derek felt that it wasn't necessary to seek revenge, Maxine was fuming.

Maxine pushed herself to a standing position. "You mean to tell me Derek isn't going to do anything?" She felt her fists bunching at the side. "Oh, hell no!"

Jamaica turned to Maxine. "He did fire her—"

"Yeah, but that was because she was swindling his money. Right?"

Jamaica contemplated the question. "Yep, that's about right."

"We need to find that ho and beat her ass down," Maxine suggested.

"I would love nothing more," Jamaica smiled.

"Nope, no more beat downs, beat ups or anything like that." Tillie intervened. She looked at Jamaica. "Honey, you have to handle this differently."

Maxine pushed the chair against the wall and sat on the opposite side of Tillie's bed, and Tillie was in her world. She had her girls by her side, where they should be at all times.

"What do you have in mind?" Maxine asked.

Tillie looked over Jamaica's shoulder at the door, making sure no one was entering, especially Randy. When she whispered the plan, Maxine jumped to her feet and yelped in excitement, while Jamaica asked, "When are we going to do it?"

She brushed her thumb against her nose. "Just as soon as I break out of this joint."

They all fell out with laughter.

# 51

Upon his return from the cafeteria, Randy cracked the door to Tillie's hospital room enough to peek through. He smiled and closed the door. He decided not to interrupt the women's bonding and with a springy bounce, he headed toward the seat in the small empty waiting room at the end of the corridor. He fell into the forest green leather sofa, nestling in the corner and closed his eyes.

He smiled at the idea of the resolution between Jamaica and Maxine. He hated it when they fought like wildcats, but considering the circumstances, he completely understood Jamaica's position. However, he wasn't quite sure about his position. On the one hand, he felt as if something had died inside of him. On the other hand, he felt relieved. When Tillie broke the news about her pregnancy, he was one hundred percent against it. After all, what did he know about being a father? He loved Tillie with all his heart, but he was terrified about becoming a father. It wasn't like he had the best role model . His father was a deadbeat, leaving his mother to fend for herself with him and his three brothers. She did the best she could, raising four hardheaded boys was no easy task, but she did it without any child support or weekly visitation from his father.

Derek stepped off the elevator. He couldn't remember the room number he was given by the receptionist at Patient

Information, so he stopped at the nurse's station to ask. He noticed Randy seated in the waiting area. He motioned and smiled to the nurse and approached Randy.

"Sup, man?"

Randy raised up and yawned. "Everything is everything. Sup with you?"

"Came up to check on Tillie and Jamaica. Everything okay? Why you sitting out here?"

"Yeah, it's cool. Jamaica and Maxine are in with Tillie."

"They are? You think we need to get in there?" Derek inquired, looking over his shoulder.

"No, have a seat. They're laughing, which means everything is cool now."

"Maybe I should let Jamaica know I'm here," Derek stated.

Randy chuckled. "Don't go getting' henpecked and shit."

Derek shrugged and sat on the sofa next to Randy. "You know, man, you're good. I don't know if I could be so cool if that was my woman in there."

Randy's firm mouth curled like he was on the edge of laughter, while the five o'clock shadow of his beard gave him an even more manly aura. "I'ma tell you, man. It took all I had. I felt like choking her ass to death, for real."

"I know you did," Derek chuckled. "So, how're you feeling now about Maxine?"

"Well, truth be told, Maxine was never really my favorite person. I dealt with her because Tillie and Jamaica were my girls. You know, just like my boys. For the most part, I never paid her much attention. But when she came to my house, man, and—" he paused, contemplating whether to let sleeping dogs lie or tell Derek everything. He didn't care if Derek knew, but he wasn't sure if he could trust him. Randy was very selective when it came to choosing confidants. He learned long ago to never immediately place your trust into anyone, before they prove themselves worthy. "Let's just say that Maxine, in the past, didn't make very good decisions."

Derek nodded. "But I congratulate you on the way you handled the situation. You were calm, cool and collected."

"I had to be calm for Tillie. She didn't need all that bullshit around her. Know what I mean?"

Derek nodded and remained silent. He had gotten the feeling that Randy had a lot on his chest he needed to release and Derek was a good listener.

"Deep down in my heart, I'll never forgive Maxine. I know Tillie has forgiven her. That's more her style than mine. Tillie is a strong woman, which is one of the reasons why I love her so much. She keeps shit in order. She keeps me in order. She keeps my ass fucking grounded. You know what I mean?"

"Tillie sounds like a good woman," Derek said, leaning up on his elbows. "I still would've had to pop Maxine upside the head or something," he chuckled.

Randy chuckled. "Shit, I've been feeling that way for years."

"I would've had to release some anger on some damn body. You feel me?"

"Uh-huh, I feel you on that one. But hey, your girl took care of it for us both," Randy laughed. "Maxine's eye is jet black." They both fell out with laughter.

# 52

*It feels good to be home*, Tillie thought as she propped her feet up on the sofa.

"Now, I don't want you to lift a finger, sweetheart. Whatever you need, let me know and I'll get it for you."

"Thank you, honey, but I'm just fine."

"The doctor says you need to stay off your feet for a few days."

Tillie nodded in agreement. "I plan to do just that too. I am going to take advantage of the company's short-term disability, gonna milk it for as long as I can." She stretched her arms above her head. "Yes indeed, a vacation."

"I'm going to take a few days off too."

One corner of her mouth pulled into a slight smile. "For what?" Tillie asked Randy. "So you can worry the hell out of me," she chuckled. "Nope, I'll be fine."

"But, Tillie—"

"No buts, Randy. Besides, I like to spend some time to myself.

"Okay," Randy smiled as he sat down in the chair across the room. The glow of his smile warmed her.

" All I want to do is take a hot shower, grab a glass of wine and curl up with a good book," Tillie said, standing up. "Join me, baby. I could use some company right about now."

Randy's smiled quickly turned to a lust in his eyes. He needed to caress her and love her like never before. "Can we do that now?"

"What, take a shower?"

"No, have sex."

Tillie smiled. "Be creative."

Randy and Tillie showered. The hot, steamy water pulsated against her firm breasts and his taught muscles. Lathering the cloth, Tillie thoroughly cleaned Randy's penis and the crack of his butt several times before he returned the favor. They stepped out of the shower and into the bedroom, followed by matching wet footprints.

Tillie crawled on the bed and rocked on her knees, lowering her face to the bed and tooting her ass in the air. Randy sucked her butt cheek as hard as he could, leaving a passion mark the size of a silver dollar. Tillie hissed at the good feeling pain he inflicted. Randy's tongue circled the passion mark, forming a trail of saliva down the crack of her ass to her rectum. His tongue teased her rectum, flickering above and below the opening. Randy inserted his tongue inside her rectum, while his finger flicked her swollen bud, until she gasped for air.

"Ooh, that feels so damn good, boo," she said, winding her ass around on his tongue.

Tillie turned over onto her back and spread her legs wide. Randy grabbed hold of her clitoris and fiercely sucked it, just the way she liked it — hard and rough. She raised her hips in the air and fucked his face, her juices waxing his face, leaving a shiny coat.

"Damn, you gon' make me come, baby," she panted. "Oh shit, Randy!"

"Let it flow, baby."

"I feel like I have to pee."

Randy sucked harder and with more force, inserting his finger inside her rectum, causing her to retract her muscles and place a serious tight hold on his finger.

Her body began to shake, her legs shot out straight before her, then wrapping around Randy's neck, locking down a tight hold.

"Oh shit, motherfucker! Don't you stop! Don't. . . you. . .sto. . .oo. . . op!

Randy did not stop and Tillie experienced the big one, her heart racing. She felt light-headed.

"I feel like I'm about to pass out," she said, her voice shaky.

"You'll be fine. That's must've been a big one."

"Yeah, I guess." Tillie rolled over and climbed up under the covers. "Could you please get me a glass of water? My throat is so dry."

Once Tillie climbed beneath the covers, Randy knew he was going to have to take care of his own business if he wanted to release the build up from weeks of lack of pussy. When he returned with the water, Tillie was softly snoring and curled up in the mist of a bed full of throw pillows. Randy hovered over her, placed the glass of water on the nightstand and kissed her on the forehead.

"I love you, sweet baby," he whispered in her hair as he inhaled her scent.

"I love you too, sweet baby," she said, partly asleep. "Did you come?" she asked, inserting her thumb into her mouth.

That must have been one hell of an orgasm, because Randy can't recall ever seeing Tillie suck her thumb. Randy smiled in achievement and headed to the living room sofa to take care of himself.

The picture of Tillie that sat on the end table was Randy's inspiration to regain erectness. He stroked his dick in a slow, but methodical rhythm. Experienced men knew the art of masturbation. Jacking off was for the younger, inexperienced generation. Real men knew to start stroking slowly. Randy was a veteran.

He closed his eyes and thought about the great sexual moments he and Tillie had together. His mind raced through the myriad of positions and sweet moments. He finally settled on a thought of Tillie sucking his dick and her mouth swallowing him whole. He loved when she got in a rhythm, her head bobbing up and down, seeing the head of his dick disappear in her mouth, followed by the whole shaft disappearing.

His stroking increased and his mind drifted to him fucking Tillie from behind. He loved when she leaned forward, her face buried in the pillow and her ass raised high. He could see the many times he grabbed her ankles and raised them as far as he could, enabling his dick to go deeper. His rhythm was faster, a steady pace and he felt his dick throbbing like he was actually fucking Tillie. He could hear her moaning and panting, begging him to go deeper.

"Shit, shit, shit," he grunted. His dick was throbbing hard as though it was growing in size. The same feeling he got when he was inside of Tillie's hard, sopping wet pussy. His stroking was more intense as his face distorted to the good pain he was feeling.

"Gooooddamnnnn. Shit, shit, shit," he groaned as sperm shot out of his throbbing dick. Randy's head fell back as he continued to stroke his dick at a slower pace. Beads of sweat had formed on his forehead and chest. His mind was moving at a walker's pace now. He could see Tillie's head resting on his shoulder after he had tried his best to fuck her silly.

"Shit. Damn, I needed that," he stated as he smiled and felt the call of sleep come over him. With the thoughts of his future wife on his mind.

# 53

Jamaica tossed and turned, unable to sleep. She had night sweats. The back of her head was soaked and she had to pee. She tossed the covers off her and swung her legs over the edge of the bed. She stepped down on the wooden step stool, used to climb into a bed that was more befitting of someone six feet tall as opposed to her five-foot-three stature, and walked sluggishly to the bathroom.

She pulled her panties down around her knees and sat down on the toilet. She looked into the tub and decided to take a shower. Still seated on the toilet, she reached over and turned the shower knobs. She pulled off her damp nightgown and tossed it to the floor. She pulled her panties down around her feet and kicked them across the floor toward her nightgown. She drip-dried, stood to her feet and climbed into the shower, immersing herself beneath the massaging waterfall.

Lathering her hand with soap, she caressed her breasts, massaged her nipples and made a trail of soap down toward her belly button, where she played in it with her pinky finger. She continued her travels through the forest, resting between the thickness of her pussy lips, where she played around, stroking the insides. She tossed her head back under the running water, while she massaged her clitoris and cleaned under the hood. Her fingers traveled up her sides to her armpits, around the edges of her C-cup breasts.

She reached for the removable showerhead, placed one foot on the ledge of the tub and the showerhead between her legs. She fell back against the shower wall and breathed deep and heavy as the hot water pulsated against her clitoris.

"Oooh, shit," she moaned. "Yes…hmmm."

Her leg propped up on the ledge of the tub began to tremble, the tremor moving rapidly up her body, causing her to shake. She held the showerhead in place and released the urged to explode. The sensation of urinating left her as a small stream of her juices flowed from her body and onto the floor of the tub. While she enjoyed the pleasure she was giving herself, it just was not enough.

She stepped out of the shower, dried off and pinned her tresses back into a French roll. She moisturized her face, applied mascara and glossed her lips.

She stood inside her closet and looked around. She needed the perfect attire for what she had planned. She slipped into her beaded pumps. She moisturized her body with Vaseline Intensive Care lotion and sprayed *Sung* by Alfred Sung on her breast, back, abdomen and around her thighs. She pulled her Black Diamond mink from the hall closet, grabbed the keys to her Chevy Tahoe, and headed toward Fox Hall Road.

Using the spare key Derek had given her, in case of an emergency, she entered the foyer and tiptoed up the staircase. She stood in the doorway of the bedroom and watched as he slept peacefully, with an occasional toss or turn.

"Hey, baby," she softly called out.

Derek did not budge.

She walked toward the bed, opened her mink coat and raised her knee to the bed. "Hey, baby," she said again, this time a little louder.

Derek stirred from his slumber and looked up at her. He could not believe his eyes. He smiled, but said nothing, pulled back the covers and turned over onto his back.

She was a woman on a mission, which was to bring her man to the ultimate climax. Something she knew he would never want to get from another woman, especially Leslie. There was another woman in the picture now and although Derek had not had any relations with Leslie long before he met her, she needed to remind him that she was the Queen Bee in his life. Besides, if you fuck your man right, he will not stray. If he does stray, then he is not a man, rather a four-legged animal looking to stick it and quit it, without even licking it. It was the credo every young sistah knew at an early age. The same credo every young sistah disregarded in their search for love and the right man, which usually meant *any* man.

The sexual tension between them was already thick as cheesecake and hard as ice.

The throb between her legs hungered for the thickness of his penetration. There would be no lovemaking, cuddling or fondling. No kissing and not even a smile, only a good old fashion fucking.

She dropped her coat to the floor and straddled him. Her erect nipples begged for his touch. As he raised his hand toward her breast, she slapped his hand. "Don't fucking touch me," she said, every word enunciated, sounding like a dominatrix. "Put your hands under your pillow and leave them there. You understand me?"

Derek nodded and obeyed, anxious to play the game. His dick was pointing toward the moon, ready for blast off.

"Let me grab a condom," he said, trying to move, but she would not budge.

"Not tonight," she whispered. "Oooh," she cooed as she slid down on his bareness. "Damn, baby!" She raised her arms above her head and wrapped them around the back of her neck. "Whew," she said, her breast jutting upward as her hips ground vigorously on his dick. "Damn, you feel so fucking good," she whined, with a deep arch in her back.

"Yeah, fuck me, baby," he said, grabbing her around the hips.

"I told you not to fucking touch me!" she yelled, slapping him in the face. He loved it. "You'll have your turn in a minute."

She leaned down on him and grabbed him around the neck, her ass pumping up in the air, fucking and pounding against him, hard and quick.

She pulled a groan from deep within and said, "Yes, yes, yes—"

"That's it, fuck me, baby," he egged her on. "Give me all of that sweet pussy."

"Call me bitch," she demanded.

He shook his head. "I can't do that."

"Do it, motherfucker!" She slapped him again, this time igniting a sexual rage inside him.

He gave her exactly what she wanted, maybe more than what she bargained for. "Fuck me, bitch!" he said between clenched teeth. He grabbed her by the back of her head and covered her mouth, his tongue breaking through.

Jamaica pulled away. "I told you don't—"

"Shut the fuck up, whore, and fuck me, you bitch!" He flipped her over. Still inside her, she wrapped her legs around his waist. He pumped vigorously inside her pussy, trying to knock a hole in her back. "Whose pussy is it?" he yelled, followed by a few grunts.

" It…it's…yours," she managed to say as her head tapped against the headboard.

"Ah yeah, bitch. This is my pussy," he said, his body tensing up. "This…is…my…oh shit!" He felt the blood rush from his head, down to his dick. It grew larger inside of her. The harder he fucked her, the louder she yelled. The louder she yelled, the deeper her nails dug into his flesh. The deeper her nails dug into his flesh, the harder he fucked her, hitting the tip of her uterus. "Shit! Shit! Shit!" he growled, his face distorted, his pumps quickened as he pushed her legs back behind her ears. "Uh! Uh! Uh!" he groaned, pulling from deep within with each pump.

Jamaica grabbed onto the headboard and held on for dear life, trying not to get a concussion, as her head banged against the headboard with each hard thrust, his balls smacking against her ass.

"Oh, fuuuuccccccck! He yelled, as his dick exploded inside her. He collapsed, panting from exhaustion.

Derek rolled off her and lay flat on his back, barely able to catch his breath. "Did you come," he asked.

Jamaica pulled herself up on her knees and straddled his face. "No, but I will in just a few minutes, baby."

He wrapped his lips around her clitoris and sucked profusely, as her hips gyrated.

"Don't stop sucking me," she begged. "Oh please, don't...don't...you...dare stop, motherfucker."

She held on to the headboard and fucked his face until she could not take it anymore. "Oh yes! Oooooooooooooh!" She squirted inside his mouth. She dismounted him and kissed him, tasting her juices.

"I love you, baby," she said, slipping into her coat and left Derek with a smile on his face.

# *54*

Jamaica tossed her mink coat on the sofa, kicked off her shoes that were killing her feet, and made a beeline for the shower. While showering, she decided it was time to give Leslie a taste of her own medicine, *Jamaica style*.

Stepping out of the shower, she wrapped up in a thick terry cloth robe, sat at her desk in the alcove of her apartment and set out to put her plan into action. First things first. Despite all that had recently taken place, Maxine and Tillie were still her girls. She always had room in her heart for forgiveness when it came to them.

She reached for the phone and placed a three-way to her partners in crime. "It's time. Be at my place in an hour," she said, pacing the floor. "All black, from head to toe," she instructed. "And don't forget your skull caps."

"What the hell? Skull caps? We're not robbing a bank, Jamaica," Maxine said, yawning. She looked out the window. The moon was still lighting the earth. "What time is it?"

"It's five in the damn morning," Tillie chuckled. "Jamaica what is wrong with you, girl?"

"Early bird catches the worm," Jamaica replied. "Now get your fat asses up out the bed and let's rock and roll."

"I don't believe this shit," Maxine mumbled. "Hey, shouldn't your ass be mounting Derek about this time?"

"I'm gonna ignore that one, Max, because I have an agenda and I plan to complete it today," Jamaica snapped. "Now get your ass up!"

"All right. Damn!" Tillie slammed the phone back into the cradle.

Jamaica hissed at Tillie's attitude, then asked, "Maxine, are you up?"

"Barely, but I'll be there with bells on."

"No bells, just all black."

"Do we need black face paint too?" Maxine chuckled.

Jamaica hung up in her face.

Sitting in the chair, Jamaica pulled her knees up to her chest and rested her chin between her knees. How was she going to find Leslie? She knew getting information out of Derek would have been like snapping your fingers to make a blind man see—impossible. However, she recalled Derek mentioning how Gina did not care for Leslie. Bingo!

It was approaching six o'clock and she knew she had no business calling Gina, but she did not think Gina would mind either. She dug inside her purse for Gina's business card. Derek had given it to her after the attack. In case she could not reach him, she could contact Gina.

Punching in the number on the keypad, she pressed the receiver against her ear, closed her eyes, and took a deep breath. The phone rung several times before Gina answered.

"Hi, Gina, this is Jamaica."

"Oh," she said, her voice sounding foggy from a deep sleep. "Is everything alright?"

"Yes and I'm so sorry to call you so early in—"

"Oh, girl, don't worry about it. I need to get up anyway. What's going on?"

"I really need a—" she paused. She was not sure if she wanted to continue the call. For a split second, she thought about letting sleeping dogs lie.

"Jamaica, you there?"

"Yes, I'm here. Could you please give me Leslie's address?"
Gina cleared her throat. She was silent.

Jamaica continued. "I can't ask Derek for it."

"Why?"

"Because—"

"Because what?"

"Gina, I can't let that bitch get away with what she did to me."

"Oh, I see," her voice trailed off, as if in deep thought. "Yes, Derek did tell me something about that. I am so sorry that happened to you. But do you think pay back is in order? I mean, after all, you would only be stooping down to—"

"Yes, I do believe it's in order," Jamaica interrupted firmly. "I did absolutely nothing to deserve being attacked by someone who was fucking your brother."

Gina sighed. "Derek is not going to like this one bit."

"I am asking you not to tell Derek."

"I'm sorry but I would never deceive my brother, not for anyone, Jamaica."

"I am not asking you to deceive him. Just don't tell him I asked you for her address or anything we have discussed."

"I won't give you that woman's address," Gina said firmly. "And I would advise that you leave it alone. If there is anything that needs to be handled with Leslie, allow Derek to take care of it."

"Yeah, well, he has yet to do shit about her attacking me," Jamaica yelled into the phone. "Therefore, I'll have to do it my goddamn self!" She slammed the phone into the cradle and tossed it to the floor.

Jamaica rushed into her bedroom and opened the dresser drawers, pulling out black sweats, a fitted tee shirt and black socks, and threw them onto the bed. Standing before the mirror, she pulled her partially wet tresses into a bun a top her head.

She slipped into her clothes and sat by the door, waiting for Maxine and Tillie.

# *55*

Gina, eyes wide opened, couldn't get back to sleep. She knew she didn't have to be at Derek's place for another four hours. The phone call from Jamaica worried her. She knew Leslie all too well, and it was not her first time at the poker table. Leslie knew how to play the game and play it well, which is why she picked up the phone and called Derek.

"Houston," she said, before Derek could say hello. "We have a problem."

"Hey, sis, what's wrong?" he whispered, not wanting to wake up yet.

"Your girlfriend called me."

"Jamaica? What'd she want?"

"Leslie's address."

Derek shot straight up in the bed. "What?"

"Uh-huh. I don't know what she has up her sleeve, but she was very adamant. Derek, you and I both know Leslie."

"I know."

"I'm worried about her, brother. That is why I called you. You need to call her or do something before she does something crazy."

"I'm on it."

"Call me back and let me know if you need back up."

He chuckled. "I'll do that," he responded sarcastically.

Maxine was the first to arrive. "Why do I feel like Peggy Lipton from The Mod Squad?" she chuckled, plopping down on the sofa. She laughed out loud. "What is that shit under your eyes?"

"Mascara."

Maxine shook her head. "Jamaica, do you think you're going a little too far?"

"Nope. In case she tries to sucker punch me, then her fist will slip off of my face."

Maxine fell over sideways on the sofa with laughter. "You fool! You need Vaseline, not no damn mascara!"

"Shut the hell up!" Jamaica snarled.

Maxine looked at her watch. "Tillie's late."

"Yeah, I know. Want some coffee or juice?"

"No thanks. My adrenaline is pumped up."

"Mine too, but I think it's more nervousness. The butterflies are having a field day in my stomach."

In the early morning, Leslie stood with her shoulders hunched under the candy apple red raincoat in the middle of Watkins Plaza, waiting for the black Hummer to pass so she could dart across the street. "Come on, damn it!" she yelled, her face grimacing at the driver. The Hummer sped up and splashed splotches on her wool salmon colored slacks. "You son of a bitch!" She raised her fist in anger, sticking her middle finger in the air.

Inside the CVS Pharmacy, she came out from under the raincoat and shook it briskly, before tossing it over her arm. She looked down at her pants and swore like a sailor on leave who was getting drunk in the local town's bar.

She browsed each aisle, looking for several items. She filled her arms with what she needed and headed toward the register.

"Do you have a CVS card?" the clerk asked.

Leslie shook her head no and remained silent.

The clerk picked up the green clear bottle. "We have a sale on Citrate of Magnesium, five for two dollars," she smiled.

Unconsciously, Leslie's brow furrowed. "If I had wanted five bottles, I would've picked up five bottles. Don't you think?"

The clerk frowned, thought twice about snapping at a customer and returned to ringing up the items.

Leslie paid the clerk, dashed out the CVS and hurried down to the Safeway. She grabbed a cart and rushed down the aisle toward the pet food. She tossed ten cans of Pedigree dog food in the cart, done a one-hundred-eighty-degree turn and stormed down the aisle. She made a right turn, then another quick right and searched through the frozen vegetables. She grabbed two bags of mixed vegetables, tossed them in the cart and rushed to the register. The line was long and she was agitated.

"Damn it," she mumbled under her breath. "I hate this damn store. Every time I come in here, it's always a long ass line. It's seven in the damn morning! Why aren't these people at work or some damn place?"

The woman in front of her looked over her shoulder.

Leslie continued fussing. "Only one damn cashier."


Tillie rapped and tapped her fingers on the front door until Maxine flung the door open.

"You're late. Massa gon' get you good," Maxine smiled.

"Girl, I feel like crap. I ain't thinking about Jamaica."

Maxine frowned, her brows drew together. "Are you okay? You should be home and off your feet."

"I know, but I owe the bitch a payback too."

"Good, we're all here," Jamaica said, walking out of the bedroom. "Let's meet in my office."

Maxine and Tillie looked at each other with wide eyes. "Her office," they said in unison. They stood in the arch way of the small alcove. "Where are we going to sit in *your office*," Maxine said, her arms folded across her chest.

"I am going to sit right here," Tillie said, taking a seat in Jamaica's favorite chair. "I'm sure you don't expect for me to sit on the floor, after what I've just experienced."

Jamaica playfully popped her upside the head. "Of course not."

## *56*

Derek sped up Wisconsin Avenue NW, burning rubber, making a right onto Military Road, before he realized he was going in the wrong damn direction.

"Shit!" he cursed, slamming on the steering wheel. "Goddamn it, Jamaica. What in the hell are you getting ready to do?"

He made a quick right up a one-way street. So what if he was going in the wrong direction? He needed to get to Jamaica before she did something she would later regret.

He flipped open his cell phone and used voice command. "Call Jamaica," he said into his phone.

"Aren't you going to answer that?" Tillie asked, somewhat engulfed in *One Love*, a novel by Bill Holmes.

Jamaica stared at her caller ID and shook her head briskly.

"Who is calling you so early?" Maxine asked.

"It's Derek and I'm not going to answer it. I know he's only calling me because Gina called him and told him that I called her, probably."

Tillie flipped the page of the book. Her concentration moving from the warmly sensual words on the pages to what was going on around her. "Who is Gina?"

"Derek's sister," Maxine answered. "Don't you remember her from the party?"

"Oh, uh-huh," Tillie said. "Jamaica, may I borrow this book?"

"Yeah, as long as you return my shit. It's personally autographed to me by Mr. Holmes."

Tillie nodded. Jamaica's house phone stopped ringing and her cell phone started singing.

"Damn," Jamaica said.

"He knows," said Maxine.

"Yep," Tillie agreed.

"I'm not going to answer it. He's not going to talk me out of it, that's for sure."

When Jamaica's voice mail picked up, Derek didn't bother to leave a message, closing the phone and tossing it onto the passenger seat. As he sped through the pot-holed streets of the nation's capital he tried to calm his nerves and take his mind off of Jamaica by thinking of different cities he'd traveled to — Boston, Philadelphia, New York City, Atlanta — where he had relatives. He wanted to take Jamaica to those places, to meet his family.

Derek's thoughts turned back to Jamaica, then to a fiery inferno of anger. He asked her not to do anything stupid and she disregarded his wishes. He was in the middle of rush hour traffic and there was no way he was going to get to her place in time. If she didn't answer the phone, maybe she had left already.

He wasn't sure. Actually, he wasn't sure of anything. Maybe if he had did something about Leslie a while ago, he wouldn't be driving like a mad man trying to save his lady from doing something stupid.

He figured if Gina did not give up the address, then she must be going to the office. Most likely, she had her partners in crime with her, Maxine and Tillie. On second thought, Tillie wasn't in the condition to be acting a fool with Jamaica. But he still needed reinforcement. He reached for his cell phone, when he hit a pothole and his fingertips pushed the cell between the seat and the car door. "Fuck!" he yelled. He leaned over further, not taking his eyes off the road.

The young boy, on his way to school, found himself straddling the double mustard yellow line as he stood in the middle of the road, surrounded by pedestrians yelling at him to run across the street. As if in a slow motion frame from a movie, the Mercedes swiftly swerved toward him at a high rate of speed, the driver no where in sight. He tried to move, but his feet felt like they were buried deep in concrete.

"Oh my God!" a woman hysterically cried, frantically calling out to the young boy. "Move, baby, move! Run!"

He heard the words but the young boy felt something he had never felt before—grave panic. Panic like he'd never known before welled in his throat. His eyes were wide, staring blankly at the oncoming speeding vehicle. Fear overtook him— a fear that makes most people lose control of their bodily functions. A fear that made him piss on himself.

The car continued toward him. It was now close enough where he could see the driver's face, his eyes bulging out of his head, his face distorted with fear as he desperately tried to stop the car and regain control. The driver pumped the brakes, sending the car into a tail spin, smoke billowing from the tires.

Derek's eyes widened and his pulse raced faster than a car speeding around the track at the Indy 500.

"Oh my God!" The woman's screams were horrific and spine tingling, filling the deserted park as the silver Lexus connected with the young boy, dragging his small body a good hundred feet, before colliding into a telephone pole.

Smoke exuded from the smashed, folded hood of the car. Derek's head rested against the deployed air bag wheel as the opened gash down the side of his face gushed with red and protruding flesh. The little boy hidden beneath the silver metal of the once shiny Lexus.

## *57*

It was eight o'clock and the morning light spun and danced against the wall. Jamaica gulped down the last of her orange juice and the remainder of Tillie's juice, too. She was afraid, but if she did not do it now she would never be able to. She would eventually lose her nerve.

"Let's go," she said to Tillie and Maxine. "Put the damn book down, Tillie."

"Go where?" Tillie asked. "Do you even know where she lives?"

Jamaica looked back at Tillie and said nothing.

"Wait a minute, Jamaica," Tillie stated with concern. "You don't know where she lives, do you? You haven't told us anything except dress up in this ridiculous ass outfit. What is your plan? I love you, girl, but I'm not going to jail for you."

"No, I don't know where she lives, but I do know she works for Derek."

"We're going to go to her job?" Tillie inquired.

Jamaica said nothing.

Maxine looked at Jamaica, then at Tillie, and back at Jamaica. "You've gotta be shittin' me! I am not doing that shit, going to someone's job. That's too much."

Jamaica propped her hands on her hips. "What exactly do you propose we do?"

"I propose we leave that woman alone," Tillie answered. "That is Derek's battle—"

"Bullshit! That bitch included me in this battle when she attacked my ass at the fucking bus stop."

"Call the police, Jamaica," Tillie retorted. "Report her ass. Have her arrested. Do something. Anything. As long as you're not stooping down to her level and embarrassing us in the process."

"Well, ain't this about a bitch," Jamaica said, falling back onto the sofa. "Tillie, I don't believe you. I practically knocked Maxine's eye out because you—"

Tillie raised her hand to silence her. "Hold on now, Jamaica. I *never ever* asked you to react toward Maxine in any way, shape or form. That was my battle, of which I was well equipped to fight. *You* chose to do what you did. Don't you *dare* blame your actions on me."

"Come on, y'all. Let's not travel down that bumpy ass road again," Maxine pleaded.

Jamaica raised her hand in surrender. "Whatever, Tillie! You handle your shit the way you want and I'll handle my shit the way I prefer. Cool?"

"Uh-huh, real cool, which is why I am taking my black ass home. This shit here is for kids. Somebody needs to grow the fuck up. That's all I'm saying."

"I see your lips flapping, but I don't hear you saying much of anything," Jamaica taunted.

"Okay, chill out, ladies," Maxine ordered. "Tillie have a seat."

Tillie shot Maxine a cold glare.

Maxine continued. "Please, Tillie. Have a seat. We're not going to do this anymore, leave angry." She looked at Jamaica. "Jamaica, if I could make a suggestion."

"I'm not changing my mind."

"You don't have to. But, I would like to suggest we do something—"

Tillie interjected. "*We*? Who in the hell is *we*?

Maxine ignored Tillie and continued. "There are other ways to get back at someone other than causing them physical harm. I've always been told the best way to get at someone is through their pockets."

Jamaica folded her arms across her chest. "Hmmm, you make a good point. Derek found her in the park, living out of a box."

"Are you serious?" asked Tillie.

Jamaica nodded. "That's what he told me. He gave her a job, fixed her up and ended up fucking her. How fucking noble of him."

"I say we fuck up her credit," Tillie said.

"Exactly where I was going," Maxine cosigned.

Jamaica listened intently.

"If we fuck up her credit, she'll be ruined and end up back on the streets. I've heard the biggest fear for someone who used to be homeless is being homeless again, no matter how much money they have."

"It's agreed. OCF is in business," Maxine announced.

"OCF?" Jamaica chuckled.

"Operation Credit Fuck up!" Tillie exclaimed.

Maxine laughed. "See? Great minds think alike. How did you know what it meant anyway?"

"A lucky guess," Tillie said. "Now, I am *hungry*."

"Me too," Maxine said.

"I hop, you hop, we all hop to IHOP!" Tillie sung, grabbing her purse. "Let's rock and roll, baby."

"Okay, let me grab a pad and pencil real quick."

"Jamaica, why do you need pencil and paper?" Maxine asked.

"So we can write down how we are going to destroy that bitch!"

"Well, the first person we would call is my cousin Darlene. She is a professional at that shit," Maxine laughed.

## *58*

Derek wasn't wearing a seat belt, his face buried into the deployed air bag. Onlookers rushed toward the car, yelling and screaming, hysterically. "Call 9-1-1! Call 9-1-1!"

An elderly man looked under the car to see the mangled young boy. He wasn't moving. It looked as though he wasn't breathing.

"We've gotta get him out of there!" the man yelled, reaching underneath the car.

"Don't move him. Let the paramedics get him out," a woman yelled. "You may cause him more harm."

"Hey mister, can you hear me?" another man yelled through the shattered glass at Derek. "Can you hear me?"

Derek faintly moved his mouth.

"He's alive," the man yelled. "He's alive."

Rushing up the street was a young woman who looked to be in her mid to late twenties, wearing a bathrobe, fuzzy yellow slippers and her hair in rollers. "Oh my God! No! Not my baby!" she screamed and cried at the top of her lungs. "Oh sweet Jesus, not my baby!" She frantically approached the car. "Where is he? Where is my baby?"

The crowd of onlookers fell silent. An elderly woman pointed toward the bottom of the car. "He's there," she whispered, her voice cracking, tears streaming down her cheeks. "He's under the car."

"Oh my God, Jason! Baby, come from under there. Come out, Jason! Please baby, come out!" She dropped down to her knees and reached under the car. She cried hysterically as she frantically pulled her child from beneath Derek's mangled car and cradled him in her arms, her face buried in his chest. "Please, God, don't take my baby! Oh God! Lord please, not my baby, not my baby, dear Lord."

The conversation with Jamaica had Gina in a ball of nerves. Her talk with Derek didn't sit too well with her either. She called Jamaica's home and got no answer. Maybe Derek had gotten to her. She hoped. She prayed. Unable to wait for Derek to call her, she dialed his cell phone. It was on automatic answer.

Sirens blared and people screaming at the tops of their lungs scared the hell out of Gina. "Derek!" she yelled. "Hello!" she cried. "Oh no, Derek, please answer me!"

"Break the glass," she heard someone yell.

Gina held the phone to her ear and rocked back and forth, her heart in her throat, tears flowing down her cheeks and around her mouth. "Derek," she cried. "Please answer me. Derek, please."

She listened intently at the sound of breaking glass and what sounded like saws cutting through steel.

She hollered. "Somebody please! Pick up the phone. Hellooooooo," she cried. "Hellooooooo!"

"Okay, pull him out gently," she heard someone say, assuming it was the paramedic. "Watch his neck."

Gina went numb. Her heart sank and the fear of her brother being dead overwhelmed her. She yelled through the phone, loud and hard, catching the attention of the paramedic. "Hello, that's my brother. What's going on? Please talk to me!" she yelled.

The paramedic picked up the phone and stated, "Please calm down. My name is Richard Tucker and my badge number is T0199B. We're taking your brother to Howard University Hospital. Get there as fast as you can."

Before Gina could thank the paramedic or say anything else, Richard had hung up the phone. She immediately grabbed her purse and headed to the hospital.

The white sheet covered the young boy's face. "Noooooooo!" his mother screamed. "Why take my baby?"

An elderly woman wrapped her arms around the mother's shoulder. "The angels have him now."

The mother fell into the woman's embrace. "I want him here with me," she cried.

Doctors battled for two hours to try to save his life, as he lay with massive bleeding from injuries to his chest. During the vain and desperate battle, surgeons opened his chest and massaged his heart, in a last, yet desperate, attempt to save him.

# *59*

Less than four hours had elapsed when Derek's death was announced at 11:00 Monday morning. Gina cried nonstop, curled up in Derek's bed. When she left the hospital, she drove by the accident scene. Derek's car was still wrapped around the telephone pole. She drove to his house, in a daze, not sure how she got there in one piece.

"Why?" she cried, repeatedly. "What am I going to do without my big brother?"

There was so much to do, so many people to call. She wished she had someone she could turn to. Another brother or sister. She was it. She was all Derek had and he was all she had. She sat up in the bed, wiped her nose with the hem of her sleeve and reached for her cell phone. This was one call she dreaded making.

She inhaled deeply and blew it out as if she was smoking a cigarette. "Hello. Jamaica."

"Hey girl, how are you? Listen, I'm really sorry about this morning. It was really stupid of me to want to—" she paused. Any uneasiness came over her. "Is everything alright, Gina?"

Gina quietly sobbed and sniffed. "It's Derek—"

"What about Derek?"

"He. . .he—"she burst into tears.

"Gina! What's wrong with Derek?"

Gina could not get the word out. The more she thought about it, the more the memories came rushing to her. The pain was unbelievable; it hurt to even think about it. "Dead," she whispered. "My brother is dead!" The tears streamed down her face as she lost it.

"What do you mean?" Jamaica began to cry. "What are you

about, Gina? Gina, please get it together. Please. Please tell me what's going on."

Gina was hysterical but she felt for Jamaica as she heard her crying and could feel her sorrow. It was the tears of loss— the loss of a loved one.

"Jamaica, Derek was in a car accident this morning and it's all my fault! He didn't make it."

Standing in the kitchen, Jamaica leaned against the refrigerator and slid down, her butt planted to the floor. She needed to pinch herself. It all felt like a bad dream. "What. . .what—"

"It's all my fault. I called him this morning after I got off the phone with you and told him that you called me—"

"He was coming over here?" Jamaica whimpered.

"Yes, he was."

Jamaica held the phone and just looked at it. She didn't know what to say to Gina. One thing she did know—it wasn't Gina's fault. She knew who was responsible for the death of the man she loved. She hung up the phone, pulled her knees into her chest and buried her face between her knees, crying for hours.

# *60*

The sanctuary of Union Wesley Methodist Church was large and conservative, with beautifully colored stained glass windows. At the foot of the altar was Derek, laid out in his best Armani suit, surrounded by an assortment of flower arrangements: roses, carnations and lilies. Thoughts of rest in peace and cards of sympathy and safe passage to the other side were beautifully arranged around the casket and flower arrangements. Gina stood in the pulpit, before the mourners. As she gazed down at Derek, she smiled and spoke into the microphone.

"He looks peaceful," she whispered. She cleared her throat. "I loved my brother very much and there is so much I will miss about him — his smile, the way he laughed, the way he would rub his bald head when he was stressing out about something—" she paused, followed by a soft chuckle. "He always seemed to rub his head when I was around."

The mourners sent soft chuckles toward her, slightly easing her pain, which kept her from breaking down.

"I am not much of a speaker. That was always Derek's thing, being the center of attention." She used a Kleenex to dab around her eyes and nose. "I would like to thank each and every one of you for coming today. I know Derek is looking down from heaven and smiling—" she paused again and looked down at the front row. "Especially you, Jamaica. Derek really did love you. More than you will ever have the chance of knowing. I love you too. You'll always be a member of our family and my sister."

Gina looked toward the back of the sanctuary as the doors opened and Leslie entered, dressed in black from head to toe. Although a black veil covered her face, Gina knew who it was . A silent rage overwhelmed her. She closed her eyes and silently counted backward from ten. This was Derek's homegoing service and Leslie was not going to get an ounce of attention from Gina, as far as she was concerned. However, at the repast, as God was her witness, she would not be responsible for her actions.

She opened her eyes and spoke eloquently. "My brother was a kind man, a gentle man and probably the most righteous man I know." Her gaze aimed toward the back of the sanctuary, at Leslie. "He was not a selfish man. He gave of himself. Honestly, probably too often, but that was Derek—a man with a good heart, a blessed man. I know why the Good Lord blessed him so. Because He knew Derek would be there for others, even the lost souls. He helped so many people. He took a homeless woman from the park, gave her a job and a place to live. He never ever asked for anything in returned."

Leslie lowered her head and dabbed her eyes beneath the veil.

Gina continued. "He had so much love in his heart for things and people, that weren't always good for him. I miss you, Derek—my big brother. Thank you for being my angel on Earth and now, I know you will be my angel in Heaven. Know that I love you and—you will be sorely missed. By all of us."

If Gina had looked at the congregation, she would have seen the whole church with tears in their eyes. She stepped down from the pulpit and stood before the casket. She placed her hand on his chest and cleared her throat. When she opened her mouth, the escaping sound was beautiful and soothing. *His eye is on the sparrow, and I know he watches me.*

Jamaica stared at the casket, her head shaking from side to side, still unable to consume all that was going on. *This has to be a bad dream*, she thought, closing her eyes tightly, squeezing out rivers of tears.

Maxine and Tillie sat in the pews behind Jamaica, their eagle eyes glued on her, waiting to rush to her rescue.

Gina took her seat beside Jamaica and wrapped her arm around her shoulders, pulling Jamaica into an embrace. She whispered in her ear. "I can't believe she showed her face."

Jamaica looked up and gave her a quizzical look. "Leslie."

Gina kissed Jamaica on the cheek. "Let it go. I don't want to lose you too."

Gina knew how Derek was about his home. It was his palace, his world. He never allowed many people inside his world. Therefore, the repast was held in the downstairs dining hall of the church.

"Honey, you have to eat something," Maxine said, "or else you're going to make yourself sick."

Jamaica held on to a blank stare. "No thank you."

"But you haven't eaten anything in—"

Jamaica's head jerked around, facing Maxine. "Am I fucking speaking French or some shit?" she snapped.

"Jamaica, you're in a church," Tillie scolded in a hushed tone. "I know you're upset, but please mind where you are."

Jamaica's anger turned toward Tillie. "You don't know how I feel, Tillie. My man is dead," she gasped.

Tillie and Maxine looked at each other and remained quiet.

Leslie watched Jamaica from across the room. Remorse had set in and she wanted so badly to apologize, although she knew it would not do any good. Besides, she was hurting too. Jamaica was not the only woman who loved Derek. When he died, a part of her died too. A part of her that felt safe. For five years, she had Derek to lean on. Now she had to stand on her own two feet. Moreover, she knew if Gina had anything to do with it, she would be back on the streets in two shakes of a duck's tail.

She worked up her nerve and slowly walked toward Jamaica. She stood behind her and spoke. "Jamaica?"

Maxine and Tillie looked up and smiled.

Leslie pulled out the empty chair beside Jamaica and took a seat. She inhaled deeply and held it for what seemed like forever.

Jamaica's eyes squinted, her head tilted to the side.

Leslie exhaled. "I am Leslie."

Maxine and Tillie's smiles turned to angry frowns. They looked at each other, but kept their eyes on Jamaica.

Jamaica's jaw dropped. She was at a loss for words. The other day, she had sought out vengeance. Today, she felt sorry for her. She felt sorry for herself.

"What I did to you was wrong. I hope you can find it in your heart to accept my apology. If not, I completely understand." She looked at Maxine and Tillie. "I wouldn't forgive me either. We both have lost someone we loved very much. I'd like to put this all behind me and move on with my life."

Jamaica, still speechless, turned her back on Leslie and stared into Maxine's eyes. "I don't have the strength," she whispered.

Maxine smiled. "It's not worth it, baby girl."

Tillie felt sorry for Leslie. Maxine felt sorry for her too, but that was about it. All Jamaica needed to do was give her the sign and she would beat Leslie as if she stole something.

Jamaica faced Leslie. "Thank you," she said with a forced smile. "I appreciate your apology and accept it."

Leslie smiled, stood up and walked toward the doors and out of the building.

"So much for the big payback," Maxine said to Tillie.

Tillie shook her head and drew her brows together. "I think there has been enough suffering. No more is needed. Don't you think so, Jamaica?"

Jamaica remained silent. She did not know how to feel about what had just happened, but she was relieved to have brought closure with Leslie. In her heart, she wished the closure had come sooner. In her mind, Derek would be alive and they would be planning their life together. Only if closure would have come sooner.

## *61*

For the past three weeks, since Derek's funeral, Harmony Hills Cemetery was where Jamaica spent most of her afternoons. As the cold and dampness from the ground seeped through her denim pants, she leaned forward and kissed the headstone.

"I love you, baby," she said, pulling herself up from the ground and wrapping her coat up around her neck. She stared blankly at the grave, wondering if he was cold. "I will try and come back tomorrow."

As she walked away, she looked over her shoulder and cried. Leaving him there—alone, in the cold damp ground was the hardest thing she'd ever had to do in her life.

Curled up on the sofa, Jamaica sipped her third snifter of Cognac as Etta James belted *At Last* on MAJIC 102.3, followed by Heatwave's *Always and Forever*, and Luther Vandross' *Dance With My Father*. Tears flowed as she closed her eyes and fell off to sleep, and the snifter glass fell to the floor, shattering.

Lightly, a loose tendril of hair was fingered from her cheek. "Hey sleepy head," the familiar voice sung out, stirring her from her slumber. "Hello, Jamaica," he smiled, the silvery white light adorned his head, making him look like Jesus Christ.

Jamaica blinked her eyes several times, before she realized what was going on. She shot up on the sofa and scurried into the corner of the sofa. "Oh my God. Is that really you?" she asked, eyes wide and large, expanding to the size of golf balls.

"I am okay, baby," Derek said, his spirit setting the room aglow. "I am worried about you though. Thank you for visiting me every day, but you don't have to do that, babe. I want you to move on with your life."

She shook her head and cried. "Oh, Derek, I miss you so much. I can't make it without you."

He hushed her. "I'm here with you. I will always be with you."

She reached out her hand and stretched her wide opened fingers. "I want to feel you again, please. I need to."

"It wasn't your fault," he said. "The accident was my fault."

"No, you were coming—"

"It doesn't matter anymore, babe. I love you and I will always love you."

"I love you too," she cried.

"When you need me, just whisper. Alright?"

The crying eased up as she nodded her head. "Alright."

"Take care of Gina for me." His spirit began to fade. "I love you, Jamaica."

"Don't leave me, Derek! Please don't leave me."

"Just whisper," he said, quickly fading.

"Nooooo! Please, don't go. I need you here with me. I can't make it without you. Please, don't go."

"I love you," he said, fading.

"Derek!" she cried, staring off into the distance. "Please don't leave me."

She dropped her hands in her lap and looked around her apartment. It felt cold and empty. There was no more life. Her man was dead. There was no more life. Something inside of her was buried with Derek.

She stood to her feet, motionless, staring down at the shattered snifter on the floor. She bent down and picked up a piece of glass. She blinked her eyes several times, before falling back onto the sofa.

"I can't make it without him," she cried, pressing the piece of glass between her fingers and holding it firmly against the inside of her wrist. "I won't live without him," she cried, dragging the sharp, ragged edge of the piece of glass over her wrist. Blood poured from her vein and onto her lap. She raised the glass to her neck and stared blankly at the wall. Her head fell over to the side as blood poured from the self-inflicted cut across her throat.

One week later, Maxine, Tillie, Randy, and Gina embraced each other as they watched Jamaica being lowered into the double plot, on top of Derek.

"I feel like I'm having a nightmare," Tillie sobbed.

Randy pulled her closer to him. "I wish it were a nightmare."

Gina leaned over and looked down into the grave at the casket. She shook her head and wiped her nose. "They are together forever now."

Maxine stared off into the distance. "You know what this is?"

They all looked towards her. "Some serious love," Randy said.

Maxine shook her head. "Fatal desire."

If you have questions or comments for Jessica,
please e-mail her at JessicaTilles@aol.com.

Visit Jessica on the World Wide Web at:
www.JessicaTilles.com

# _XpressYourself_ Novels

**QTY**

_____   _Anything Goes_ by Jessica Tilles ISBN: 0-9722990-0-9; $15.00

_____   _In My Sisters' Corner_ by Jessica Tilles ISBN: 0-9722990-1-7; $15.00

_____   _Apple Tree_ by Jessica Tilles ISBN: 0-9722990-2-5; $15.00

_____   _Sweet Revenge_ by Jessica Tilles ISBN: 0-9722990-3-3; $15.00

_____   _One Love_ by Bill Holmes ISBN: 0-9722990-4-1; $15.00

_____   _Fatal Desire_ by Jessica Tilles ISBN: 0-9722990-4-1; $15.00

**Send to:**
Xpress Yourself Publishing, LLC
Attn: Book Orders
P.O. Box 1615
Upper Marlboro, MD 20773

Please send me the books I have checked above. I am enclosing $_____ (plus $1.50 per book, shipping and handling). Send check or money order (no cash or C.O.Ds please).  Allow up to two weeks for delivery.

Name _____

Address _____

City _____State/Zip _____

Visit us online at
www.xpressyourselfpublishing.org